A
Shrouded
Spark

A
Shrouded
Spark

BRESHEA ANGLEN

ARCHWAY
PUBLISHING

Archway Publishing books may be ordered through booksellers or by contacting:

Archway Publishing
1663 Liberty Drive
Bloomington, IN 47403
www.archwaypublishing.com
1 (888) 242-5904

ISBN: 978-1-4808-3970-0 (sc)
ISBN: 978-1-4808-3971-7 (e)

Library of Congress Control Number: 2016918791

Print information available on the last page.

Archway Publishing rev. date: 1/25/2017

About the Author

Breshea Anglen is a newly published author from Ohio and a member of Delta Xi Phi Multicultural Sorority Inc. She attended Bowling Green State University and earned a Bachelor of Science in education in 2015 as well as a Master of Education in reading in 2016.

At Bowling Green State University, Breshea discovered her affinity for poetry. Thereafter, with the help of two friends and a mentor, she founded BGSU's first spoken word poetry group. Her love for poetry kick-started the completion of her first novel. The poem, "Eloisa to Abelard", by Alexander Pope, greatly inspired her work.

Young Adult fiction of the fantasy genre has been Breshea's favorite for much of her life. Breshea loves reading fantasy because it feeds her captivation with every day magic, mysticism, and discovering the secrets of the universe.

Now, Breshea is a 5th grade English teacher. She's always had a passion for the English language as well as for working with children. She enjoys writing, reading young adult fiction novels, performing spoken word poetry, watching independent films, and spending time at local animal shelters.

Breshea lives in Cleveland, Ohio, with her family and one particularly lovely dog, Rocco.

For my Nanie,
who gave me the stories first.

For Tyell—
I will give the stories to you.

"How happy is the blameless vestal's lot!
The world forgetting, by the world forgot.
Eternal sunshine of the spotless mind!
Each pray'r accepted, and each wish resign'd"
- From "Eloisa to Abelard" by Alexander Pope

Chapter One

Noni caught glimpses of light. She heard voices; some of them called her name. There was always a strange feeling in her chest, a certain tightness, whenever she heard them. The voices had no faces. Her memories would never play back for her. Her thoughts were a fog inside her consciousness.

The first time that a voice broke through, strong and clear, was the first time that Noni could call upon some memory.

"Noni."

The pain and tightness rose behind her ribs. Glimpses of faces flew past her eyes as she tried to match the voice with the face that it belonged to. It wouldn't click. The voice just wouldn't attach.

"I think she's opening her eyes…"

Flames overwhelmed her chest. Her lungs, her throat, her eyes—the ache inside her grew like a brush fire. Light began to spill into her limbo, shining through the darkness, bringing her back to the places that hurt. She breathed. She saw. She ached.

"Call a nurse! Tell the doctors to get in here! She's waking up! She's waking up!"

The first thing in her line of vision was a set of prayer beads—a rosary—dangling above her face, glistening underneath the fluorescent lights. Each bead was a deep shade of red; a set of dark, wrinkly hands held the rosary. She wanted to swat it out of her face, but her arms wouldn't move, and neither would any other limb.

There was too much soreness, too much pain. She looked away from the beads, and that was when she saw a face all too familiar to her.

Noni's aunt Deidre stood beside her, eyes sunken in, tears rushing down her brown, hollowed-out cheeks. Her hair was no longer the same black that it had always been; it was almost ashen, sticking out every direction from underneath a tattered, red bandana. Her honey-colored eyes bore into Noni's so intensely; the stare was too strong for the younger girl to endure. This was not the woman she remembered.

After a series of rapid health checks, the doctors removed Noni's breathing tube, and she began to take in air on her own. Her throat was sore, raw from having the intrusive tube inside. Noni felt slow, drowsy. When the doctors began asking more questions, Noni could only manage one word.

"Water."

Deidre brought a small cup of ice water for Noni. But before the woman could even let her drink it, she was hugging her, rubbing her face, kissing her all over. Noni wished she would stop so that she could tell her aunt that she was dying of thirst, but she just couldn't get the words out.

Eventually, Deidre helped Noni drink the water, tipped the plastic cup against her lips, and made sure not to spill a single drop. The water only made Noni's throat burn even more. As soon as the cup was empty, one doctor returned. Noni's eyes met hers, and the woman smiled warmly.

"My name is Dr. Cohen. I'm the attending neurosurgeon, and I'm going to be taking care of you, okay?" she said. She sat down on the edge of Noni's bed and began asking her a series of questions. "What's your name?"

"Noni Grace," she mumbled.

"How old are you?"

"Eighteen."

"What year is it?"

"2017."

"Where do you live?"

"Morrison, Ohio."

When Dr. Cohen stopped questioning her, Noni was relieved, and even more so when the woman stepped away from her bedside.

Deidre nearly collapsed into a chair beside the bed. "Oh Noni, I'm so glad you're awake. So glad." Deidre was crying again, holding Noni's hand so tightly.

Noni would've hugged her back if she wasn't so sure that she'd fall out of bed if she tried. Whatever medication they'd given her had thrown her off completely. She had no idea how long she'd been lying there, but her muscles were in knots.

"I knew you would wake up. I just knew you would," Deidre wept, kissing Noni's forehead repeatedly. Noni leaned into it carefully, sighing as she did. Her aunt swiped Noni's curls away from her face and took a deep breath.

"How do you feel?" asked the doctor.

With a raspy voice, dry from lack of use, Noni answered, "Tired. Confused."

The doctor offered Noni another drink of water, but she declined, not thinking her stomach could handle anything else yet. "How long...how long have I been asleep?" she asked.

The doctor sighed sadly, shaking her head. "Noni, you've been in a coma for two weeks."

Noni's eyes flew open wide with disbelief. "Coma? What— why was I in a coma? What happened?" She noticed her aunt watching her sadly, face contorted into an expression of fear and confusion.

"You mean you don't remember?" Deidre asked.

Noni remained silent and shook her head. She couldn't remember a thing. Deidre looked to Dr. Cohen as if to gain permission to speak. Noni tried to relax. She waited for an answer. Her aunt, nerves wracked, wrung her hands together as she began talking.

"You and Bianca were in a car accident. You were hurt very badly." She paused, closing her eyes and mustering up the courage to find the right words—words that would not jar the memory of the crash. "Bianca is fine. She has a broken arm and a few bruised ribs, but that's all. It's you we were worried about, baby."

Noni gripped the rails weakly, trying and failing at pulling herself into a more upright position. Frustrated, she let her arms fall to the side and heaved out a heavy, tired breath. "Where's Bianca?" She clutched at the side of her head, irritated by her lack of coordination, and let her head fall to the pillows.

The older woman stood quickly. "She's here, Noni. I'll bring her."

When her aunt left, Noni let her eyes fall shut. She wracked her brain for glimpses of what she'd been through, for memories, for *something*, but in the end, she found nothing. She couldn't call to mind a single moment from the crash, but body held tight to every memory. She could feel every ache in every bone, every bruise on every inch of her skin. She could barely move without feeling pain. There were bandages across her head; she could almost smell the blood underneath—that, mixed with the hospital stench invading her nostrils and the mixture of medication in her body, caused a lurch in her stomach. Sick, she covered her nose with the edge of her hand. She breathed deeply and concentrated on the sound of the heart monitor beside her bed.

When Bianca finally came, she wept immediately upon the sight of her cousin. She rushed to Noni's bedside, wrapped her good arm around Noni, and sobbed into her shoulder.

"I'm so glad you're awake," she sniffed, using her sleeve to wipe her eyes. "Don't ever scare us like that again."

Noni, dazed and aching, muttered a promise into Bianca's shirt to never scare anyone like this again.

Dr. Cohen wanted to keep Noni under close observation. Though

Noni was conscious and lucid, Dr. Cohen still wanted to be sure of her condition. Comas were not to be taken lightly, and the doctor couldn't send Noni home without being completely sure.

Hospitals made Noni anxious. She'd spent more than enough time in them as a child. The stench of antiseptics, the squeak of slip-resistant shoes, the tired faces of worried relatives roaming the halls—all of it made her squirm. Noni's father had been a surgeon. Her mother had been a nurse. They spent all of their time in the hospital, and she spent all of her time in the hospital day care. It had been something of a second home.

During Noni's recovery, her days in the hospital blurred together. The medicine spun her in and out of consciousness. There were times when she woke and forgot why she was in the hospital, but she would find Deidre or Bianca at her side, and they would always explain. Only one person outside of her family visited Noni, and she was lucid when he arrived.

Terrell rushed into the room with a bouquet of flowers, grinning wildly. He was still in his work uniform: black pants, white shirt, and green vest. He was grinning in the doorway, his brown eyes sparkling as they found Noni.

"You're awake," he said. "Thank goodness."

It took her a few seconds to register his face, but when she did, she smiled. "Yeah," Noni replied. "It's something, right?"

Terrell came to her bedside and motioned to the flowers. "I bought these." He said. "You don't seem like the type to like flowers, but you know, it's the principle of the thing."

Noni laughed, reaching out for the bouquet. "It's the principle of the thing. Thank you."

Noni had known Terrell for a little over two years, ever since she started working at the Michael's Grocery Store. He was a few years older than her and had been working there long before she was hired. During her first few weeks, Terrell was her trainer. He showed her the ropes and helped her work through her mistakes. He knew how to do his job, and he knew how to help people.

Terrell watched Noni closely as she peeled through the flowers, examining each and every bloom in the bouquet. There were orange and red lilies and fuchsia carnations. She'd never really been a fan of flowers, but they were beautiful.

"How are you feeling?"

Noni shrugged, setting the bouquet aside on the small table beside her bed.

"Everything hurts," she told him. She paused, trying to find the words. Dr. Cohen told her that forgetting words was normal for coma patients who'd just woken up. Normal or not, it was frustrating. "Forget it," she muttered. She looked over at him. "I feel like crap."

"I think that's normal," Terrell told her.

"I don't remember it," Noni admitted. "—the accident. I don't remember."

Terrell nodded. "Maybe it's for the best?"

"Maybe," She sighed. "Thank you for coming."

"You don't have to thank me," He grinned. "As soon as I heard you were awake, I knew I had to see ya. I came a few times, you know, while you were still out."

"Was it bad?" Noni asked.

Terrell nodded once more, running his hands across his hair. "Yeah. It was. It was bad, Noni."

"Okay," She sighed, closing her eyes.

Abruptly, one of Noni's nurses came into her hospital room. The woman was smiling and spoke immediately.

"Hi, Miss Grace," She greeted. "How are you feeling?"

Noni rolled her eyes. Terrell saw her and laughed.

"Awful, but what's new," she grumbled.

The woman laughed softly. "That's normal," she said. "I'm just here to do some routine checks, okay?"

The nurse checked her vitals, her temperature, her motor skills, and just about everything else. She didn't leave before letting Noni know that she seemed completely healthy. Noni hoped that meant she could go home soon and get as far away from the hospital as possible.

Terrell stayed through the whole ordeal. He didn't ask Noni anymore questions about her condition, and he didn't remind her of the crash again. Instead, he told her stories about work and about all the ridiculous things that happened while she'd been gone. He kept her smiling and entertained until visiting hours ended.

"Hey," he asked her. "You want me to come back tomorrow?"

Noni nodded. "If you have time, that'd be...great. That'd be great."

"Deal."

Terrell left just before Bianca returned. She took his spot at Noni's bedside, laying her head on the edge of her cousin's bed.

"You ready to go home? 'Cuz I am." She complained.

Noni sighed. Bianca had no idea.

Noni remained hospitalized for a little over a week after she woke, under close observation. Still, her memories of the crash did not return. Since there was no visible damage to her brain, her Aunt, Bianca, and even the doctor believed that maybe it was for the best.

Whenever Noni mentioned the crash, Deidre would always stop her. She only cared that Noni was alive; she wanted to put the crash behind them—to forget—just as Noni had. Noni herself couldn't decide if she was thankful for her lapse of memory or not.

Nevertheless, after her last day in the hospital, they took a taxi home. When they arrived, Noni realized that she had never missed being home so much. After spending so much time in a hospital, the small two-story white house had never looked so inviting. Bianca went inside first. Deidre helped Noni out of the car, but she didn't let her walk inside.

"Noni, sweetheart," She spoke.

The teenager looked up at her Aunt curiously, awaiting her words.

"Thank you for pulling through." Tears brimmed the corners of Deidre's eyes but they never fell. "I don't think I could've handled losing you, too. So thank you for pulling through."

Noni hugged her Aunt tightly, softly resting her head on the woman's chest. "I'm not ready to be with Mom and Dad just yet."

Deidre carefully helped her niece into the house, opening the door and leading her in. She turned on the lights, and that's when it happened—

"SURPRISE!"

Balloons were everywhere. There were streamers hanging from the archways and confetti twirling through the air. At least ten people stood in their living room, clapping and smiling at Noni as if she had been gone for years. A banner hung across the doorframe that said *Welcome Home!*

Through the haziness in her head, Noni smiled.

"You know how Ma is." Bianca sighed as a small grin made its way onto her face.

Deidre guided the two girls into the living room and carefully sat Noni down on the couch while everyone, all of their neighbors, crowded around Noni. Noni stared around at them, not sure how to feel. Thankfulness and anxiety were all mixed up in her head, in her chest—she tried to sit as still as she could as their smiling faces bore down on her.

"So glad you're home, and well." Their neighbor, Kathy, smiled a red lipstick smile that stretched across the expanse of her face. Kathy had been a good friend to her family for as long as Noni could remember, so no one ever mentioned her lipstick. She handed Noni something, wrapped tightly in newspaper. "And happy graduation!"

Noni unwrapped it, slowly, careful not to tear any of the paper. Her eyes teared up when she finally saw the gift. It was a picture of Noni and Bianca outside their highschool, wearing their white cap and gowns. They looked so happy, with wide smiles plastered across their faces. Noni and Bianca stood, side by side, arms interlocked, grinning wildly. Noni thanked Kathy and hugged the older woman as she fought back happy tears.

The rest of their neighbors showered Noni with love and gifts until Deidre ordered them into the dining room where she'd laid out a feast. Noni wasn't sure where Deidre had found the time to cook so much food, but then again, Deidre was known to create time out of nowhere.

Alone, Noni sat on the couch with the picture frame in hand and found herself near tears. She couldn't remember anything about the graduation. It should have been one of the most important days of her life, but she couldn't recall a single thing about it. Noni had graduated, walked the stage with her classmates—there were pictures to prove that much.

She remembered nothing. The only thing that she could dredge up was being in the car with Bianca, heading toward the hall where the graduation ceremony was held. She couldn't recall the ceremony. She couldn't recall the pictures or the moments. She couldn't recall the crash that followed. Now, her brain was foggy with loss and medication, and all she wanted to do was sleep until her clouded head had cleared.

Noni couldn't rest, at least not with everyone fawning over her the way that they were. Hugging her, kissing her, doing everything but talking about what happened. They kept telling her, "Welcome home," and, "We're so glad you're alright," but no one dared to mention the actual event. Noni wondered: had it been that awful? So gruesome that no one could find the guts to say a word about it? Perhaps they knew that she couldn't remember and didn't want to remind her of it.

Unfortunately, her scars were a permanent reminder. One long stitch across her hairline, another from her temple to her eyebrow, and one under her right eye. That was the extent of the damage, save for her loss of memory. She would've thought that since she had been in a coma she would have sustained more severe injuries. Many things didn't make sense; she wondered if this was a normal side effect.

"Hey, why do you look so sad?"

Noni glanced up to see Bianca looking down at her. The girl knelt down in front of Noni and smiled. "Girl, you're thinking way too hard," Bianca said.

"I'm just tired." Noni replied, flicking her eyes to the dining room where everyone had begun to gather.

Bianca shrugged. "Go to bed then. Nobody would blame you— not after the beating you took." Bianca regretted her words as soon as they came out of her mouth. "My bad."

Noni shook her head. "It's cool," she said. "You're the only person who's not afraid to admit that it happened."

Bianca folded her one good arm underneath her broken one. "Ma told me not to talk about it with you," she scoffed. "As if I wasn't in the car when it happened."

That, Noni thought, *wasn't hard to believe.* "Figured as much." She looked to Bianca. "Do you remember it? All of it?"

Bianca nodded. "Yeah, most of it," she admitted, averting her eyes. "You really don't remember anything?"

"Nope," Noni answered, "not a thing." She lowered her voice then, so that only Bianca could hear her. "Was it really that bad?" she asked.

Bianca stared down at her feet, shrugging one shoulder before looking up at Noni again. She nodded. "Yeah." She looked around, as if to check whether any of the adults in the other room could hear them. "I mean, everybody thought you *died*, Noni."

"*What?*" Noni hissed. Bianca held her index finger to her lips and shot Noni an accusatory glare.

"You looked half dead when you got pulled out of the car," Bianca spoke, as softly as she could. "I mean—it was scary, okay? Nobody thought you were gonna make it. Noni, I—It's probably better that you don't remember, anyway."

Noni stopped pushing. "Probably," She agreed.

"We're all just glad you made it." Bianca stood up from her space on the floor and hugged Noni with one arm, careful not to squeeze.

Noni smiled. Bianca released her and nodded. "I'll get you something to eat, okay?"

Although Noni knew that she wasn't hungry at all, she nodded.

Bianca began to walk away, but before she could, Noni spoke once more.

"Bee," she began. "You said someone *pulled* me out?"

Bianca's expression darkened, filled with worry and apprehension. She nodded silently.

"So what?" Noni whispered. "Did the rescue workers come and pry me out with the jaws of life or something?"

Bianca sighed. "No—I mean, Ma told me that the rescue workers were there and they were like, you know, rushing to our car, but by the time they even got there, some guy was already pulling you out." She paused. "The rescue workers got me out after that."

"Some random guy," Noni repeated, disbelievingly. "Some guy—"

"Noni, Bee!" The sound of Deidre's voice, booming from the kitchen, startled the girls. "Come in here and get y'all's plates!" Bianca turned immediately, rushing into the dining room. Noni carefully stood. She made her way into the dining room, taking an empty plate from her Aunt's hands before the woman placed a quick kiss on her forehead, careful to avoid the bandage covering her stitches.

"Feeling alright?" her Aunt asked.

Noni shrugged slowly. "As good as I can feel, I guess."

Deidre nodded, brushing Noni's curls from her face and resting her hand against her niece's cheek. "Well sit down, eat as much as you can, and then head to bed, hmm? It's a lot, having the whole neighborhood in one house," she chuckled.

It wasn't the guests that made Noni tired, but she knew what Deidre meant.

Noni went into the dining room where everyone sat around the table, and sat down between Kathy, who was going on and on about the potato salad, and Bianca, who looked at Noni as if she'd done something awful.

"You've never had a good poker face," Noni muttered, rolling her eyes as she sat down next to Bianca. "Eat—it's not that serious."

It's a good thing Kathy's so loud, Noni thought. It kept the attention off of Bianca and Noni.

Bianca shoveled potato salad into her mouth. Noni took a bite as well, trying to focus on whatever was happening at the table. She didn't know how to feel, mostly about the fact that no one wanted to talk about the crash.

Had it really been that gruesome?

Noni spent the next few days at home with Bianca. Because of their injuries, they'd been granted time away from work. Unfortunately, Deidre, as much as she wanted to stay and take care of the girls, had to leave them at home alone. She worried herself sick each day and called them during every lunch break. Noni was still taking medication that gave her random bouts of drowsiness, so it was nice to have Bianca around to make sure that she didn't pass out in the middle of the living room floor.

Occasionally, friends from school would visit. They all heard about what happened to the girls; it'd even made the news station. Both Noni and Bianca had received many gifts—flowers, teddy bears, and get well cards—the usual "car accident" gifts, they supposed. All of the stuff took up a lot of space in the living room.

On Noni's third day at home, she received a card in the mail from her Math teacher. A small, purple envelope. She opened it with the tip of her fingernail, careful not to make reckless tears in the paper. It was a white card with the words "Get Well" embossed on its face. She opened it and read the personal message on the inside. As she was reading, her emotions overwhelmed her.

You were lucky to get out of there alive, Noni. We are all glad that you are okay. Don't take this lightly—make use of the second chance you've been given. Live your life to the fullest.

She held the tiny card in her hands, turning it over and then reopening it again just to read the message one more time. She carried it, rereading it, as she made her way into the kitchen where she found Bianca, struggling to put away leftovers from the lunch that Deidre had left for them.

"What's that?" Bianca questioned. "Another get-well card?"

"Yeah, from Mr. Richards," She replied. "Didn't know he cared."

"Everyone cares when something bad happens—besides, everyone loves you. Of course he cares." Bianca turned to the fridge again, trying to organize things with her one good hand.

Noni watched her cousin, sighing heavily as she closed the card and tucked it back into the torn purple envelope. "Bianca," she began. "I know—I know that you don't like talking about the crash. But I really need you to tell me what happened." Noni could almost sense Bianca starting to decline, so she kept talking. "Everyone knows *exactly* what happened except for me, and they just keep tiptoeing around the subject like I'll break when I hear it. Can you just—can you just be real with me for five seconds, Bee? Please?"

Bianca listened to her every word and watched her carefully. Noni breathed heavily, her chest heaving up and down.

Bianca rolled her eyes, exasperated. She tossed her braids behind her shoulder before she spoke. "You can never just leave it alone, " she sighed. She closed the fridge and sat down at the small kitchen table. "Fine. I don't know why you want to hear this so bad, Noni, I really don't. Don't you think it makes me crazy, talking about it?" She shook her head. "We were late to lunch, leaving the ceremony. And you were driving. And, I don't know Noni, we were listening to some stupid song on the radio and dancing." She paused. "Literally, out of nowhere, a truck came right at us. From the driver's side. Smashed right into us. Right into *you.*" Bianca averted her eyes.

Noni suddenly felt awful for bringing it up at all.

"Noni," Bianca said. "you know I never really jumped on the miracle-bandwagon, but … I don't think there's any other way to explain how you survived. You...I was sure that you weren't gonna make it, and I mean *sure*. I mean I didn't think I would either. We were stuck in that car for at least ten minutes. I was scared—well I was scared you'd bleed out."

Ten minutes. Noni knew that those had to be the longest ten minutes of her cousin's life.

"The whole car was upside down.," Bianca continued. "I was calling out for you, but you weren't conscious and I couldn't even get myself loose to try to get to you. Then, I don't know—I don't know; it was like a miracle. Like a *real* miracle. This guy, this *one* guy came and dragged you right out of the car. Like it was nothing." She shook her head. "Call me crazy, hallucinating because of the pain or whatever, but I swear that guy pulled the car apart just to get to you. And right after he got you out, the rescue workers got there and took you to the ambulance. And then me. And that was when I passed out."

A long, heavy silence surrounded the two girls, settling in the air around them. Noni wrapped her arms around herself uncomfortably, trying to process her cousin's confession. Her own words were thick in her mouth, stuck behind the arch of her tongue. There was so much to say, so much to digest.

"I'm sorry," Noni finally spoke. "I didn't...I'm sorry for making you remember all that."

"S'alright. You have a right to know what happened."

Noni shrugged. "It's just hard not knowing. Not being able to remember." There were so many things that Noni had the displeasure of not remembering—years' worth. "But it would've been nice to remember graduation, you know?"

Bianca nodded. "Mom was so upset that she didn't tape it for us," she said. "Just give it time. There's always hope that you'll remember at some point. You've barely been upright for a week, you know?"

"Yeah, I know."

Noni's body sagged with exhaustion. She quietly left the kitchen as Bianca resumed her rearranging of the refrigerator's contents.

Noni walked through the dining room and up to her bedroom, going straight to her bed and lying down. Sleep had become all too necessary. She placed the get-well card onto her dresser and buried her face in the white pillows at the head of her bed. They smelled like the fabric softener that Deidre used, like flowers and rain. It was Noni's favorite scent and the only scent that her Aunt ever bought ever since Noni was a child. Noni liked it because it was familiar. Something she could remember. She wrapped herself up in the knit blanket that lay across her bed, one that her mother had knit for her while pregnant with Noni. It was soft, purple and white, and it too smelled of flowers and rain.

As she drifted off to sleep, Noni thought about all the things that Bianca had told her about the crash, and what she'd gathered from the conversation was that she shouldn't have been alive—more or less. Judging from the placing of the scars on her head, she should've at least been in a coma longer. Stuck in a car wreck for ten minutes with critical head wounds—there was no way that she should have lived. Noni wondered how many run-ins with death could she survive.

She shut her eyes, trying to wipe away her worries.

Silently, she began to question—who was the man who saved her life? Who was this man and why had no one mentioned his name?

Noni wondered how Bianca and her Aunt had survived, for those two long weeks, of her being in a coma. She wished that she could tell them that even though she remembered nothing about the crash, she remembered things about being in a coma. It had all felt like a dream to her. She wondered if that was normal. Did all coma patients remember? It was supposed to be a complete loss of consciousness. Noni didn't think she was supposed to recall anything, but she did— being clothed by absolute darkness, senses numbed—she remembered it. Always feeling like someone was beside her, but knowing fully that she was alone.

Noni rationalized that feeling by believing it was her Aunt who sat beside her while she was in the coma. Deidre at least told Noni

about that, and about how she'd never left her side. One day, Noni
thought, she would actually tell them about it, even though they
might never believe her.

She fell asleep then, and oddly enough, she remembered her
dreams. She dreamt of gardens, vast, never-ending gardens. Flowers
of all colors, a plethora of flora that overshadowed even the grass
from which it grew. Noni dreamt of thick storm clouds, closing off
the whole sky. In her dream, she was waiting for something, and she
thought that maybe she could have been waiting for it to rain. When
she woke up the next morning, she swore it was because of the fabric
softener.

CHAPTER TWO

Noni found his name in the police report online. The report listed him as one of the witnesses. His name was Alexander Albright, and he lived fifteen minutes outside of their city. The report was very useful, listing even his address. The only thing missing was a picture of him.

Noni doubted that Bianca remembered what he looked like, and she doubted that Deidre wanted to remember him because it would only bring back bad memories. Noni really didn't want anyone else to have to remember that day, but she couldn't keep the knowledge to herself. She had begun to feel much better, so she took it upon herself to do something daring.

It was the weekend, early in the day and both Deidre and Bianca were home. Noni found them downstairs chatting together in the living room. She stopped in the archway, leaning against its frame as she watched them. Deidre was the first to notice her.

"Feeling alright?" The woman asked.

Noni nodded. "Yeah. I feel pretty good."

Deidre gave Noni the once-over and quirked an eyebrow. "Something on your mind?"

Noni shrugged quickly. "Kind of. Yeah. It's just—okay, I was on the internet."

"Always a good start," Deidre smirked.

Noni rolled her eyes. "And I looked up the police report from the crash," she said. Deidre's eyes widened and Noni held up her hands quickly. "Not because I wanted details on that. Trust me. But I wanted," Noni hesitated. "Well I wanted to know the name of the guy who got me out of the car." She paused, taking a breath and letting Deidre and Bianca absorb what she'd said. "It's just that I was thinking that maybe I could, you know, send him a thank-you letter or something. And maybe…ask to meet him and say 'hey thanks for saving my life'?"

As soon as Noni finished, Deidre smiled and she started nodding. "I think that's a great idea, Noni. I really do," she said.

Noni could finally breathe.

"It's thoughtful. It would be a very, very good thing to do." Deidre shook her head, smiling proudly.

"Took long enough to think that up, huh?" Bianca questioned, glancing up at Noni. "I would've thought you'd have done that forever ago!"

Noni shrugged. "I've been thinking it over for a while I guess."

Bianca grinned. "I'm sure he'll be really glad you did."

Noni did exactly what she said she'd do.

She wrote him a letter, a short letter. She sent it off the same day that she wrote it and found herself to be giddy once she sent it off. She couldn't understand why, but she was excited and couldn't shake the feeling. She wished she would have done it sooner but she had been living in a cloud of fear and medication ever since she left the hospital. She finally felt clear and could concentrate on the real things in her life, things like thanking someone for making sure that she still had a life to begin with.

She wondered what kind of person he was to be brave enough, strong enough, to pull a dying girl from a car wreck, he must've been something amazing. Noni wondered how the crash had affected him, if at all. Did he have nightmares? Bianca had nightmares. She didn't want Noni to know about them, but sometimes Noni heard her wake up screaming in the middle of the night. Noni chose to ignore it, for Bianca's sake, not her own. She wondered if the letter would come as a surprise to him. She wondered if he thought she was dead. To him, she could very well be dead. Noni spent more time thinking about this, about who this man could be, than she intended. After mailing the letter that morning, she couldn't stop herself. All through breakfast and lunch, she kept bringing it up, kept thinking. The sense of giddiness and excitement never really left her.

Noni lay sprawled out on her bed, staring up at the ceiling. She closed her eyes for a brief moment, but as soon as she did, there was a knock at her bedroom door. Her eyes met the door. It swung open only to reveal Bianca, grinning.

"I'm tired of being in the house," Bianca said. "Let's get dinner and go see a movie or something. Might as well use the rental car while we have it. I'll drive!"

"With one arm?"

"With one arm."

"That can't be safe," Noni sighed.

Bianca shrugged. "Better than you having a flashback in the middle of the road or something. We'll be fine—it'll be fine. Come on, Noni, get dressed. Let's go!"

Noni couldn't refuse. She hadn't left the house since she'd come home from the hospital. She actually felt good today, and she hadn't felt good in a while, so she decided that leaving wasn't such a bad idea. As soon as Noni was dressed, donned sunglasses and all, they left. Even with one arm, Bianca was a good driver. Thankfully, neither of them had any aversion to cars, even after what they'd been through. If anything, Bianca was a bit more careful than she usually was.

Noni chose the restaurant. They went to a small diner about ten minutes from their home. It was called *Rhonda's*, and it was one of their favorite restaurants because of its homey, comfortable feel—and because of their peach cobbler—it'd been named the best in all of Ohio, and Noni went there every chance she got. As soon as they sat down in the restaurant, Noni ordered fries and an entire peach cobbler for the two of them to share and take the leftovers home when they finished. When their food came, Bianca pulled her hair back into a ponytail and Noni rolled up her sleeves before they dug in. They ate as much as they could, as fast as they could. Bianca was much slimmer than Noni, but she could sure pack it away.

Bianca laid her head down next to her empty plate. "I don't think I can move." She sighed. "So good."

Noni smiled. "I haven't had cobbler in forever. It was better than I remembered." She licked her fork clean for good measure.

Bianca flinched and made a gagging sound; she hated when Noni did that.

"Last week when Auntie made some, I couldn't even hold it down."

"Eh, Ma never made the best desserts anyway," Bianca joked.

Noni laughed aloud, clutching her too-full stomach. "She'd kill you if she heard you say that!"

Bianca shrugged. "Probably," she laughed.

Noni sat back and took another deep breath. "So today," she began, "after I sent that guy, Alexander Albright—that's his name—after I sent off the letter, I was thinking, he probably thinks I'm dead or something."

"Morbid, " Bianca responded. "but understandable."

"I know," Noni said. "Auntie thinks we should make him a gift basket or something."

Bianca chuckled. "That's so boring. A gift basket? Just thank the guy and show him you're alive. I think that'll be enough."

"Auntie is still making the gift basket; there is literally nothing I can do to change her mind," Noni said. Bianca muttered "Figures," before she laughed a little.

"So do you really think it's a good idea that I tried to contact him?" Noni asked.

Bianca nodded fast, grinning widely. "Of course, yeah! I think it's great. I mean, you might get to meet the man who saved you. I think that's wonderful. I think it'll be cool. I mean—imagine the questions you could ask! Like, what made him save you? Why was he at that place, at that time? How'd he find the strength to do what he did, you know? Man, that's wild," she sighed. "wild."

After lunch, Bianca chose the movie. They saw an action flick, which was her favorite genre. By the time that they left the theater, it was early in the evening and sweltering. It certainly hadn't been that warm when they got there, and so they were left wondering what had changed. The sun still hung in the sky, still beating down on everyone, heating up the sidewalks and the streets. Noni could see heat waves rising from the ground, and she suddenly felt dizzy and nauseous.

She leaned up against the closest wall, the outside of the theatre, just to catch her breath and try not to be sick.

Bianca rushed to her side. "Whoa—you okay?"

"Yeah," Noni mumbled, suppressing the urge to unleash the contents of her stomach all over the pavement. "Side effects of my medicine or something," she groaned.

The two girls found seats outside the theatre at small, circular tables on the sidewalk. Bianca sat Noni down and pushed a large cup of soda toward her. "Guess that head of yours isn't all that better huh?" Bianca said.

Noni shrugged, pushing the drink back toward her cousin. "Could be the food. We ate a lot."

"True." Bianca sighed. She watched her cousin, careful not to sound overly concerned. "Tired?"

Noni nodded. "Exhausted." She was so used to sleeping all day and eating small meals, and so she assumed that their outing had taken a lot out of her—not to mention the sweltering heat of the day. She sighed and reached out for Bianca's drink before taking a long sip. "Thanks for bringing me out," she said. "It was nice."

"Not a problem," Bianca replied, smiling. "I missed having my partner in crime!" She reached out, touching Noni's hand. "Hey, seriously though. I'm glad you're better. Even though you're not one-hundred percent yet, it's just good to be able to get you out of the house."

Noni smiled back, nodding slowly. "Thanks, Bee."

They headed home. Deidre had dinner prepared when they returned: roast chicken, mashed potatoes, greens and cornbread. Her Aunt insisted that she should eat, but Noni couldn't bring herself to take one bite. She spent the rest of the night in the living room on the couch watching old reruns of *I Love Lucy*. Eventually, Bianca came out to join her, curled up on the couch right beside her, never saying a word.

On the verge of sleep, Noni's mind wandered. She breathed in the scent of the pillows on the couch. They didn't smell of the fabric softeners that her Aunt used. In fact, they smelt of cigarettes, which her Aunt wasn't supposed to be smoking. She fell asleep inhaling the scent of tobacco.

Noni had the same dream that she'd been having for at least a week. She stood in the garden full of flowers underneath a sky full of clouds, anxiously waiting for rain, or the sun, for something, for anything.

This time, as she waited, she noticed that the flowers began to wilt. All at once, they shriveled up, lost all of their color, and withered away to nothing. As they died, Noni realized that she wasn't breathing. She grabbed at her chest and throat, fighting to take a breath. There was no air to breathe in. The flowers turned to dust and the ground turned black, dead and dry. She fell to her knees then, fingers digging into the ground as her lungs caved into themselves. Flames rose from the dirt like weeds, engulfing everything.

She was on fire. Every inch of her skin was burning. Through the crackling of the flames, she could swear she heard her mother, shrieking. This was the first night that Noni woke up screaming.

The scream scared Bianca awake, and sent her into a panic. She jumped away from Noni, who was in a frenzy, thrashing back and forth on the couch. With one arm and all the strength she could muster, she held Noni still and called her name repeatedly until she finally opened her eyes. "Nons—Noni are you awake?" she questioned frantically.

Noni felt the weight of Bianca's arm restraining her. She sat up quickly, pushing her hair out of her face, wiping the sweat from her forehead.

Cautiously, Bianca sat on the chair across from her, eyes wild and wide with confusion. "Noni," Bianca repeated. "are you listening?"

"I think I had a nightmare," Noni finally spoke, still trying to catch her breath. "I don't feel good," she announced.

Bianca took a deep breath. "Well you don't look good either."

Noni's skin felt like it was still on fire, and her stomach churned with every move she made. She pulled her knees up to her chest, resting her head atop them.

"Is it your head?" Bianca asked quickly. "Should I wake Ma up so she can call your doctor—"

"—No," Noni shot. "No. It was just my dream. And I haven't been feeling well since earlier." She stood up quickly, ignoring the head rush that followed. "I just need some water. Just some water."

Noni shuffled to the kitchen, tore open the refrigerator and pulled out a bottle of cold water. She ripped off the cap and threw it aside before turning the bottle upside down and emptying it of its contents. Once she was finished, she realized that Bianca had followed her to the kitchen and was standing in the doorway, leaning against the frame with her good shoulder.

"Was it about your parents?" Bianca asked quietly. "About the fire?"

Noni sighed, shaking her head. She hated to dig up those memories. "No," She spoke quickly. "It was weird. I don't know." She threw the plastic bottle into the recycling bin. "I don't want to talk about it."

Bianca nodded. "Okay." She backed out of the doorway, giving Noni enough space to walk out.

Wordlessly, Noni headed upstairs to her bedroom. Her body was still trembling and she felt completely out of sorts. When she got into bed, she tossed and turned all night, trying to shake the remnants of her strange dream. The overwhelming feeling of breathlessness shook her. It was almost as if she could still feel the weight in her chest, drowning her. She couldn't put a name to the feeling she'd experienced, but she could still feel it.

She thought that maybe it was because of the crash. Maybe her head was still so shaken up that it was causing the strange, recurring dreams. That had to be the reason.

The room was too quiet. Noni couldn't sleep; all she could do was lay there in bed and think. She didn't want to turn on the television, she didn't want to leave the bed, and so she lay there, still and silent. She lay there long enough to watch the sunrise. She was shaking even though she wasn't cold at all.

When Deidre came into her room that morning to check to see how she was feeling, Noni lied and told her Aunt that she was fine. She didn't tell her about the dream, nor about the tremors that still wracked her body. Minutes later, Bianca showed up at her door. She didn't speak, only brought in a bowl of oatmeal and a glass of milk, setting it down on Noni's nightstand. Noni pretended to be asleep.

The scent of the oatmeal filled up her room. Noni ended up shoveling it down just to get the smell out.

Suddenly, Bianca's words echoed in Noni's head. *Was it about your parents?*

Noni hadn't dreamt about her parents in ages. She tried her best not to think about them. Not because it hurt, but because there were just things that she couldn't remember. Important things. There were too many things she couldn't remember. There were too many things that didn't make sense anymore.

She couldn't remember the night they died. She only knew that there had been a fire. Noni had been very young, and she had been in the house, too, but she couldn't remember any parts of that night. She hadn't been harmed, but she saw doctors after the fire. She saw therapists after her parents died, neurologists to make sure that her brain hadn't been damaged by the smoke or by the fall from the window that she'd apparently taken. Nothing was wrong—she just couldn't remember. Some of her doctors said it was lacunar amnesia. Some of her doctors said it was just trauma.

After the crash when Noni found out that she couldn't remember a single detail about that day, it didn't come as a surprise to her. There was only disappointment.

When they finally got the family car back from the dealership, Noni and Bianca were more than ecstatic. Deidre told the girls that the car looked beyond repair when it'd been towed away. The mechanics must have worked magic to get the vehicle running again.

Nevertheless, on the day the car was returned, Deidre offered to take her girls out. Noni especially had been cooped up in the house for the last three days, and Bianca had an itch for adventure. She took them into the city, which was a bit of a hike from their modest town. They left the car in a parking garage and started their journey through the city.

"Where should we go first?" Deidre asked.

Bianca was the first to answer, raising her one good arm in the air. "Oh! I heard there was a new shoe store somewhere down here!" Bianca grinned devilishly.

Deidre touched her daughter's head lovingly and rolled her eyes. "Okay, baby—lead the way.

Bianca dragged her mother and cousin to Shoe Playground, a shop on the edge of 4th street. She rushed into the store, tearing through tennis shoes like a tornado. Noni had never, in her life, seen someone try on shoes that quickly. She and her Aunt Deidre followed behind Bianca dutifully, offering opinions when warranted and carrying boxes of shoes. Bianca left the store with at least three new pairs of shoes.

As they exited the store, Deidre tapped Noni on the shoulder and pointed across the street.

Noni looked. Through the glass windows, Noni could already see the white, empty canvasses and wooden easels. She grinned at her Aunt. "Good eye!" She clasped her hands together happily.

Deidre ruffled her hair. "Let's go."

The craft store, Morello's, was a new addition to the downtown area. In fact, the store wasn't even completely unpacked. However, the window display was enough for Noni. She walked directly into the aisle with painting supplies and found exactly what she wanted. Full canvasses, an array of paint, and a multitude of brushes. Noni traced lines on the blank canvas with her fingers, smiling to herself. She picked up a new pack of paintbrushes, two medium sized canvasses, and turned down the aisle with determination. Abruptly, she ran straight into another person, dropping the brushes and letting one of the canvasses slip through her hold. Swiftly, the woman caught the brushes with one hand and steadied the canvas in Noni's arms with the other.

"Oh! Thank you so much!" Noni exclaimed, gathering up the canvases in her arms. The woman smiled warmly, brown eyes meeting Noni's. The woman's black, wavy hair was pulled back into a tight ponytail. Her skin was brown and seemed to glow under the lights. Instantly, an overwhelming sense of nostalgia washed over Noni. She eyed the woman intently. "I'm sorry, do I know you from somewhere?"

The woman watched Noni, blinking slowly as she answered.

"No, I don't believe so." She answered, handing Noni the paintbrushes hurriedly. "Have a nice day, and be careful next time." She smiled, nodded, and shuffled past Noni as she quickly gaited down the aisle.

Noni secured the items in her arms before she walked away. She found her Aunt and Bianca admiring picture frames at the front of the shop.

"Ready?" Deidre asked.

Noni nodded, setting her things down on the counter. She went to pull her wallet from her pocket but her Aunt swatted it away.

"Aunt Dee!"

The woman shushed her. "Don't worry baby girl, I got it."

Noni, against her better judgement, did not protest.

They spent most of their day downtown. Deidre found a bookstore and bought an inhuman amount of trashy romance novels, Bianca found at least three new outfits, and Noni brought them all to the best burger joint they'd ever experienced. Still, as much as they ran around distracted by all of the attractions, Noni still couldn't shake the sense of nostalgia that had enveloped her at the craft store.

Once they got home, Noni went straight to her bedroom. She pulled her easel from the closet and set up one of the new canvasses. She carefully poured paint and got fresh water for all of her new bushes. She pulled her desk stool over to the easel and, with a relieved sigh, picked up a brush. Noni closed her eyes, and oddly enough the first thing she pictured was the face of the woman from the craft store. Noni dipped her brush into the brown paint and outstretched her hand toward the canvas. Suddenly, her hand began to shake. Noni lowered her hand for a moment and wiggled her fingers to shake off the nerves. The last time she'd painted anything had been for an art show at school. That'd been months ago—she was rusty. Noni picked up the brush and started again. Brown paint touched the canvas and splattered. Her hand shook violently. Noni dropped the brush and flexed her fingers, clenching her hand into a fist repeatedly. She tried one last time before giving up, but the result was the same. Maybe she was tired. Maybe it was her medication. She didn't know, but something was definitely wrong. Noni went over to her desk and picked up a pen. Opening an old notebook, she began to write down her name. Her handwriting was smooth until she wrote the last letter of her last name. Her hand trembled, causing the pen to skirt wildly across the page. Noni threw the pen and began massaging her hand with the other.

"Maybe it's just because of the crash. It'll go away," She told herself. Noni began packing away her supplies. Suddenly, her bedroom door swung open and her Aunt Deidre walked inside.

"Aren't you painting, baby girl?" Deidre asked.

Noni shook her head, forcing a smile. "No I...I can't right now."

"Why?"

Noni tightened the cap on the paint bottle hastily. "My hand, it's—I don't know, it keeps shaking. I think it's a side effect of my meds or because of the crash. I don't know. I think it'll go away."

"Honey, that doesn't sound good. Maybe we should go see Dr. Cohen."

"No," Noni protested quickly. "No more doctors. It'll be fine, Auntie. I swear."

Deidre didn't argue. "Okay. But if it gets any worse, you tell me. Noni Grace—you tell me if it gets worse."

"Yes ma'am."

Deidre left without another word. Noni stuffed all of her supplies to the back of the closet.

CHAPTER THREE

Days had passed in silence with no reply from Alexander Albright. Noni had spent more time waiting for the mail carrier than she'd like to admit. Every day she'd hear him slip letters into the mailbox, but none of them was what she was expecting. Bills, get-well cards, shady advertisements—none of it was what she wanted.

Bianca caught Noni one day, just waiting at the door. "Noni, this is pathetic."

Noni whipped around, glared at her cousin, and rolled her eyes. "Didn't ask for your two-cents."

"You never have to. *Anyway*, don't you have something better to do? Anything better? Better than waiting at the door for the postman? He's gonna get creeped out, sis."

Noni heaved an exasperated sigh. "Would you go?" she mumbled. "I really don't have time for this—"

A knock at the door startled them both.

Noni looked to Bianca. "You expecting a package or something?"

"No. Is Ma?"

Noni shrugged. She looked at the door, then to Bianca. Bianca shook her head. Noni walked up and stared through the peephole, but all she saw was a tan neck. Quickly, she unlocked the storm door. A tall, plainly dressed, brown-skinned man with a warm smile greeted her.

"Hi," she said. "Can I help you?"

"I'm looking for Noni Grace," he answered, speaking through the glass. He reached into his jeans' pocket and pulled out a folded up envelope. "I got her letter."

The envelope, Noni noted, had her handwriting on it.

"I'm Alex," he said.

Noni took a step back from the screen door. She couldn't believe her eyes. She couldn't believe what was happening. The man looked unsure of himself.

"Am I at the wrong address? I could've sworn—"

"Yes, this is the right house!" Bianca pushed past Noni and unlocked the screen door, opening it for their guest. "This is Noni—she's a little slow on the uptake."

When Alex laid eyes on Noni, a wide smile came across his lips. "Noni," He said her name, relieved. "You look well—may I come in?"

Noni nodded, smiling. She and Bianca both stepped back and let him inside. They marveled at the size of him; he had to be at *least* six feet tall. Noni noticed his hair after his height, the curliness of it, coarse and pulled back into a tight ponytail. He stood, shoulders squared, gazing at her from the doorway, and for a moment, Noni was almost afraid of him, of his presence, of his stance, which seemed to demand regard. But when he spoke, when he *smiled*, all the worry in the room disappeared, and Noni was overcome by a sense of ease.

"When I got your letter I was ecstatic. That was extremely kind of you; I'm glad you're okay."

Taking a deep breath, Noni shook her head and laughed a little. "It was kind of *you* to save my life." She laughed again as she watched him smile, taking in all of his unexpected glory. Dressed in nothing but faded jeans and a white t-shirt, there should have been nothing magnificent about him. But to Noni, even to Bianca, he was a hero, and he was glorious. The sight of him filled Noni's chest with joy.

"Come—" Bianca gestured. "Come, sit. I'll get you something to drink. I'm sure you're thirsty—it's awful hot outside."

The two girls led him into the living room. Bianca went to the kitchen to prepare drinks, but not before she called her mother down from her bedroom.

"I-I can't believe you're actually here, in my living room." Noni stumbled over her words, unable to control the shock racing through her body. "Thank you. Just...thank you."

"There's no need to thank me," he spoke. "You were in danger. It was my job to help you as much as I could."

"She has every need to thank you." Both Noni and Alex looked up to find Deidre standing in the doorway to the living room. She stepped forward and extended her hand to their guest. "Deidre Harris. It's an absolute pleasure to meet you."

"Alexander Albright—the pleasure is mine, Mrs. Harris." He beamed. "Thank you, all of you, for inviting me into your home."

"Have a seat Alexander, please." Deidre insists.

"Thank you, ma'am," he smiled again. "And Alex is fine, please."

Noni and Alex sat down together on the couch. Alex's eyes met Noni's.

"Your letter," he began. "It was amazing. Really, such a heartfelt message. Thank you." He told her. "I never expected such gratitude."

"You *saved* my *life*," Noni reiterated. "I had to thank you. Without you, I wouldn't be alive. I wouldn't even be here. You deserve every bit of thanks and more. I don't know how I'm ever going to repay you for that."

Alex shook his head quickly, staring directly into Noni's eyes as he spoke. "Life is priceless, Noni. There's no way you can repay me. As I said, I'm just glad that you're okay. Don't even think about trying to repay me," he insisted. "And you *are* okay, right?"

Noni nodded. "Right." She was okay and it was all thanks to him.

Bianca soon brought out a pitcher of ice-cold lemonade. She went back and brought four glasses on a tray. Deidre filled each glass and handed them out. Alex thanked her graciously, bowing his head to her as he did so. Deidre never seen such manners and so she smiled and thanked him for being so polite. She asked him many things, asked for him to tell them about himself, about where he'd come from, how he'd come across the accident on that day, and about how Noni's letter had brought him to their home.

Alex told them that he was nineteen years old and from New York. He said he came to Ohio for college with his sister. They attended Morrison University, both with full rides. On that day, Alex told them that he had been walking home from classes, heading toward the shuttle stop. When he'd seen the crash, he hadn't even hesitated before running toward the wreckage.

"The EMT hadn't arrived yet," he told them. "and I was worried that they wouldn't get there in time. The fire station was so far, and I knew that if someone didn't act, it would be too late. Knowing that, I went in and did my best to get you out, Noni, without doing too much damage. It took a while, you know, I had to be as careful as I could. I'm not a doctor and I didn't want to hurt you. But by the time I had you out, the firemen showed up with the jaws of life and were beginning to pry you," he motioned to Bianca "out of the car." He looked to Noni for a reaction.

Her eyes had glazed over, as if she were looking, searching for some semblance of a memory to grab hold of. But, as always, there was nothing.

"They took you away in the ambulance then, and I gave my name to the police." Alex glanced at Noni's Aunt and cousin and then looked back at her. "I was always hopeful that you'd live through it. And now here you are, alive and well!"

"Just a few scratches," Noni smiled. And lost memories. She couldn't keep track of her lost memories.

Alex drank his lemonade and Noni marveled at him. How could she have ever imagined that this person, the person who saved her life, would be sitting in her living room, drinking lemonade from a *Mickey Mouse* glass? That he would, despite his contagious smile, be so outstandingly ordinary? It wasn't as if she'd expected G.I. Joe to come through her doorway, guns blazing and muscles rippling. Alex, however, was not what she'd expected at all. A nineteen-year-old college student, who'd just happened to be walking to the bus stop on the right day at the right time, was all that he was.

"I just can't thank you enough," Bianca spoke. "For saving my cousin. She means the world to me, and I don't know what I'd do without her," she smiled. "Thank goodness the EMT showed up so ya didn't have to drag another body out of the car, eh?"

Alex chuckled, setting down his glass. "You sure have a way with words."

Bianca took the compliment with a smile.

Noni rolled her eyes and cut in, laughing anxiously. "Seriously though, what can we do for you? Anything, honestly?"

"There's nothing," Alex told her again. "Just knowing that I did some good by getting you out of that car is reward enough."

There was truly, truly no reward that Alex would accept. Noni, who was still in awe at this miracle of a person, chose to accept this fact, for the time being. He stayed for two glasses of slowly sipped lemonade. When he finally left their household, it was not before scrawling down his phone number and handing it to Noni, telling her to "call, if there is ever a reason." As she tucked the piece of scrap paper into the pocket of her denim shorts, she wondered if there would ever be a reason.

Noni heard the car from the living room. The sound of screeching brakes and rattling speakers couldn't be mistaken. She hollered for Bianca to come downstairs and hurriedly slipped on a pair of ratty tennis shoes. Bianca galloped down the stairs with Deidre trailing behind her, lecturing her about cleaning her room before she left the house. The lecture was useless. The words "clean room" would never appear in Bianca's vocabulary.

"Aunt Dee, it's a lost cause," Noni laughed, hugging Deidre after she got her shoes on. "You might as well let her get buried under a mountain of clothes. Maybe then she'll learn."

Bianca laughed mockingly as she walked out the door.

Deidre kissed Noni's forehead.

"Take care of your cousin, will you?"

"Always," Noni smiled.

Terrell waited outside, hanging out of the window of the driver's side.

"Hello, ladies!" he greeted the girls.

"Good afternoon, kids!" The three of them turned to find the girls' next door neighbor, Kathy, waving at them.

"Hi Miss Kathy!" Bianca and Noni spoke simultaneously. Bianca climbed into Terrell's back seat quickly. Noni walked over to the passenger's side and waved to Kathy before getting inside.

The old woman pointed to Terrell and grinned. "What a handsome boy!" she exclaimed.

Noni's face began to heat up and she just waved at her neighbor one last time.

Terrell doubled over the steering wheel, laughing so hard that his shoulders shook. As he pulled out of the driveway, he turned to Noni with an eyebrow raised and said in a faux-seductive voice, "Do you think I'm handsome? Hmm?"

Noni rolled her eyes. "No, you're the worst," she teased.

"It's okay, Noni—you can tell me I'm handsome."

"Another word and your face is going through the steering wheel."

Terrell zipped his lips. Noni resisted the urge to stick her head out of the window to cool her heated cheeks.

They were headed to the town square. Terrell heard about an art show happening that afternoon and had known that Noni would be interested. He had texted her that day, asking if she and Bianca wanted to go. Noni was beyond ecstatic. The last art exhibit she'd seen had been hosted by their high school, and it had been extremely lackluster. Noni was ready to see some real art. Most of the attending artists were local, and Noni was excited to see what their small town had to offer.

When they arrived, Terrell parked as close as he could so they wouldn't have to walk very far. The chatter and music could already be heard from the square.

"Hey," Bianca began, unraveling a piece of bubblegum. "maybe one day you can get your art in a thing like this, huh Nons?"

Noni smiled. "Yeah, maybe." She still hadn't told Bianca or her Aunt about the tremor in her hand. It hadn't happened lately, but it was still something that scared her. Noni wasn't sure when she'd be able to steady her hand enough to paint, but she could hope.

The square was jam-packed. There were booths upon booths, art stands, even people sitting on the ground showcasing their creations. Not only were there paintings, but there was also pottery, jewelry, woodwork, sculptures, and more. The amount of talent and art contained in their tiny town square was astronomical. The three of them didn't even know where to start. Bianca, naturally, wanted to go straight for the authentic jewelry. Terrell vowed to follow Noni wherever she went. Noni, who was not interested in jewelry at all, decided to visit the painters' booths first. They all promised to meet up at the fountain in the middle of the square within the hour.

The first painter she met was a surrealist. She was almost ninety years old, and all of the paintings she had displayed depicted different stages of her life. From her childhood to her retirement, she'd painted it all. Her style was similar to Salvador Dali, from what Noni could tell. She'd learned a great deal about Dali in school and could recognize his style almost anywhere. The artist confessed that he was one of her favorite painters.

The second tent Noni and Terrell visited belonged to a man who painted portraits for a living. He did caricatures as well and offered to paint one for Noni and Terrell. Initially, Noni declined, but Terrell immediately retracted her refusal. He hooked his arm around hers, sat her down on a stool, and told her to smile. She couldn't stop laughing though the whole ordeal. When they finally received their caricature, Noni was even laughing in the picture—little word bubbles with "Ha! Ha! Ha!" surrounded her huge head.

The third tent that they visited was unlike anything that Noni had ever seen. The art style was uncommon, completely unique. The artist had at least thirty framed paintings hanging inside of his tent, and none of them were small. The paintings depicted a place that looked like a different planet. There were two suns in the sky, in each painting, and the ground was red, like Mars. None of the people in his paintings had faces. They were all just silver, full of light.

"They're strange, I know."

Noni nearly gasped at the sound of the artist's voice behind her. She turned to see him. He was tall, muscular, and couldn't have been a day over thirty. When he smiled, his whole face lit up. His hazel eyes seemed to light up too.

"No," Noni replied, "Not strange—different—but not strange." She noticed that there were no price tags on the frames. "Not selling?"

The dark-skinned man laughed. "Selling. Letting people name their own prices." He shrugged. "I don't need the money—my art just needs to breathe." He smiled at her and outstretched his hand. "Sugen."

"Interesting name. I'm Noni—Noni Grace." She shook his hand. "I paint too—well, I try to. I'm nowhere as good as this," she laughed.

"Don't sell yourself short, Miss Grace. You have an artistic aura about you," He grinned. "Have you ever gotten to showcase your art?"

Noni shrugged. "A few art shows at my old high school, but nothing beyond that."

Sugen nodded, inhaling deeply. "Well, if you want to get better, you may want to get your art breathing."

Noni clenched her hand, flexing her fingers and ignoring the subtle tingling in her tendons. "Maybe you're right." She bought one of his paintings before she left the tent. It was medium sized, and she knew it would fit on the wall just above her headboard.

"You know," Terrell began as he walked alongside Noni, carrying their caricature, "If you love art so much, why don't you do that for a living?"

Noni shrugged. "Don't know if I'm good enough to make much of a living," she admitted. "Besides, I'm good at Science and Math too. I think anatomy is neat. I...think medicine is the right path for me. My mom was a nurse. She loved it."

"Yeah, but do *you* love it like you love art?" Terrell asked.

"I'm good at it," she pressed. "I don't have to stop painting. I can do both."

Terrell nodded. "Well one day, I'd like to come to an art show that *you* host," he grinned.

Noni shook her head, smiling. "Keep dreaming."

They met Bianca at the fountain a little bit past the hour. She lay across the rim, dangling a necklace above her face. It consisted of a pink crystal hanging from a thin chain. The crystal reflected the sun's rays in every direction.

"You like?" she asked Noni.

"It's beautiful." Noni sat down next to Bianca and Terrell followed suit. "I mean *really* beautiful."

"I think I'm going to give it to Mom." Bianca grinned. "I think it'll look better on her."

"I think she'll love it." Noni folded her legs up on the edge. "Get anything for yourself?"

"Some bracelets." Bianca answered. "Nothing like this though. What'd you get?"

"This kick-ass caricature!" Terrell exclaimed, showcasing the picture of he and Noni. Bianca broke out laughing when she saw it.

After she calmed down, Noni showed her the painting she'd bought. Bianca thought it was weird but complimented the colors. Noni herself couldn't get over the painting. Something about it drew her in. She couldn't wait to hang it in her room—it belonged with her.

CHAPTER FOUR

Life went on, uninterrupted. Noni resumed her job at the grocery store as a greeter—it was something to keep her busy. The crew she worked with kept life amusing.

Of course, Terrell was there, being the resident comedian. He was constantly cracking jokes, never doing work, and doing it wrong when he did it. There was Casey who spent more time in the bathroom fixing her makeup than she did working. Finally, there was Elijah, who was as quiet as a church mouse. He started working with them about three months prior. He never really spoke to anyone, just worked silently, doing mostly janitorial tasks. Noni stayed away from him; he had a bad habit of staring at her and it didn't sit well with her.

Several others worked that day; Noni greeted customers with Terrell at the front.

"Do you ever get a day off, Noni?" Terrell asked, feet planted, leaning against the cart basket that should've been grouped with the others. "I feel like you've been here every single day since you got out."

"Got nothing better to do," Noni replied. "It beats sitting at home doing nothing."

Terrell shook his head. "What I'd give to sit at home and do nothing," he sighed. "What kind of high school graduate are you, eh? No pre-college parties to go to? No wild road trips?" he joked.

Noni just shrugged. She'd already received multiple acceptance letters to colleges and she'd already chosen where she wanted to go. "I'm just going to enjoy being home while I can. I'm sure there are tons of parties in my future."

Terrell laughed, "Man, college was the place to be." He shook his head, smiling and staring off into the distance. Noni watched him reminiscing about his days in college. Terrell had gone to college for a year before coming back home. Noni had never asked him why. "Enjoy it while you can," he said.

Noni nodded. "I'm sure I will."

A crowd of customers strolled through the sliding doors. Noni put on a smile and waved to them. "Good morning and welcome to Michael's!" Noni greeted. "All dairy items are half off today!" Pretending to be excited about half-priced milk was hard work.

Noni organized coupon books while she waited for more customers to greet. Terrell stacked a few carts here and there. Casey came over and had him watch her register while she went for a bathroom break. When he returned, he continued his conversation with Noni about college.

He talked to her all about where she'd applied and planned to go. She told him all that she could. The college that Noni had chosen, Oak Brooke University in California, was about as far away from home as she could get. It was one of the top-ten nursing schools in the United States. She'd been accepted months prior to her graduation and— for the most part—was excited about leaving.

Terrell asked if Noni and Bianca were thinking of going to the same university together. Noni said that Bianca planned to stay closer to home. Noni, on the other hand, had bigger plans. As much as she loved her Aunt and cousin, she wanted out of Morrison. She'd spent her whole life there, shadowed by memories of loss. After her parents died, the shine of Morrison died out, leaving Noni to live out her days in the dark. As much as she loved Bianca and Deidre, she would never be able to shake the loss of her parents. This town and everything in it was a constant reminder, and Noni needed out. There was an entire world waiting for her, and more than enough time to make new memories in a place that didn't haunt her.

She needed out. She wanted to know what the world was really like.

They talked more, ignoring most of their duties. Terrell was so interested in Noni's life, more so than any other person she knew. He watched her intently as she spoke, taking in every word. He watched the way she smiled and touched her face when she talked about things that excited her, watched the way her eyes lit up when she mentioned Bianca and her Aunt. She was so lost in her story that she didn't know that his stare had gone from interest to deep intrigue.

"Hey Noni," Terrell began, "Is there something wrong with your eye?"

Taken aback by his question, Noni paused. Then, realizing that he was staring directly into her right eye, she laughed.

"No," she replied. "Nope, it's always been like that."

He referred to the splash of hazel in her right eye. Normally, it blended in and no one could see it, but in the light, the discoloration brightened.

"I've noticed it before. It just looks bigger."

Noni shrugged. "Maybe it's just the lighting. It's just a genetic flaw."

Terrell laughed shortly, shaking his head at the girl. "Just about the only flaw you have, huh?"

Noni took her lunch break—leftovers from last night's dinner. Half an hour was enough time for her to rest her legs and prepare for the next half of her shift.

After finishing lunch, she went back to greeting. It wasn't very eventful, but then it usually wasn't. A few old women stopped to talk to her about their half-off dairy, but that was the extent of the excitement.

Bianca left work before Noni but made her promise to come straight home after work to have a "Girls' Night," which usually included snacks and movies. Noni, who had picked up an extra half of a shift, promised Bianca that she would get home as soon as she was done. Noni didn't want to miss the shift; she'd almost had to beg her boss to let her stay longer. Seeing as how it hadn't been long since she'd returned to work, and her boss still treated her like a wounded bird, Noni wanted to prove that she was still capable of doing her job.

She stayed late into the evening, cleaned with the night crew, and made sure that all items were back in their appropriate sections. Customers had a knack for leaving things in the exact opposite place they'd found them. Noni couldn't count how many cans of peas she'd had to take out of the bread aisle.

Toward the end of cleaning, Noni got a call on her cell phone. It was Bianca. Noni answered the phone, unsurprised.

"Are you on your way?"

Noni rolled her eyes. "Still cleaning up. Give me an hour—I'll be there."

"An hour. Right. You won't be here by the time the streetlights come on."

"Yes, okay. You're holding me up."

"Noni—"

"Bye, Bee."

Noni hung up the phone. She tried to hurry while still paying enough attention to her tasks. When she went to start cleaning the back room, Terrell stopped her.

He told her that she'd done more than enough work for the day and that she should go home for the night. 'You work too hard, Noni' he told her.

Noni couldn't argue—she was beat. Throwing on her jacket, Noni prepared to leave. She left the store, waved to her coworkers, and walked out. She jogged clear down the street and stopped only once she'd reached the nearest bus stop, and she was out of breath when she got there. Seeing as how she still didn't feel fit to drive, and since Deidre had the car, Noni had started taking the city bus more often.

She waited only two minutes and was thankful that she'd made it in time. The bus was never late. She boarded. There were at least seven people on the bus, minus the driver, whom she greeted warmly before searching for a seat. Three teens sat in the very back of the bus, all talking and laughing loudly at something on one of their phones. A woman and her baby sat in the first row and she shushed lightly to get the child to sleep. An old man sat sleeping with his head tilted back, snoring through the hat that covered his face, and beside him sat a young man who didn't seem to be much older than Noni. His head was down, and he seemed to be sleeping too. Noni sat across from the mother and child.

The ride home, back to Noni's side of town, took only twenty minutes. When Noni left the bus, a few of the passengers left with her. She began walking down the street. Her house was only a ten-minute walk from the stop. It was dark and late, and Noni really wished she would've told Bianca to meet her at the stop. She kept along. The sound of footsteps echoed in the night. The thought of movies and snacks kept her hopeful for a quick walk.

Halfway down the street, Noni noticed that there was still someone behind her. She glanced back and saw that it was the young man from the bus. His head was still down and he was at least fifteen feet back. She faced forward and kept walking. She supposed he must live somewhere close.

Passing the abandoned apartment buildings and old diners, Noni noticed—after some time—that the man was still following her. Taking a deep breath, she quickened her pace. Her pulse sped up; she was nervous but she didn't know why. She'd walked home from the bus stop countless times and had never felt this way. But tonight, there was something eerie astir.

The man quickened his step.

Noni panicked. She wouldn't look back. No. Her legs started moving faster than ever.

Behind her she could hear his swift footsteps. Noni was no runner and had no track or cross-country in her past, but she ran as fast as she could. He was closing the gap. Gaining on her. She heard the rustling of his clothing. She tasted the sweat falling from her brow. The wind whipped at her skin, deafened her ears, cut at her eyes.

He grabbed her backpack first.

She tried to wrestle her way out of it, but he pushed her harshly and dragged her into the alleyway between the decrepit apartment buildings. Noni could taste her own tears.

She fought. "Who are you?!" she yelled. But before she could say another word, her breath left her.

The man brandished a knife, held it against the skin of her throat. "Scream again and I *will* use this."

She couldn't see his eyes, only the shape of his mouth and, from it, she smelled the foul stench of his breath.

Noni didn't move. Didn't breathe. Didn't speak.

In a split second, she raised her leg and aimed right between his. The man caught her knee with the palm of his free hand. He clenched the hand in which he held the knife, only to rear back and strike her, a punch that sent her head bouncing off the wall behind her. He took Noni by the shoulders, and slammed her against the bricks. She heard herself scream, felt the sickening crack of her skull against the brick; her eyes crossed and her vision blurred.

She hit the ground. Tasted the dirt and gravel in her mouth. Though she tried to sit up, her arms were too weak. Noni gave up, laid there in the filthy alley and awaited whatever was to come. She felt him approaching and shut her eyes.

He stopped, mid-stride.

A light, brighter than any Noni had ever seen, illuminated the sky. As she opened her eyes, she had to squint just to see. Headlights? She couldn't be sure. Nevertheless, her captor seemed to cower and shrink as it washed over him.

Another man stepped out of the light and toward Noni's attacker. She couldn't see his face, but his shadow was intimidating.

The two men exchanged no words, but tension was thick and heavy in the air between them. Neither of them made a move. Noni's vision blurred, but she was awake long enough to see two things: first, the defeat of her attacker.

The second man charged at him, grabbed him by his neck and lifted him into the air. He flung him onto the ground—limbs flailing, his body crashed into the ground.

Her savior's voice echoed and reverberated throughout the alley. "Leave this place."

Noni heard her attacker's weapon clatter to the ground. Through her spotted vision, she watched him run off into the darkness and disappear as if he never existed. Through the haze, she could not understand how a man could disappear like that. Noni groaned aloud, trying and failing at turning over. Her savior stepped over the knife and came to kneel beside her.

The last thing that Noni saw surprised her most. Before her eyes fell shut and her body went limp, she realized that she knew this man. And she spoke his name.

The last thing that she saw was Alexander's face.

"Noni—Noni, are you awake?"

She woke slower than she would've liked to a hand on her shoulder and a cold towel on her forehead. The stifling air suffocated her; Noni could taste the sweat on her lips.

His face was the first thing she saw, and she almost screamed. She shot up, confining herself to a solitary corner of the couch she lay on. No longer were they in the dark, filthy alley. Noni lay on a white sofa, a loveseat the length of her body. She clawed the fabric with her fingers just to keep herself steady. "Where are we?"

"I'm sorry to have startled you—this is my sister's apartment. Do you remember me?"

"Of course I remember you. I'm not that—" she stopped. "My

head." Reaching back, Noni ran her fingers along her skull, feeling for pain and tender spots. She found nothing.

"What about your head?"

"What happened? I know I heard something. I know I *felt* something break."

Alex moved toward Noni and she jumped back immediately, moving like a caged animal, skittish and terrified. Alex held his hands up in surrender, standing from the wooden chair beside the loveseat Noni lay on. He took a few steps back, giving Noni space to breathe.

"You're okay, really," he assured her. "I know that you must be very startled, and I do apologize for that. But you're safe. You've only been out for about half an hour—you're fine."

Noni reached up and gently removed the wet cloth from her forehead. She never took her eyes off Alex. " Thank you. Again," she spoke. "You really have a knack for saving me, or something."

"I think I just have a knack for being in the right place at the right time." Alex smiled softly. He reached out for the cloth that Noni held and she quickly handed it over. "Sorry about the heat. Thought this'd help." Carefully, he folded the cloth and set it down on the small coffee table behind him. "This apartment is only a few blocks from your house. My sister just moved in a few weeks ago. Our old place was too small for her I guess."

"Far too small, actually."

Noni looked up then to see a woman standing behind the sofa. She had long black hair, brown skin just like Alex's, and a smile that rivaled his. In her hands, she held a glass filled to the brim with ice water.

"I'm Ileana, Alex's sister," she introduced herself. "You must be thirsty—here." Ileana handed the glass to Noni, and she gratefully received it.

"Thanks. I'm Noni, but you probably knew that already, huh?"

Ileana nodded. "Oh yes. I'm familiar with my brother's heroic escapades."

Noni almost laughed. She hastily drank the water, gulped it down without even taking a breath. She watched Ileana as she walked out from behind the couch and stood next to Alex, who had finally taken his seat again.

"I'm so sorry about what happened, Noni," Alex said. "I know you must have been terrified, having a stranger attack you like that."

"I called the police as soon as Alex brought you here." Ileana chimed in. "Hopefully they'll catch that man before the night is out. Things like this happen far too often, and the perpetrators need to be punished, sorely."

"Thank you," Noni replied. She took a deep breath, closed her eyes, and tried to forget what had happened. It wasn't as hard as she thought it would be. The events of the night were foggy. She could only recall bits and pieces of what happened: running away from the man, the knife against her throat, being slammed against the brick wall. Then Alex showed up. He showed up and saved her just like before. And the man who attacked her had disappeared. Noni was sure that she'd hallucinated his disappearance. She remembered him vanishing, but with the way that her head had been injured, from the crash and from tonight, she was sure that she'd blacked out before he ran away.

"Is there something wrong, Noni?" Alex asked.

"Would you like something more to drink?" Ileana inquired. "Anything you need."

"Thanks, but I'm fine," Noni told them. "Could I have a minute alone to make a phone call? I need to let my family know I'm okay."

"Absolutely, of course," Ileana answered. They stood in unison.

"We'll just be in the other room. Shout if you need anything." Alex said.

Noni quickly nodded. "Sure. Thanks."

Once the two of them were out of the room, Noni could breathe easier. She noticed that her knapsack was lying on the carpet beside the sofa. She reached into the side pocket, grabbing her cell phone.

Nine missed calls and seven texts, all from Bianca. Quickly, she called her cousin. The phone only rang once before Bianca picked up, frantic as ever.

"Noni?! Where are you?" She exclaimed. "I've been worried sick! I called work and they said you left hours ago!"

"I know, I know. I'm fine. I promise." She took a deep breath before she spoke. "I was on my way home from the bus stop, and I was—well, I was attacked. He didn't take anything." She left out the part about the knife. She didn't need Bianca to freak out even more.

"*Attacked*? Oh my God Noni. Did he hurt you? Do you want me to call the police? Where are you now??"

"He hit me but nothing hurts, I feel fine. They already called the police and I'm…well it's all really complicated. I'm with Alex. At his sister's apartment."

Silence filled the line. Noni awaited the well-deserved outburst.

"How the hell—what?" Bianca paused. "Alex. As in Alexander? As in the same bizarro strongman that saved your friggin' life already—*what?*"

"He was in the right place at the right time. Again. Which is weird but I'm willing to overlook it because, hey, I'm alive."

"Point taken," Bianca sighed heavily. "I'm glad that you're okay, and safe. Are you *sure* you're not hurt?"

Noni's mind flew back to the blows she'd taken during the attack: a fist to the face, head slammed against a brick wall. But she felt no pain. Nothing was sore, nothing bleeding; she didn't even have as much as a headache. "I'm sure."

"Okay."

Noni could hear the worry in Bianca's voice. She was more concerned than even Noni herself, surprisingly.

"Mom still has the car. I can walk to wherever you are—I'll come get you."

"No, I don't want you walking alone. It's not safe." She glanced back at the kitchen, where she saw Alex and Ileana talking. "I'll be fine; I'll have Alex bring me home."

"Okay," Bianca responded. She didn't sound pleased. "I'll call Ma and have her come straight home. Hurry, okay?"

"Alright."

She hung up. Noni slipped the phone into her knapsack again. Tiredly, she ran her fingers over her hair, pushing the curls from her face as she sighed. She stood up and walked quietly through to the kitchen where Alex and Ileana were still deep in conversation.

But once they heard her approaching, the talk ended immediately and Alex spoke.

"You okay?" he asked.

Noni nodded. "Would you mind taking me home?" She questioned. "It's getting late and my family's worried."

"Of course, I wouldn't let you leave alone," Alex told her. "A short drive and you'll be home."

Noni smiled graciously. "Thanks a lot."

"Is there anything else I can get you before you go, Noni? Anything at all?" Ileana asked.

Noni shook her head. "No, but thank you. For your hospitality, and for being so concerned. You're very kind."

"It's the least I could do."

Noni gathered up her things—jacket and knapsack—before leaving with Alex.

Though the distance from Ileana's apartment to Noni's home was short, neither Noni nor Alex was comfortable with walking that night. He drove her home.

On the way to her house, Noni was able to breathe again. Although she was still very much shaken by the attack, she hid it well. Nevertheless, she felt safe with Alex. She looked over to him, her second-time savoir, and smiled. "Thanks again. For everything," she told him. "I still don't understand how you manage to keep saving me like this, but I'm beyond grateful."

"I don't understand it myself, but I'm glad that I could help you more than once," he replied.

Noni smiled and shook her head. "We can't keep meeting like this, you know. One day it's gotta be something normal. A movie. Ice cream. Something non-life threatening."

Alex couldn't help but laugh. He nodded as they came upon Noni's street. "Yes, something normal would be nice," he grinned. "Please, let me know when you'd like to do normal things." They wheeled into the driveway, and Alex stopped as close as he could to the house.

Noni could already see Bianca waiting in the doorway. She glanced back at Alex. "I will," she promised. "Thanks again, Alex."

"Everything looks fine to me."

Noni, her doctor, and Deidre looked over Noni's X-rays. Deidre had insisted that, after hearing everything that'd happened, Noni should see her doctor about her head.

"That's a relief," Deidre sighed.

Dr. Cohen nodded. "Yes," she smiled. "That head of yours is fragile, you know?"

Noni managed a polite laugh. Her eyes ran over the X-rays, repeatedly, searching for some sign of injury. She supposed that if there were anything wrong with her skull though, she would've landed herself in the hospital the night of the attack.

"Even though nothing's wrong, I'm still glad that you came in," Dr. Cohen told Noni. "It's good to know that everything is as it should be. If anything were wrong, we'd have caught it here."

Noni just nodded. Deidre thanked Dr. Cohen and they began to talk about future appointments that Noni may need, just to make sure she stayed alive, awake, and healthy. Noni, still perturbed about the whole ordeal, tuned most of it out. Here and there, Dr. Cohen asked her questions, clarified things for her, but Noni didn't do much talking or even listening. Lost in her own thoughts, she sat quietly.

She was awarded two days off work to recover from the attack. Though she had no physical scars, the memory of it was enough to deserve a rest.

Noni tried to think of all the good things instead of focusing on the bad and the fear. She still had a job, thanks to her boss, who was beyond amazing and always understanding of her situation. Ileana, Alex's sister, had been more than helpful and had gone so far as to call Noni the next day to make sure that she was alright. Noni hadn't heard from Alex, but she had a feeling that he may have had something to do with that phone call. Things weren't as bad as they could be—she'd escaped an attack with all of her possessions and her life as well. Everything could have gone much differently, but it hadn't, and that in itself was a blessing.

"Thank you, Dr. Cohen." Deidre spoke as they left the doctor's office.

Noni smiled and waved. "See you next month."

Dr. Cohen returned the gesture. "Be safe, Noni."

Noni could only hope that she would be safe from there on out.

They left the doctor's office and went straight home. Deidre had taken leave from work for half the day and in a few hours would have to return. Noni could never express her admiration for her Aunt; the woman worked almost fifty hours a week at a job that didn't pay nearly enough. She worked to support the entire household without a complaint. She hadn't always been alone. Her husband, Bianca's father, died almost eight years ago. Before his death, Deidre had been a stay-at-home mom. Her husband had a good enough job that she didn't have to work. However, once he got sick, all of that money went into paying for hospital care. Cancer, as it turns out, is an expensive disease.

After his death, Deidre was forced to pay off the rest of the hospital bills, funeral costs, and to find a job to support the family. For a while, she had two jobs. However, once Noni and Bianca were old enough to work on their own, she was able to quit one. Deidre was a hard-working woman; she did what she had to in order to make sure that she and her girls were always taken care of.

Once she and Noni returned home, Deidre nearly collapsed on the living room couch in exhaustion. Noni was on her way to her bedroom when the woman called out to her. "Noni? Did you take this out?"

"Take what out?" Noni walked back into the living room. In her hands, her Aunt held an album. A photo album. It was extremely old, leather bound, with dust around the edges. Noni stepped forward, sat down on the couch with her Aunt. "I didn't." She responded. She wouldn't have done that. Bianca must've; she probably wouldn't admit to it, though.

Deidre opened the album and examined the first picture. Her hands graced the faces of her sister and brother-in-law. Noni's parents.

Noni's eyes glanced over the faces in the picture. Her mother and father stood in front of their old house. Her father's arm was wrapped around her mother's shoulders and they smiled brilliantly, proud of their accomplishment: their first house. They were happy.

"This picture was taken before you were born." Deidre spoke. "Your mother might've even been pregnant with you." She smiled thoughtfully. "I haven't seen these in years."

"I don't take them out much," Noni admitted. She remembered things about her parents—bits and pieces—but couldn't recall a lot of things—things like her mother's touch and her father's voice, had all been lost to her faulty memory. When they passed, she had been only seven years old. Pictures were all that she had left. Almost twelve years passed since her parents' death. When she was younger, she dreamt of the fire that swallowed their home.

She was young when her parents died, but Noni remembered. She remembered her father's screams. She remembered her mother's tears and the scent of burning flesh. She remembered climbing out of the second story window on a sheet while her mother held the opposite end. Noni's mother had promised she'd come down right after her.

She'd promised that she would get Noni's father and come down right after.

The fire swallowed them whole; it swallowed everything.

They never came downstairs.

Grief welled up in her throat. Moments. Noni could remember moments. All the beautiful moments that she'd spent with her parents and even the moments that hurt. Though the small details were lost to her, she could still see the flashes, and their faces— faces that never left her memory.

She pushed it down. It hurt to remember. She swallowed it all. All of the grief. It was hard enough to live day by day, haunted by the things she *could* remember. "Auntie, I'm going to head upstairs now." She announced.

Deidre looked up from the photo album and smiled at her niece. "It's alright to be sad, Noni," she said. "It hurts—that won't ever go away. We just learn to live with it after a while. But it's okay for it to hurt sometimes."

Noni spoke no more, only nodded as her Aunt finished speaking. If Bianca were here, it'd be easier. She'd quietly crack a joke about how she didn't even believe in heaven and Noni would just listen to her humorous rants. But Bianca was at work and Noni was alone, alone to wonder what kind of benevolent God would take her parents at such a young age, leaving their daughter to grow up without them.

In her room she sat, away from her Aunt and the pictures that would haunt her for the rest of the night. Unfortunately, she couldn't escape the thoughts. Or the grief. But she could try.

"Are you sure you don't want to come with me, Nons?"

Noni watched as Bianca ransacked Noni's closet, tearing out item after item and haphazardly tossing them across the room. She always had trouble finding things to wear. She was headed to the music festival; the city held it every year, and Bianca went every year. More often than not, Noni would accompany her.

"Nah," Noni replied. "I don't really feel like it." she lay back onto her bed and sighed. "Wouldn't mind getting out of the house, but there's going to be way too much going on there."

"So go do something!"

"Nothing to do." Noni replied.

Bianca rolled her eyes and turned to her cousin, red shorts in hand. "Well, I'll have my cellphone on me. So if you get too bored, I'll come back and get you or something," she replied.

Noni, who had changed back into her pajamas after her doctor's appointment, just laughed. "Sure, sure."

Bianca changed clothes and began searching for jewelry on Noni's dresser. She picked up a pair of earrings and traded them for the ones she was already wearing. While she did this, her eyes grazed the dresser's surface, stopping when she found a folded up piece of paper. She picked it up, unbeknownst to Noni, opened it and read what was written inside. Grinning furiously, she turned to Noni with the piece of scrap paper in hand.

She cleared her throat. "Have you called him yet?"

Noni sat up from the bed, eyes squinted to see what Bianca held. Once she realized what it was, she rolled her eyes and lay back down. "Nope."

"Why not?"

"Because every time he's around, something bad happens!"

Bianca couldn't help but laugh. "What, you think he's bad luck or something?"

Noni shrugged. "Maybe."

Bianca walked over and sat down on the bed, throwing the paper in Noni's direction. "First of all, luck doesn't exist. Second of all, you should be thankful that *he* exists."

"I am thankful. I am."

Bianca nodded. "He seems really nice."

Noni smiled softly. "He is. Extremely nice and polite too. It's unreal." She recalled the last conversation they'd had in his car when

he'd brought her home. The thought of it brought an even wider smile to her face.

"Maybe you should give him a call, huh?"

Noni lay there, shrugged a bit. "Maybe."

Bianca ruffled Noni's curls before jumping up from the bed. "I could always still come pick you up for the festival. Let me know what you do!"

When Bianca finally left, Noni found herself alone with her thoughts again. She held the paper Alex had given her, staring at the ten digits that he'd hastily scrawled down. She remembered what he'd said to her. *Please, let me know when you'd like to do normal things.* She remembered that she told him she would. Noni wondered if it was the right time, if there was any such thing as a "right time." She had agreed, wholeheartedly, that she would see him outside of him saving her life.

Currently, her life was in no imminent danger. Her cellphone sat on the table next to her bed. She picked it up and dialed the ten digits, waiting anxiously. Standing from her bed, she paced around her bedroom as the phone rang. One ring after another. She considered hanging up. Hanging up and pretending as if she'd never called in the first place.

The line clicked. "Hello?"

Noni had to breathe before she replied. "Alex. Hi—hey, it's Noni."

"Noni," she could hear the smile in his voice, "I thought you'd never call! Are you well? Better?"

"Yeah, I'm all good. Went to the doctor and everything checked out."

"Fantastic. That is so good to hear!" he rejoiced.

Noni smiled at his elation. "Yeah, I guess it is." She paused, collecting herself before her proposal. "So I was calling about what we talked about the other night. And I was wondering if you'd like to do, you know, normal things. Things that don't involve me being in mortal danger. Normal stuff. Fun stuff," she rambled.

Alex laughed; the sound of it brought a foreign heat to Noni's face. "Yes, absolutely, of course," he replied. "What did you have in mind?"

"Oh nothing, exactly. I don't know I-I was just calling on a whim, honestly. No planning went into this. Literally none."

He laughed again, a light chuckle. "Well, it's very warm out today. How about we go for ice cream? Something simple. Normal, right?"

Noni smiled. "Right."

CHAPTER FIVE

His favorite flavor of ice cream was pistachio. He stacked four scoops inside a waffle cone that was bigger than Noni's head. She marveled at his appetite. He was totally and completely enamored with the taste of the treat in hand, like he'd never tasted something so amazing in his life.

He bought Noni a double scoop of strawberry and vanilla ice cream. Noni, spoon and cup of ice cream in hand, followed him out of the ice cream shop and out to one of the small tables. Together they sat and enjoyed their ice cream in the midst of the blistering heat.

"You know, I could never find pistachio ice cream this good back home," he sighed, staring longingly at his treat. "This is a day to behold."

"I wish I enjoyed everything as much as you're enjoying this," Noni laughed, shaking her head as she watched him.

Alex grinned. "Sorry about that; I'm easily pleased. It's the small things that get me."

"S'alright," Noni returned, adjusting her sunglasses. "You're not high maintenance—it's admirable." She swiped a corner of her ice cream with her spoon, tasted the sweet mixture of strawberry and vanilla, and sighed happily. "This was definitely a good idea."

"Agreed," Alex replied. "I'm happy you finally decided to call."

Noni ate more. "Me too." She accomplished smiling with a mouth full of ice cream.

"So where's your cousin? I assume you two must spend a lot of time together."

Noni nodded. "We do," she started, "but Bianca is way more of a people person than I am. She's down at the festival with some of her friends. She invited me, but I decided not to go."

"Understandable." Alex took another bite of his ice cream. "I've always found festivals to be very entertaining for a short time, and then extremely overwhelming."

"Couldn't agree more," Noni responded. "How's Ileana?"

"Good." Alex answered. "When she heard that you called, she was quite excited. She really likes you!"

"She's sweet," Noni smiled. "You both are."

"Thank you," he grinned. "So tell me about yourself. We haven't really had a chance for normal conversation," he joked. "What do you do?"

"Mostly I just work," Noni told him. "Bianca and I work at this grocery store on the west side of town. It's pretty small and the hours aren't amazing, but it's a job. I don't know. My senior year just ended and since I'm not focused on school or getting into a college anymore, I guess I just—don't really do much of anything. After the crash, things just sort of slowed down."

Alex watched her intently as she spoke, never taking his eyes off her for a second. "What did you do before it all happened?"

"School was my main priority. I was in Art Club. Used to cheerlead with Bee but it was never really my thing," she laughed. "I guess I didn't do a lot this year. I was so focused on college that I forgot about all the fun things!"

"Well what sort of fun things?" Alex questioned.

Noni sighed as she ate. She smiled. "I don't know. I used to dance. Used to read a *lot* more than I do now. Painting—I really miss painting. And movies; honestly, I could watch movies from sun up to sun down."

"Why don't you paint anymore?"

Noni looked down at her ice cream. "Time," she lied. "just don't have the time."

Alex nodded. "You should do more of the things you love. Work is important, but happiness is fleeting."

Noni glanced up at him, caught herself smiling at his words. "You're right," she spoke. "I'm having a lot of fun right now, just so you know. So thanks for that."

Alex smiled in response. "Me too."

Noni dug into her ice cream, savoring the taste and the few moments of silence. She looked up at Alex who was focused on his waffle cone, carefully biting around the edges so that it wouldn't fall apart. She could see the joy in his eyes as he ate; small things truly did excite him. When he caught her watching him he just smiled, laughed despite himself.

When she finished—way before he did—she started to ask him questions. What did he like to do? What was it like back home? What did he like most about Ohio?

Alex told her that his favorite thing to do was running. The sensation, he explained, of running, of feeling his heartbeat pound in his chest, the sound of his footsteps pounding in his ears, the adrenaline pumping through his veins, the sights, the smells, was incredible. "I didn't have a lot of time to run for leisure back home," he admitted, "but now, I run every day. It's magnificent."

Back home, Alex and his sister lived with their father. Their family was small, just the three of them—Alex's mom had died when he was young, too. He told Noni that his and Ileana's father suggested they come to school as a pair and stick together. Much like Noni and Bianca, Alex and Ileana were closer to one another than they were to any of their friends.

"What I like most about Ohio?" he mused. "First of all, there are many fewer people," he joked, causing Noni to laugh. "No, no but really. I like the people here. Especially in Morrison. They're very kind. And I like the atmosphere, the slowness of it all. It's very busy, where I'm from. Lots of noise and so much happens all the time. It's not like that here. I can think. I can breathe." He smiled. "Also, I'd never seen a cow in real life until I came here—they're such majestic animals."

At that, Noni nearly toppled over laughing. Alex almost looked confused.

Once they finished their treats, Alex suggested they take a walk around town together. Noni almost protested—the heat was unimaginable—but she was having such a good time, and she didn't want it to end. They walked together all the way to the park and through it. Alex seemed to be unaffected by the heat and sun, but Noni was thankful for the shade.

"So what's college actually like?" she asked him. "Do you like it so far?"

Alex shrugged. "It's alright," he told her. "Honestly, it's no harder than anything else."

"And you live with Ileana, not in the dorms?"

Alex nods. "A lot less expensive that way." He watched her while they walked. "It's great, really!"

"You make it sound so easy!" Noni laughed. "I'm just so nervous about it. I've been accepted into all the places I want to go. And I *do* want to go— can't wait to get out of here. But it's the leaving that scares me. Bianca, my Aunt...leaving them is going to be hard. But I'm sure you can understand that."

He nodded slowly. "It's tough," he admitted, "but I think you're strong enough to handle it. I can tell that you love them very much. You won't lose them by going away. If anything, your bond will grow stronger."

Noni smiled. "For only just having left home, you seem pretty well versed on the subject," she noted.

Alex shrugged. "I learn quickly, I guess."

They walked for a long time. Through the entire park, they made their way along the pathways. They strolled past birds squabbling over breadcrumbs, children playing on the merry-go-round and parents watching over them. Noni quietly realized that she had never done this before. As long as she'd lived in Morrison, she had never come here with anyone just to walk and talk. It was surreal how comfortable and safe she felt with Alex. She'd even felt this way the first time they'd met. Even then, she'd been overcome by a sense of comfort. It was as if they'd been friends this whole time. It wasn't hard to find things to talk about and when there was silence, it was welcome. He wasn't anything like anyone she'd ever met. So calm, down to earth, and wiser than any other person their age—it was hard to believe that he was just a college student.

When the sun set, the heat subsided. They were able to sit on the benches, underneath the setting sun, to rest for a while. Noni liked it when Alex talked; it gave her a chance to observe him even more. Other people's stories interested her. Like books, she catalogued them in her mind. These were the things she could always count on herself to remember, unlike other details of her own life, which had been lost within the faults of her mind. This, the lives of others, she could always remember.

"Am I talking too much? Please, stop me if I become boring."

Noni only shook her head. "Nope, not at all. I like listening," she said. "You're interesting. Plus, you've got this funny accent." She paused. "Which really isn't a New York accent at all, I noticed."

"Didn't live there my entire life," he confessed. "Alas, I am not an authentic New Yorker. You caught me."

She laughed at his comment before she could reply. "That's alright, no judgment." She giggled. "You know, you're really different—not like anyone I've ever met."

"I doubt that," Alex replied. "No one is ever really that different. I'm sure you've met someone just like me somewhere."

"Nah," Noni placed her hands in her lap as she looked up at him. "I'm sure you're one of a kind." Alex just smiled at her.

He took her home before the sun completely set. Noni was sure that Deidre would've had a heart attack had she come home any later. Since Noni's attack, she didn't want either of the girls out past dusk. Bianca would break this rule. Noni would not.

As Alex dropped her off, Noni told him that they would have to get together another time. He promised he would if she could promise to stay out of harm's way for at least a few days. Noni, laughing, crossed her fingers and promised that she would. Once out of the car and at her doorstep, she waved and watched him drive off.

Inside, Deidre was back home. The scent of dinner wafted through the warm air, making its way to the front of the house.

"I'm home!" Noni called to her Aunt as she took off her shoes at the door. She could hear Deidre rummaging through the kitchenware. She headed toward the kitchen. There, she found her Aunt kneeling in front of the open cabinets underneath the sink.

"What's for dinner?" Noni asked. The rich scent of fish baking in the oven rose to Noni's senses. "Salmon? Please say its salmon."

Deidre chuckled lightly, "Nothing, if I can't find my saucepan."

"Need any help?"

After finding the pan buried deep into the cabinet, Deidre stood and shook her head. "No sweetheart," she replied. "Call your cousin. It's getting dark."

Noni nodded. "Right."

She left the kitchen to call Bianca. Bianca answered after two rings and told Noni that she would be home late. Traffic was backed up because of the festival and the baseball game at the stadium downtown. Unsurprised, Noni told Deidre what to expect. Deidre put aside dinner specifically for Bianca and told Noni to eat while everything was still hot. Together, they shared dinner at the table. Deidre asked about Noni's day, knowing that she had been gone with Alex.

"It was nice," Noni told her, cutting her salmon into small squares as she talked. "We got ice cream, then walked around the park for a while. Talked a lot. About college and whatnot." She took a piece of the fish into her mouth. "He's an interesting guy. Really, really nice too. I had fun."

"That's good, Noni." Deidre answered. "I really did like that boy. Such good manners. Not like anyone Bianca's ever brought home."

Noni nearly choked on a fishbone. "First of all, I didn't really bring him *home*," she laughed, "but Bianca really *does* meet some weird people." Wiping her mouth with her napkin, Noni continued to laugh. "You're right though. He's almost scarily well-mannered. I don't think I know any guys our age who are like him."

"Well his mother raised him right, that one."

Noni agreed.

They finished dinner. Noni cleaned up all the plates and put the food away. Deidre—absolutely exhausted—went to bed early. She, unlike Noni, wasn't often awarded time off work and had to rise early in the morning. Noni made sure that the kitchen was spotless so that her Aunt wouldn't have to clean a thing. With the kitchen clean and food put away, Noni plopped down on the sofa in the living room and popped in the first DVD she could find. *Pretty in Pink* was on top of the DVD player and so she chose that. It was one of hers and Bianca's favorite movies, so she wasn't surprised that she found it lying about. Maybe if Bianca got home early enough, they could finish it together.

While she was waiting, Noni fell asleep. Try as she might to fight the exhaustion, her heavy eyelids won the battle. She snuggled up to the nearest pillow and buried the side of her face in it. The fabric, cool to the touch, helped her to stave off the heat and sleep. Her dreams were all but pleasant. Lately, they'd been fitful. She'd found herself waking up drenched in sweat with screams on the tip of her tongue more often than not. But that night, Noni dreamt of her parents.

She was a child. Her mother and father were running in front of her. Their legs were much longer than hers, and she could barely keep up with them. She reached out as far as she could, but they were always, always beyond her touch.

They headed for a tree.

In the middle of a field of high grass, the massive tree stood with not a leaf on a single branch. Her father reached it first, began to run around it with her mother. Noni chased behind them, her hands almost touching the burned, singed hem of her mother's white night gown. They laughed, full of joy, and reached back for her as they raced around the thick base of the tree. Noni, running as fast as she could, tripped over her own small feet, falling to her knees before them. The sound of their footsteps ceased.

When Noni looked up, they were gone. The only thing she could hear was the wind whipping past her face; it deafened her. Standing, Noni grabbed hold of the tree's base to help her up. It pulsated beneath her fingertips. Just like a heartbeat, the pulsation thudded rhythmically. One beat after another. The base shook with every pulse. Noni watched her hand shaking as it pulsed; she brought her right hand forward, warily touching the base. Rays of light exploded from beneath her hands, blinding her, burning her skin. Noni screamed.

A knock at the door roused her from her sleep.

Noni shot up, chest heaving up and down as she grabbed at her heart.

"Nons, open the door! I forgot my key!"

She heard Bianca calling from outside. Pausing the movie—which was nearing its end— Noni unsteadily stood up from the couch and walked to the front door. Her hands shook as she unlocked the door and opened it for her cousin. Once the door was open, she expected Bianca to burst in.

Bianca wasn't there.

"Bee?" Noni called out. She left the front door open and walked outside, barefoot into the grass. She searched around the bushes. "Bianca, this isn't funny. Come inside." Noni walked out further into the driveway and around the edge of the house. Still, there was no sight of the other girl. Suddenly, Noni felt a presence behind her. She turned, expecting to find her cousin.

It wasn't Bianca. A shadow of a person stood before her. Noni opened her mouth to scream but the figure grabbed hold of her throat before the sound could escape her. "I've been looking for you everywhere," it hissed.

Noni was lifted off her feet by her throat and then slammed into the ground within seconds, all the air knocked out of her lungs. The figure sat atop her, hands closed around her throat and smiled. Noni was losing air, her throat caved into itself. She reached up, tried to fight back, clawed and grabbed at its face. She couldn't breathe, but she would fight until the last bit of air left her. With both hands, Noni grabbed hold of the face of her attacker.

Her eyes closed.

No more air.

And that's when she felt it.

The burning beneath her fingertips.

An overwhelming heat came over her. Noni felt like her hands were on fire, felt it scorching her chest. Every breath fed the flame.

With her last bit of energy, Noni opened her eyes in time enough to watch the light leaving her hands, blinding herself and the shadow that attacked her. It screamed, a terrifying noise, released Noni's neck as it tried to fight at the light. Noni, too, could feel herself crying out. Afraid of her own hands, she thrashed back and forth in the grass, horrified. It was all she could do to crawl away, screaming.

It was then that she heard the voice, calming and soft. It quieted her screams as the light behind her hands subsided. Noni didn't know where it came from, if it was in her head or all around her. But she heard it clearly, and it sounded just like Alex.

Everything is fine, Noni.

She shook her head, tried to banish the sound of it. But it rang out just as well.

Everything is fine. Just close your eyes and all will be well.

Noni closed her eyes.

Thrust into the darkness of her own mind, Noni felt herself slipping away. It was like spiraling into sleep. Like fainting. Like falling.

"Noni? Noni wake up."

She opened her eyes.

Bianca hovered over her, smiling. "You fell asleep waiting for me! Aw!"

Noni's eyes scanned the living room. The movie still played in the background. She touched her neck, her collarbone, stared down at her shaking palms. She looked back at the TV. The movie had barely reached the middle.

"Noni—you okay?"

She looked up, her eyes meeting Bianca's. "Fine. I'm fine," she lied. "How long have you been here?"

"I just got here. That's why I woke you up. So you could, you know, sleep in your own bed instead of this old—"

"And I was right here when you came in? Asleep right here?"

"Yeah, I told you, I just got here."

"And you didn't forget your keys or anything?"

"Girl, what the hell's the matter with you? You're freaking me out."

"I'm sorry," Noni ran her fingers through her hair, trying to understand what she was feeling. Her heart kicked at her chest, beating her ribcage black and blue. She held a hand to her chest, tried to breathe. "I'm sorry I just—I just don't understand I...I don't understand."

Bianca gingerly touched Noni's forehead. Her hand came away drenched with sweat. "You've got a fever."

"Bad dream. It was a bad dream," Noni began to mumble. Bianca dismissed her words.

"You have a fever. Come on, let's get you up to bed. Come on."

Bianca all but dragged her cousin upstairs. She helped Noni into bed, brought her a cold towel to place on her neck to quell her sudden ailment. She brought her a glass of water and two ibuprofen pills, coaxing her into taking them. Noni, delirious with fever, just lay in bed and stared out the window in her bedroom. She heard the trees shaking, branches scraping the paneling of the house. The wind howled, deep and hollow. "Noni, you're scaring me." Bianca whispered, touching her cousin's shoulder lightly. "Should I get Ma?"

"I'm fine," Noni said. "I just had a *really* bad dream." *It was a dream, wasn't it?* Noni asked herself. She woke up just where she'd fallen asleep, curled up on the couch, in front of a movie she'd barely watched. "It was just a bad dream."

"Well your dreams have been getting worse lately."

Noni turned and watched Bianca, saw the guilty expression on her face.

"I hear you at night. I hear you wake up almost every night. Whether it's gasping or crying, I hear it. And I don't know what's going on but...ever since the crash it's gotten worse. I know you used to have nightmares when you were little but—"

"—It's not like back then," Noni shot. "I don't really feel like talking about it. I feel sick. Please."

Bianca gave up. "Okay," she replied. "Just call me if you need anything." She rose from Noni's bed, sighing. "I love you, Noni."

Noni closed her eyes and sighed. "I love you too, Bee."

Bianca left.

Noni, alone in her room left with nothing but her thoughts, kept her eyes closed and listened to the howl of the wind outside. The rustling of the trees sounded like claws, like animals outside her window. Despite what Noni told Bianca, these dreams *did* remind her of the night terrors she had as a child. She dreams of monsters, black like shadows, always surrounded by fire.

She wondered if it was the fever that made her hallucinate.

Her temperature would not subside.

Bianca told Noni that exercise was the cure to most sicknesses.

Noni, however, wasn't sick, despite what everyone else thought. That next morning before she left for work, Deidre checked her temperature: no sign of a fever. She made Noni take more ibuprofen and sent her back to bed. Unfortunately, Noni couldn't spend another minute in bed. After a sleepless night, she'd grown sore and tired of staring at her four bedroom walls. Bianca, who had the weekend off, suggested that Noni come with her for a run. Noni, who was not a runner by any means, agreed under one condition: the word "run" needed to be substituted with "brisk walk." Bianca settled.

They dressed for the activity. Bianca was an avid runner and had a plethora of exercise gear. Her doctor had even given her a brace to wear on her arm—which was almost completely healed—so that no more damage would come to it. Noni had to borrow multiple items from her; she at least wanted to look like she was serious about this.

The heat outside was as stifling as ever. Fortunately, Bianca was sane enough to suggest that they take the car to the park. It was too hot to consider running all the way there. Noni, knowing her stamina, probably wouldn't make it past the first half mile.

Once they arrived at the grounds, Bianca parked the car and they prepared for the run. Noni attached a bottle of water to the exercise belt that Bianca loaned her. When they began to run, all she could hear was the water sloshing around inside the plastic.

Bianca was a better runner by far. For the entirety of high school, Bianca had been on the cross-country team. She'd never been their best runner, but she was one of the valued team members. It was the only sport, besides cheerleading, that she'd ever stuck with. Deidre had been proud that she even did that—Bianca wasn't much of a team player. Noni, on the other hand, could never find a team on which she fit. She never tried cross country—or track—because running was never a desire of hers. Though she loved to swim, the swim team hadn't seemed right for her either. None of the other sports teams interested her; sports, as a whole, were not her place of expertise.

Bianca was the athletic one in the family; Noni preferred leisure above all else.

They jogged slowly, at a leisurely pace, for Noni's sake. The two girls didn't speak. Instead, they let the sound of their feet pounding against the grass be the noise between them. Noni was thankful for that. After the way she'd behaved last night, she was surprised that Bianca even asked her to come that morning. But Bianca was forgiving like that. She probably wouldn't ever bring up the ordeal; she'd forget about it—as she did most things—forgive, and move on. It was a gift that only she and her mother possessed; Noni would dwell on situations until she'd broken them down into the smallest of incidents. It was hard for her to move forward sometimes.

Noni gained a new appreciation for trees that day. The canopy above sheltered them from the sun's rays, which would normally have been beating down on their backs by now. Though the shade shielded their skin, the humidity still crawled up behind them, snaking into their lungs and filling them with hot, moist air. Sweat stuck to them, sticky like molasses. Their hair, dampened with the salty moisture, clung to the back of their necks, molded to their skin.

After ten minutes of steady jogging, both girls were drenched with sweat. Bianca still had it in her to keep going strong, but Noni was too tired to continue. Her lack of sleep and lack of exercise caught up to her, and she slowed down, falling behind Bianca. Bianca turned around, stopping to see to her cousin.

"It's fine," Noni told her. "Go ahead, I'll catch up. Promise."

Bianca didn't argue. "Okay. But you call me if you need me. Five minutes. Catch up."

"Path's right in front of me. I won't get lost; I'll be fine," Noni assured her.

Bianca nodded and began running again.

Noni, trembling fiercely as she stood, stumbled over to the nearest tree and fell down against it. Her chest was tight and heavy, and her shallow breathing didn't help her any. She wiped the sweat from her brow, raised her arms above her head so that the air could reach her lungs.

Letting her head fall against the tree, Noni stared up at the canopy above her. Shards of sunlight fell through the trees all around her. She reached out, let the sun hit her palm. It was warm against her skin. She folded her hands behind her head again and let her eyes close for just a second. She focused on her breathing. She brought a wave of calm to her chest. She kept her eyes closed until she could finally manage deep breaths.

"Noni?"

When Noni opened her eyes, she could only smile. "Alex!" she beamed. "What are you doing here?"

"Running—well I *was* running until I saw you here. You okay?"

"Yeah," she nodded. "I'm fine, I'm just a little out of breath. I was running with Bianca, but I let her go ahead."

"Never would've pegged you for a runner."

Noni shrugged, laughing despite herself. "I'm not," she admitted.

Alex reached out to take her hand. Noni carefully wrapped her hand around his and allowed him to pull her up from the ground where she sat. She brushed off her shorts, unhooked the water from the belt and took a long drink. When she did, she had to close her eyes and take a step back to lean against the tree again because of the sudden head-rush.

"You don't seem to be okay," Alex noted.

Noni shook her head. "Just tired. Didn't sleep much last night." She confessed.

"You must rest—you know that. You'll pass out running in the heat like this." He hooked his arm around hers. "Come on, I'll walk with you."

She cringed at the feeling of her sticky skin against his. "But I'm all sweaty."

Alex laughed aloud. "It doesn't bother me, trust me," he told her. "Besides, you'll need something to steady you. Let's go; I'm sure Bianca is worried about you."

Noni leaned against him, sighing deeply as they walked. She kept her eyes on the path ahead of her. "You know, you always seem to show up at just the right time."

Alex shrugged. "Coincidence, really. Who would've known I'd find you running in the park?"

"True. This isn't a normal occurrence." She drank more of her water. Some of it spilled against her chin. "I suppose I'm just trying to keep my mind off things."

"What sort of things?"

Noni stopped speaking for a while. She wondered if she should admit to all of what had happened. *No.* She thought. *He'd think I was crazy.* "Bad dreams," she finally spoke. "They've been keeping me awake at night. I'm not a stranger to nightmares but these have been the worst of them."

Alex didn't respond. He kept his eyes on the path before them.

Noni continued speaking. "Last night I had the most vivid dream, it was like...I could swear it actually happened. And I know lots of people say they have dreams like that but I could swear I was sleepwalking or something." She shrugged.

Alex was stiff as they walked together. He still didn't speak but his eyes began to scan the area around them rapidly.

Noni, perturbed by his behavior—and the silence—spoke more to fill in the gaps. "So anyway, Bianca thought it would be a good idea to come out and run with her this morning. And I guess it was; I'm honestly too tired to think about anything else—"

"—Noni." Alex stopped her. "I'm going to ask you to do something and you must not ask questions after." His voice was firm, demanding. This wasn't a request. This was an order.

"Alex what's the matter?"

"Get behind me. And when I tell you to run, *run*. And don't look back."

He swung around, one hand shoving Noni behind his back. He towered over her and she could hardly see what was in front of him.

Terrified, she cried out to him, "Alex! What's going on?"

A hollow voice spoke out. "So you've finally found her?"

This female voice was not one that Noni recognized. It sounded sinister, like the hissing of a snake. The sound of it made her body tremble, made her sweat and shake. She held tight to the back of Alex's shirt, clinging to him. When Alex spoke, she felt the boom of his voice reverberate through his chest. She felt it in hers.

"Leave this place." It was just like before. It was *just* like before. "Stay away from her."

"Well you didn't think you could hide her for *this* long, did you? She's in plain sight. Every day. It's a wonder she isn't dead yet." Noni trembled at the words; Alex couldn't shield her from that. She wished that it was a dream, but deep inside she knew that it was all too real. Whatever was happening, whatever had already happened, was all too real.

"Alex *please*," she whimpered, "please tell me what's going on."

"Well hello, Noni," The woman spoke. "So nice to finally meet *you*." Noni didn't look. She couldn't bring herself to look.

"Noni. Do what I told you," Alex ordered, "Run!"

Noni ran faster than she ever had in her life. Her feet beat against the grass, adrenaline burst into her veins, and her lungs expanded more and more with each terrified breath. She didn't look back. She had no idea who or what she was running from, but she never looked back. Heart racing, she sprinted down the pathway. But, even after having gotten away, from the corner of her eye she saw it; a bright flash of light, bursting in the air, breaking through the trees. With it came an enormous gust of wind, blowing branches off of the trees to which they were attached. She heard them crack and crash against the ground all around her. But she never looked back. She never stopped running.

And when she heard Alex's voice calling her name, she only ran faster.

Blinded by exhaustion, Noni stumbled through the park. She passed strangers who stared at her, eyes wide with confusion as she pushed past them. She searched for Bianca all over, trying to find her cousin just so they could make it out together.

In the distance, she saw the back of Bianca's red and white striped tank top. She ran alone; unaware of what had happened right behind her. "*Bianca!*" Noni yelled.

The other girl turned around quickly, stopping dead in her tracks.

Noni rushed up to her, falling all over herself as she grabbed hold of Bianca's shoulders. "We have to go," she struggled to breathe. "We have to get out of here. We have to go *now.*"

"What's wrong?"

"There's something—*someone*—after me. I know it. We just have to go. We have to keep running."

"Noni, you sound crazy!"

"I know what the hell I sound like but we need to go! Now!"

"Noni!" Both heads turned at the sound of Alex's voice. Noni hid behind Bianca, using her cousin as a shield as the man ran up to him. He stopped before them, hands raised in surrender. "Noni, you need to listen to me."

"You *know* those people," she accused. "How do you know them? And what just happened back there?!" she screamed. "Who the hell *are* you?!" Alex took a step forward and Noni took three backward. "Get away from me!"

Bianca outstretched her arms in front of Noni, watching Alex warily. "Look, I don't know what you did, but she's terrified and you seem to be the reason for it. Leave her alone."

"Noni," Alex began, stepping away from Bianca. "I know you're confused. I know this looks really bad, but I need you to know that you can trust me. I'm not one of them. You can trust me." He stared her dead in the eyes as he spoke. "Everything will be fine, Noni. You can trust me—you *have* to trust me."

The problem was that she knew she couldn't.

"Listen, Alex. You need to leave her alone." Bianca glanced around, seeing that there were people staring now. She moved closer to Noni, shielding Alex from her vision. "You're making a scene. Noni doesn't want to talk to you. Please just go."

Alex didn't argue. He stepped back. Solemnly, he nodded. "I'm sorry," he spoke directly to Noni, "for everything."

Together, they watched him walk away.

If it hadn't been for Bianca, Noni would've never been able to get away from Alex. How earnest he'd sounded; truth was in his mouth, but his eyes lied. As he spoke, as he begged and pleaded for Noni to trust him, his eyes were full of terror. What he was afraid of, Noni didn't know.

What he said and what he did didn't matter. What mattered was that he'd lied. He was afraid of something—he *knew* something—and he'd never said a word to her. He knew whoever it was that had come after her this time and if he knew them, that meant he knew those who had come before this. How was he connected to these people? Had everything he'd done been a game? Saving her from the man who'd attacked her in the alley, getting to know her, just so he could set her up? Noni wasn't sure what was real or fake. She was seeing things—hallucinating—and didn't know who or what to believe.

Night fell outside.

Noni sat alone in her bed with all the lights turned on around her. Bianca had been with her the whole time, to make sure she was okay. She left shortly to make a phone call.

Unsurprisingly, Noni still hadn't slept. She tried to draw for a while, to keep her mind occupied, but her hand shook too much for her to even draw something resembling a line. She gave up quickly.

As exhausted as she felt, as sore and as worn-out as her body was, she could not find peace enough to sleep. Sleeping would mean that her mind would have to rest. Sleeping would mean that her heart would stop jumping out of her chest every time she heard a sound. Sleeping would mean that she wouldn't be terrified to be alone. She wasn't sure when she would ever be able to rest. She couldn't tell Bianca the truth. The truth sounded insane. "I think I've been attacked more than once, and the guy who I thought I was becoming friends with, who kind of saved my life, is connected to it somehow" didn't sound convincing. When Bianca had asked her what happened, Noni held back. She simply said that Alex wasn't who she thought he was. It wasn't a total lie. He wasn't who she thought he was. She didn't know who he was, really. The two of them didn't tell Deidre what happened. Once they got home, they put on a good face. Deidre was too tired, too overworked, to notice the lies.

Alone in her bed, Noni curled up to her lilac-scented quilt. It was soft against her skin, comforting. She buried her face in it and breathed deeply, wanting to feel some sense of safety and comfort. Despite the heat in her room, Noni wrapped the quilt around her shoulders. She closed her eyes and lay back in her bed, trying to force herself into a calmer state. Bianca had yet to return from her own room, and that in itself made her even more nervous. Although she wouldn't talk to Bianca about what was going on, it was nice to have another person in the room.

Noni stood up from her bed. She went to Bianca's bedroom and found the door closed. She knocked twice and didn't get a response, so she opened the door and walked in. Sitting at her desk, phone in hand, Bianca lay asleep. Noni hadn't the heart to wake her. She quietly closed the door, shutting it tight before returning to her own room. She went back to her bed, wrapped herself in the comforter once more. She closed her eyes and focused on rest.

Her phone rang. Noni watched as it lit up and vibrated across her nightstand. She didn't need to look at the caller ID. She knew who it was. She let it ring at least eleven times before she picked up.

"Noni?" she heard his voice on the line. He sounded just as he did before. Terrified.

She didn't speak.

"Noni, I know you're there. Please say something."

"Who are those people?" she asked simply. "I know something's going on. I know you know them. And I want to know what you're keeping from me."

He didn't respond. Noni's anger rose.

"Are you some freaking psycho stalker or something?!" she hissed. "Because it's not a coincidence that you've been there both times I've been followed. And attacked. It's no coincidence that you always *happen* to get there just in time. I'm tired of being lied to. You either tell me or the police will be at your door tonight."

"It's not a coincidence, Noni," he finally answered. "Nothing ever is."

Noni sat silently, uncomfortably, in her bed. Her hands trembled as she held the phone.

"There are things happening around you that I can't yet explain. There are things that you don't know and I can't yet tell you. I don't want to put you in danger and I don't want to put your family in danger—"

"—I'm *already* in danger!" she argued. "I almost died in a car crash, I was attacked on the street, almost attacked in the park, and I'm pretty sure that someone came to my *house* and tried to *kill* me. So you better tell me what the hell is going on!"

For a moment, Alex was silent.

Noni's heavy breathing filled the line, confronted his silence. Her hands shook violently; she could feel her heart trying to beat its way out of her chest.

Alex finally spoke, his words slowly leaving his lips as he responded, "If I tell you, will you listen?"

Noni closed her eyes and prayed she wouldn't regret this. "Yes," she answered. "I'll listen if you tell me the truth."

"Okay," he said. "Please come outside."

"You're outside my *house?*"

"This is too pertinent of information for a phone call, Noni."

"So you knew I would agree to this."

"I assumed."

Noni took a deep breath. "Give me two minutes." She hung up the phone and set it on the nightstand. For a moment, she just sat there, staring down at her hands. She wondered if she was making the right decision. Clearly, Alex knew far more than he'd let on; he was up to something. He could be dangerous. She had no idea what would happen once she stepped outside the walls of her home. She considered waking Bianca, but something inside of her told her that this was something she would have to do alone.

She got out of bed. When her bare feet touched down on the floor, the wood creaked and cried out beneath them. She silently made her way down the hallway, stepping along the edge of the stairs so as not to make a sound. Neither Bianca nor Deidre stirred. Noni came to a stop at the front door, grabbed the doorknob and hesitated. Waves of doubt washed over her, covering her with fear and uncertainty. Her hand shook as she held the doorknob, and she closed her eyes, breathed deeply, and tried her best to keep calm. She unlocked the door and stepped outside into the night.

He was sitting at the bottom of the front steps. When he heard her come outside, he stood immediately and turned toward her.

Noni closed the door but stayed close to it. "Start talking."

Alex stood, tall and bold, just as he did the first day they met, the first day he showed up at her doorstep. He opened his mouth to speak but nothing came out. He seemed troubled, torn, and unsure of how to proceed. Noni didn't push, didn't prod, she only waited for him to say something because before the night was out, she wanted answers.

"Please take seriously all the things I am going to tell you." Alex took one slow step forward, trying his best not to intimidate the girl before him. "Do you believe that there's something else out there?"

The girl watched him warily, immediately thrown off by his question and his subsequent hand motion, arms encompassing everything around them. "I don't know?" She answered cautiously, "Like aliens, or something?"

Alex smiled nervously. "No. Not exactly." He spoke. "Not so much that as that there are things in this universe, beings, that can't exactly be explained."

"You're not making any sense." Noni folded her arms across her chest protectively. "I didn't come out here for an existential conversation—I came out here for you to tell me the truth about what you want with me—"

"—But I *am*," Alex cut in. "That is exactly what I am doing. Everything I mean to tell you will be extremely difficult for you to believe, and so I need you to be open. Open to everything. Or else none if it will matter."

Noni watched him—his eyes—and saw nothing but truth in them. And fear. She spoke again. "Okay, Alex. I can entertain the idea that humans aren't the only things out here. I mean I've read enough and watched enough to believe that we aren't alone."

Alex stepped toward her, up the stairs. He stopped two stairs below her. Still, he was as tall as she was, standing there. "I won't hide things from you anymore Noni; from here on out, I will be absolutely and completely truthful," he told her. Noni nodded.

"Okay," she said, "what's the truth, then?"

Alex took a deep breath and peered directly, deeply, into Noni's eyes. Then, as he spoke, chills ran up and down Noni's spine, cold and jarring. This was his truth. No more lies. "The truth, Noni, is that I'm not exactly from this place." He paused. "Or this Universe."

CHAPTER SIX

Noni stood unmoving at the top of the stairs. The wind howled behind her, eating the silence between them. She held her face between her hands, wide eyed, shaking her head before she spoke. "You're insane," she whispered. "You expect me to actually believe that? You expect me to believe you're some kind of alien?" she hissed. "There's no such thing—"

"—I'm not an alien."

Through the fear and disbelief, Noni conjured up a harsh laugh. "I can't believe you expect me to believe that you're *not from this universe*. How do you expect me to believe that?"

"Why would I lie about this?" Alex spoke softly. "Of all the things I could have made up to gain your trust, why would I say something as outlandish as this, were it not true?"

She folded her arms across her chest, stared at him with narrow eyes. "I don't know why you're trying to make your case here. You're obviously *crazy*."

Alex heaved a heavy sigh and started up the stairs toward Noni. She shuffled back toward the door, tried to open it fast enough but he was upon her before she could pull it. Alex stood before her and extended his hand. "Give me your hand."

"No." Noni backed herself up against the wall. "I'm not falling for whatever it is you have planned."

"I promise you, Noni. This is not a trick," Alex sighed. His body seemed to cave in as he spoke to her, in the softest, quietest voice he could muster. "Please just trust me this one last time. If you don't believe me after this, I'll never bother you again. You will never see me again."

Noni scanned him, looked him up and down, and watched for signs of deceit. She found none, and that terrified her.

Carefully, she lifted her hands. "Fine." Her palms hovered above his. "Where are we going?"

Alex shook his head. He gazed downward. "Nowhere. I'll show you everything, right here." He took her hand.

For a single second, Noni could swear that her heart stopped beating. A surge of electricity exploded her veins. She lost sight of Alex, of all that was in front of her. Her vision went dark; senses failed her and all she could feel was the hot energy flooding her.

Behind her closed eyes, she saw visions, glimpses of things she couldn't explain, memories that did not belong in her head. Everything was black, still, silent. For the longest time, nothing moved. Noni could feel the stillness in her chest. She couldn't even feel her heartbeat. Suddenly, streaks of light soared across the dark expanse. Noni felt herself jump, scared of what she had seen, and then seconds later, tens of hundreds of balls of energy soared past her once again. Orbs of light, of energy, that flew on their own. They never touched one another, just flew right alongside one another in the dark. They illuminated the darkness, and like shooting stars, they soared.

The vision shifted. Suddenly, there was only of a tree. Noni had seen this tree before. She saw it in her dreams. The massive, leafless tree that seemed dead but was filled with life. She remembered the pulsations, could see them shaking the tree at its base. She could feel the energy from where she saw it, just like a heartbeat, pulsing steadily. But it was different than it was before; the tree, on every branch where a leaf should have been, bred light, bred energy. The orbs poured from its branches, each birthed from the tree. Free from it, they ascended toward the sky.

The third and final vision appeared before her. Everything was covered in red. A dark-skinned man, unclothed, trudged along a wide, shadowy pathway, dragging his bare feet through puddles of blood. A light filled orb flew toward him, circling his head like a crown. He reached up and grabbed the orb, squeezing it in his palm. The light began to darken until it was black, dark, and sinister. The onyx glow illuminated his golden eyes.

Noni's eyes shot open. Her first breath was like the first drink of water after being stranded in a desert. She was on the ground, set against the door with her hand still in Alex's grip. She tore it away from him and stared at him as she tried to catch her breath.

"What was that?" She heaved. "What the hell was that?"

"The beginning," he told her, "of everything."

"How did you do that?" she asked. She examined her hand, turned it over again and again. "*How?*"

"I told you, Noni. I wasn't lying." Alex assured her, "I will never lie to you again."

Noni held her hand to her chest. "That tree—I've seen it before," she admitted, "In a dream. I—I've seen it in a dream. I've *felt* it."

Alex spoke slowly, picking his words carefully. "There are many names for it, but in much of your lore it is known as the Tree of Life. Some call it the Yggdrasil, and I've always been fond of that name." He tried to smile at her but Noni was clearly in no mood to see his smile. He leaned against the railing across from her. "It is the being from whence every universe originates."

"Oh my *God*," Noni groaned, grabbing at her face and chest. "Oh my God, this can't be real. This *can't* be happening."

"It's nothing to be afraid of, I promise."

"*Nothing to be afraid of?* I just found out that aliens are *real*. What's next? Vampires? Werewolves? Witches and Wizards?"

"Those are all myths. Humans are very creative creatures."

Noni held her head between both of her hands and released a long, painful groan.

Alex sighed softly and reached over to Noni, placing a hand on her shoulder. A small jolt of static traveled from his skin to hers, making her flinch. "You're going to be alright," he told her, giving her shoulder a quick squeeze. "I want you to know that you're going to be okay, because I am here to protect you."

Noni scoffed, shrugging his hand off her shoulder. "And what are you? My guardian angel?"

Alex managed to laugh. "Not quite." He stood slowly before reaching out for Noni's hand. "You need to rest," he said. "I've told you enough for today; I think it's more than you can handle right now." Reluctantly, Noni took his hand—static shock, again. He pulled her up into a standing position and then placed both hands on her shoulders as he spoke. The feel of his palms made her skin tingle uncontrollably.

"I know that you want more answers, and I will give them to you," he began, "But for now, rest—oh, and here," Alex reached into his pocket and pulled out a small necklace. A delicate, translucent orb hung from it. "This should keep your mind, and your dreams, safe."

"What is it?" Noni asked, taking it into her hands. She turned it over, examined it closely. It was so light; it was almost as if she held nothing.

Alex smiled "A gift from home, from my realm—Nova." He pointed to a small symbol engraved in the orb. "This symbol here—it means *peace* in my language." Noni's eyes shot up, curiosity filling her gaze. He wore an identical one around his neck. Alex shook his head. "Another time."

Alex watched as Noni gingerly placed the charm around her neck. She stared at it closely, thoughtfully, before letting it drop to her chest and looking up at him. "You'll sleep well tonight," he said.

She nodded silently, still touching the necklace.

"Whenever you feel ready to discuss everything, I'll be there," Alex told her.

Wordlessly clinging to the talisman around her neck, Noni watched him leave. Once he was out of sight, she returned to her bedroom, and climbed into bed before. Bianca was still sound asleep. So was Deidre. Noni quietly resumed her place underneath her blanket and closed her eyes. Her heart was heavy, chest and stomach like lead. Body trembling, she closed her eyes and focused on the dark behind them. She wrapped her shaking hands around the charm hanging from her neck and breathed deeply, slowly. After a while, her breathing smoothed out and the violent tremors of her body ceased. She found peace. Rest.

Noni never spoke of what happened that night. She knew that it was her duty to keep the secret. Besides, no one would believe her if she told them everything she knew. She'd be carted off to the nearest shrink.

The next day, she went to work as she normally would. She greeted customers at the door like normal, organized coupon books like normal, ate her lunch in the break room with Terrell like normal. Everything was as it should be.

"You look upset," Terrell noted, taking a bite from his sub. A tomato slipped out of it and plopped onto the wrapping on the table. "Bad day?"

Noni stirred her yogurt absentmindedly. She shrugged. "No," she replied. "Just a lot on my mind." An understatement. She spooned a bit of the yogurt into her mouth, not really paying attention as she ate. The break room was quieter than it'd ever been. The only sounds were of Terrell chewing and the static-ridden television playing the news in the corner. The news anchor's voice was distorted. The picture went in and out with the static. Noni stirred her yogurt.

"Noni, are you listening?"

"What?" She glanced at Terrell, who was staring at her, confused. "What did you say?"

"I asked what time your shift was over."

"Four," Noni answered. She ate her yogurt. "Four o'clock."

"Are you busy after work?" he inquired.

"No, I think I was just going to go home and—nothing. I was just going to go home and do nothing."

"Nothing sounds pretty boring," Terrell laughed. "Listen, I'm off at four too. Maybe—I mean, I thought I'd just ask for kicks but maybe—would you want to get pizza or something?"

His question hung in the air for quite some time.

"What?"

He could tell that Noni, wherever she was, wasn't really all there. "Pizza. You know, the round thing they cut into triangles. Sometimes squares. Food. Pizza."

Noni nearly smacked herself upside the head with her own hand. "Pizza," She repeated. "Yeah," she answered. "Yeah. That would be nice." She stuck her spoon into the cup of yogurt. "Don't let me forget though."

Terrell laughed as he finished his sub, picking up the tomatoes from the wrapper and eating them. He chewed with his mouth open. "Wouldn't dream of it." Terrell balled up the sandwich wrapper and tossed it in the trash on his way out. Noni uncapped her bottle of water and slowly sipped it in the silent room.

The door opened.

She turned and saw no one but Elijah walking in. He looked disheveled as usual, dressed in a baggy sweatshirt despite the summer weather. He said nothing when he saw her, only nodded, half-smiled, and shuffled toward the staff refrigerator. When he sat down at the table, he dropped his lunch and pulled a small bottle of pills from his pocket.

"Do you have a cold?" she asked.

Hands trembling, he shook his head and choked out a laugh.

"Not exactly," He responded. He swallowed the pills dry. "It's a long story." Noni tried to hide the curiosity in her eyes, but Elijah saw the spark before she could pretend not to care. "Sometimes, I see things that aren't really there. Things that don't make sense." He glanced up at Noni. She could see the dark circles under his eyes, a clear sign of sleeplessness. "I'm sure you can understand."

Noni stood immediately. "Bye, Elijah."

"Goodbye, Noni."

She tossed the rest of her lunch and hurriedly returned to her post. Today she greeted customers with Casey. When the blonde girl saw Noni return, she sighed. "Thank goodness you're back. This is so boring," She complained. "I can't see how you do this every day."

Noni laughed. "It beats cleaning or working register for six hours."

"This is true," Casey replied. "I don't know how many times I've had to listen to old ladies talk about their cats and grandchildren. Or dealing with people who bring twenty items to the twelve-items-or-less aisle. This is so much easier."

"It's definitely the easiest part of this job."

The two girls laughed together. Noni's laughter, however, slowed down and ultimately ceased when she saw Elijah coming toward them. He pushed a row of carts past them and Noni just watched him go.

Casey frowned. "That kid gives me the creeps," She muttered.

Noni watched as Elijah sluggishly straightened the carts. She remembered his dark, restless eyes. "Me too."

Until four, Noni worked relentlessly to keep herself busy and to keep her mind off all the strange things going on in her life. When business was slow, she offered to clean and to restock. She even offered to collect carts outside. She'd never worked harder a day in her life. Once her shift was over, she went to grab her things from the break room lockers. Terrell was there, too, and he smiled when he saw her.

"Still on for pizza?" he asked.

Noni had nearly forgotten. "Sure," she replied. "Know any good pizza places?"

Terrell laughed. "Do I know any good pizza places? Do *I* know any good pizza places? Ha! I can show you the *world* of pizza."

He wasn't kidding. The pizzeria that Terrell took her to was like nothing she'd ever seen. It was a few blocks from their work, within walking distance. It was a tiny restaurant—a hole in the wall—but the taste of the food was better than Noni expected.

As Noni bit into a slice of Chicago-style, deep-dish pizza, she groaned, "This is so *good.*" She chewed. "How have I never been here before?"

"No one really knows about it," Terrell shrugged. "My cousin owns the place. I come here at *least* twice a week."

"Well next time you come here you *have* to bring me." She grinned, taking another bite. She hadn't realized how long it'd been since she'd eaten a full meal. After skimping on lunch, she'd ignored her hunger. Now it was at full force and she'd devoured two whole slices of deep dish pizza before she knew it. She was wiping pizza sauce from her mouth with a white cloth napkin when Terrell began to laugh.

"You sure can pack it away!" Terrell chuckled as he watched her start on her third slice. Noni laughed as well, but her laugh dissipated as she saw his expression change. Something caught his eye—he was staring at her neck. "That necklace. I've never seen you wear it before," he noted. "Is it new?"

Noni, immediately at a loss for words and appetite, set her pizza down and pulled up her blouse. "Kind of." She used the napkin to wipe her hands.

"Doesn't really seem like something you'd wear." Terrell took a bite of his own pizza. "Not really your style."

Noni sighed. If he only knew the half of it. "It was a gift." She reached out and grabbed her glass of water; her mouth was suddenly dry.

"A real strange gift," Terrell chewed. "Looks like some kind of charm from way back in the day."

Noni gulped the water down, filling her stomach to the brim. The pizza no longer appealed to her. The cold glass of the talisman chilled her chest.

"Anyway," Terrell started again as he picked up another slice of pizza, "thanks for coming here with me. You looked bummed today, so I thought I'd do something to make you smile."

Noni did, in fact, smile when he said that. "You're always thinking of everyone but yourself," she told him. "What about you? How was your day? How have you been lately?"

Terrell grinned as he answered. He began talking to her about work, about home, and about his actual life. She knew quite a bit about him after working together for so long, but it was nice to hear someone else talk rather than her having to think and speak about her own life.

Terrell had reapplied to college. He'd dropped out just about a year before and had finally made the decision to go back. He told her that he wanted more out of life. He wanted to be able to do more for himself, more for other people, rather than just bag their groceries and return their shopping carts. "Can't afford to live on campus or be a full time student," he told her, "but I'm going to take a few classes every semester." He asked her about her college goals, and about nursing school. "So why nursing, huh? Why not a full-fledged doctor?"

Noni shrugged. "I don't really know. I mean...my mom was a nurse." She told him. "My dad was a surgeon. They helped a lot of people. I figured I should do the same, in their honor."

"But let's be real, Noni—are you passionate about it?" Terrell asked.

Noni silently stared at him. No one had ever asked her that question. She smiled politely. "Passionate isn't the right word; I guess—I'm interested. It—It sounds interesting," she stumbled, tongue-tied.

Terrell just nodded. "Well, I hope it's everything you hope it'll be."

Noni just smiled. She had no idea what she hoped it would be. She used to think she had it all planned out. She hadn't gone for her college visit yet, but she'd done enough research online and even spoken with a few nurses that frequented the grocery store. They seemed to love their jobs, and Noni hoped that she would too. She always wanted to help people, to help save people, and becoming a nurse was just the way to do it. Her parents had; she hoped she was good enough to fill their shoes.

Noni and Terrell finished eating. Terrell offered to pay for the meal but Noni wouldn't let him, offering up just enough to cover half of the bill. She did, however, accept his proposal when he offered to drive her home. It definitely beat riding the bus. When he dropped her off at home, he gave her the remainder of the pizza.

"I want you to have this," he spoke, dramatically placing a hand on his chest as he did. "It means a lot to me and I think it should be yours, now."

Noni tossed her head back and laughed as he set the pizza in her lap. "Oh my gosh," she giggled. "Thanks, I really appreciate the gesture."

"Hey, you're welcome. Couldn't think of someone more deserving of such a gift." Terrell grinned and unlocked the car doors for Noni. "This was really great, you know. We should get pizza after work more often."

Noni nodded. "We definitely should." She opened the door. "I'd do this again anytime. Thanks for the ride home!"

"Don't mention it," Terrell smiled. He drove off after Noni reached the front door.

Once she went inside, she was met by Bianca, trudging along with the sweeper. Noni frowned. "Why are you cleaning?"

"I don't know, take a guess."

She closed the door and watched Bianca travel around the living room and into the dining room. Interested, Noni followed her. Bianca turned off the sweeper when she was done, picked up a duster, and began cleaning off all the centerpieces on the table. Noni examined the house. Everything was spotless, there was incense burning, Bianca was cleaning, and Deidre was nowhere in sight. It clicked. "Bible study?"

"Bible study."

Noni stifled a laugh. "And she got you to clean for it?"

"Bribed is a better word." Bianca fastened the bandana around her hair before she began dusting again. "Told me if I cleaned she wouldn't let the old ladies harass me." She dusted the huge statue of the Virgin Mary that sat on their fireplace. "If you don't wanna get stuck here answering questions about your personal life and your religious beliefs you better go, too."

"Those ladies are harmless," Noni told Bianca.

She scoffed. "Keep telling yourself that."

Bianca cleared out of the room before any of the women showed up. They had all gone to lunch together and Deidre brought them back to their house, as she usually did. Noni greeted them one by one. Kathy from next-door, Ms. Crabtree, Ms. Jackson, and Mrs. Martinez. As they filed in, Mrs. Martinez stopped and stared at Noni.

"What a beautiful necklace," she noted. "A gift, I assume. Someone must care very deeply for you to give you such a thing."

Noni touched the necklace silently. She thought of Alex's face. She refrained from scowling. "I guess."

Mrs. Brown smiled and touched Noni's shoulder lightly. "It's good to see you, Noni Grace. Good to see you."

As they studied together, Noni stood in the kitchen, listening in every now and then. She smiled when she heard something she liked. Bianca came up beside her with a perplexed expression on her face. "Do you honestly believe in all that stuff? I'd believe in aliens before I believed in that."

I'm not an alien. Suddenly, Noni was hyper aware of the chilling metal hanging around her neck and of the echo of Alex's voice in her head. She turned away from Bianca and concentrated on the dishes soaking in the sink. "I don't know what I believe in," she replied. "I think it's nice that they're so devoted."

Bianca shrugged. "It's all too cult-like for me," she admitted, "and believing in imaginary gods really isn't my cup of tea."

A glass slid from between Noni's fingers, plopping into the sink full of soapy water and splashing bubbles everywhere. She dropped the sponge and gripped the sink.

"Jeez Nons, what the heck?"

"The cup slipped." Hurriedly, Noni picked it up again and began scrubbing away. "Anyway. I see where you're coming from," she spoke a mile a minute, "but I guess it's just nice to have faith, you know? They're old. Gotta believe in something, right?"

"I mean…I guess," Bianca shrugged. "And if you keep washing the cup like that, you're going to either break it or rub a hole into it. Chill," she chuckled lightly.

Noni rinsed the cup and took a deep breath, trying to release the tension in her chest. She closed her eyes and focused on her breathing. After only seconds, a sound sense of calm washed over her. When she opened her eyes, she realized Bianca was still staring at her.

"You looked like you were about to have a panic attack," she noted.

Noni shook her head. "Just a little anxious, that's all."

Bianca walked further into the kitchen and sat down at the small table in the corner. As Noni washed more glasses, Bianca sat quietly and began picking at the Velcro on arm brace, which she now only wore when her arm was sore. After a long silence, she spoke. "You know you've really been on edge since that day at the park," her voice was quieter than before. "What happened? You've been so weird since then."

Noni was quick with her cover story. "I took some heavy painkillers that morning. I was seeing things, imagining things, and I flipped out at Alex." She shrugged, nonchalant about her story. "Should've read the back of the bottle I guess. I wasn't supposed to be exposed to direct sunlight or whatever. Didn't drink enough water either." Noni looked toward Bianca. "I tossed the pills, anyway."

"Well good!" Bianca exclaimed. "You really scared me. I thought you were losing it!"

"I'm sorry, really. I promise nothing like that will happen again. I apologized to Alex, too, so he didn't think I was crazy or something." She rung out the sponge, draining it. "Everything's alright now though."

"Well good." Bianca smiled. "Now, you done?"

Noni drained the water in the sink. "Pretty much."

"Let's go do something."

Noni groaned aloud. "It's six-thirty," she complained. "Can't we just watch a movie or something?"

"Okay *grandma*," Bianca laughed. "It's 50 degrees outside. The *coolest* night of the summer and you want to stay indoors."

Noni racked all the clean glasses and visibly deflated. "Listen," she began, "I just want to do one normal thing today. Just one normal thing. Movies are normal and I'm going to watch one; if you wanna go out, you can."

Bianca rolled her eyes. "I'm picking the stupid movie," she grumbled. "The things I do to spend time with you."

Noni popped popcorn, they watched *Higher Learning*, and even though they'd both seen the movie countless times, the two of them were just as attentive as ever. Neither of them fell asleep or even dozed off. Noni hogged all the popcorn, as usual, and Bianca commandeered most of the couch.

When Deidre returned and found her two girls on the couch together, she made sure to kiss both of their foreheads and thank them for cleaning before heading up to bed.

Noni was thankful for the movie, for her day full of normalcy.

Work, dinner with a friend, and a movie with her cousin—what could have been more average than this? She reveled in the fact that nothing strange had happened that day because she could never be sure of what was in store for her next.

"You can't be serious." Sitting on Bianca's bed, Noni watched her cousin primp in front of the mirror. Bianca pursed her lips, cleaned up her lipstick, and then grinned.

"Stay or go, Noni. Stay or go."

Glancing nervously at the digital clock on Bianca's nightstand, Noni sighed. "It's already midnight."

"Yes, Noni, the bonfire started an hour ago. We'll be fashionably late. That is, if you ever get dressed."

"Don't you think this is a little dangerous?"

Bianca quickly turned and took Noni's face between her hands, squeezing her cheeks. "Nothing's going to happen to either of us! I promise. I'm even bringing my tazer just in case!" she grinned.

Noni wrapped one of her twists around her finger, pulling at the hairs as she looked at the clock, then at Bianca, then at the clock again. She sighed. And then, she caved. "I can't let you go alone."

"That's what I wanna hear!" Bianca beamed. "Now all we have to do is quietly escape so Ma doesn't hear us."

"I can't believe we're doing this."

"I can't believe you're still complaining."

Grudgingly, Noni went with her cousin. Sneaking out of the house wasn't something that Noni was used to, but Bianca was skilled at it. Descending the wooden stairs, they walked along the edge to avoid the weak points and keep the steps from squeaking. They left through the back door, put cotton around the lock so that the click wouldn't echo through the house. Bianca was a trained professional.

Instead of taking the car, Bianca had one of her friends pick them up. Her name was Charli, and she'd been in their graduating class. Upon seeing Noni, her eyes widened and a wide grin broke across the redhead's face. "Holy crap!" she laughed. "Not a scratch on you, huh? Ya look great!"

Noni forced a smile. "Thanks."

"From the way people talked, I would've thought you lost a side of your face or something."

Pausing, Noni shut the car door and looked into the rearview mirror, meeting Charli's eyes. "People talked about it?"

Charli nodded as she drove. "Everybody thought you died," she admitted.

"Jeez, Charli, way to lay it down softly."

The short-haired girl shrugged. "Sorry, dunno how to say it any nicer." Her eyes met Noni's through the rearview once more. "Bianca told everyone that you were alive when you came out of the coma. Everyone was really happy, naturally," she said, "but for real, I'm glad you're actually okay."

Nodding and smiling, Noni replied, "Thanks, Charli."

The ride to the bonfire was short, but eventful. Charli nearly hit two deer and succeeded in getting them lost for at least five minutes, and once they got to the bonfire, Charli demonstrated the worst parking job that Noni had ever witnessed. Bianca couldn't stop laughing.

The bonfire was at another one of their classmate's houses. His name was Ahmed and he lived in Morrison Hills and had at least an acre of land in his backyard. When they came upon the gathering, there were thirty people or so gathered around the huge fire pit in the middle of the grass. Noni recognized a few of them. When Noni, Bianca, and Charli entered the circle, four or five people ran up to Noni and hugged her, some even with tears in their eyes. Noni hadn't seen any of them since school was in session, and she *still* didn't remember a thing about graduation.

One girl in particular, from Art Club, came rushing up to Noni and threw her arms around her shoulders before Noni could get a word out."Oh my god!" she shouted. "I'm so glad you're here! The whole team was so worried when we heard about the accident! How are you? Have you been doing okay?"

Noni gave the girl two pats on the back before pulling out of her embrace. "I'm good, Chelsea," she said. "I'm doing really well actually."

"You have no idea how worried we were when we all found out. I can't believe you were in a coma! But thank goodness you came out alright!"

Noni smiled and nodded quickly. "Yeah, it was pretty much a miracle!"

Chelsea grinned and touched Noni's arm softly. "I really am happy that you're okay. We all knew you woke up, but, you know, when you didn't really come around afterward, we didn't know what to expect."

It was then that Noni realized how long it'd been since she'd seen anyone from school. It was near the end of June and their senior year ended in late April. After waking up from the coma, she'd initially been too sick to leave the house. However, even after being well enough to go back to work, Noni still hadn't reached out to any of the people that she'd known in high school. But, in Noni's eyes, she was still recovering, still needing time to recoup and reboot. Especially now, with the strange things she knew, she wasn't sure if she could get back what she had before.

But she could try.

"Let's catch up!" Chelsea grinned, hooking her arm around Noni's. "Come on, the food is on the other side of the yard!"

Around the bonfire, Noni sat with Chelsea, Bianca—who was cuddled up to Charli—and a few others who'd tagged along, and talked about what things were like after the crash. She was disappointed to tell them that not much had changed. Well, except that she'd met a self-proclaimed non-human and had visions about the beginning of time.

However, there was no way she was telling them *that*.

Everyone seemed to be pleased to see her; she received more running hugs than she could count. She couldn't remember the last time this many people paid this much attention to her.

After a while, Noni left the circle to breathe. The number of people overwhelmed her, and just stepping away to take a deep breath would be calming enough. Walking away from the fire pit, Noni went to the table where snacks and drinks were located. She grabbed a bottled water, popped the cap, and tipped it up to her lips to drink. The water was refreshing, cooling her down from being in front of a fire for so long. Noni stared off into the woods behind Ahmed's house. She saw him wandering along the edge of the woods, beer in hand, toward the rest of the group.

Then, something snatched him.

He was dragged into the dark of the woods. His beer landed in the dirt.

Noni started running. From the fire pit, over the music, she heard someone call out to her as she ran, but she ignored it and kept going.

In the woods, everything was silent. She could hear the noise from the party, the laughter and the music, but here all was still. She took a step, hearing the twigs and leaves crunch underneath the soles of her shoes. Knees quaking, hands shaking, she walked on.

"Ahmed?" she called out. "Ahmed, are you out here?"

"*NONI!*" Ahmed's bloodcurdling scream tore through the air. Noni's stomach flipped the moment she heard it. She looked back to see if anyone else around the party heard it, but no one stirred, they were blind and deaf to his scream. She started running again, racing in the direction of the scream. She wrapped a hand around the necklace, holding the talisman as tightly as she could.

"*HELP! NONI, HELP!*" Ahmed's screams erupted again and Noni ran faster. In the distance, she could see the bushes rustling. She caught sight of legs kicking.

"Ahmed!" she called to him. "Ahmed, I'm coming!"

Gripping the talisman, Noni hoped that someone, anyone would come to the rescue. Who was she to think that she could save anyone? What power did she have? What strength? The only thing she could count on was her stupid bravery.

The rustling in the brush ceased.

Noni stopped running. "Ahmed?" her voice was barely above a whisper. With trembling knees, Noni walked on. She stepped through the brush.

Ahmed lay on the ground, still and unmoving. A dark figure stood over him flaunting a knife. A line of blood traveled along its edge, dripping onto the forest floor. A sickeningly sweet voice echoed in the air. "Well hello, Noni." The woman turned, revealing her face. Sharp features, crystalline, translucent skin, and a red mouth. A red mouth covered in blood. "It's so nice to finally meet, face to face."

Noni couldn't take her eyes off Ahmed. His chest wasn't moving. "Who are you?" she demanded.

The woman grinned as she swiped her knife across her pant leg, cleaning off the blood. Clad in all black, she blended in with the dark of the night. "My name is Eifa."

For some reason, the sound of the name sent shivers along Noni's spine, and a sickness settled in her stomach. The smell of burning flesh invaded her nostrils. But nothing was aflame.

Noni took a step back, watching Ahmed while she tried to watch the woman in front of her. Eifa kept smiling at Noni, licking her lips as she did. Noni felt the sickness rising in her. She breathed, gathered enough courage to speak. "You're not human, are you?"

"Quite the observant one, aren't you?" Eifa laughed.

"What the hell are you?"

The woman grinned wildly at Noni. "Oh love, he hasn't told you yet?" She sheathed her knife and stepped toward Noni. Terrified, Noni rapidly shuffled backward.

The woman placed her hands on her hips, sighing, disappointed. "Oh, please don't run. If you get away before I deliver my message,

I'll have to kill your friend there. And I don't really want to get my hands dirty tonight, so please, do be still."

Noni stopped dead in her tracks and could only watch as the she approached her.

"What *are* you?" Noni shakily demanded.

Eifa's red grin widened. "My darling, Noni," she began, stopping in front of the teen. "I am a celestial being. I am divine." She cackled, and in a flash her hand was wrapped around Noni's neck. "I am a *god*. And my father wants me to deliver a message."

Her touch was like fire, like flames tearing at Noni's skin. Eifa lifted Noni off the ground, choked every breath out of her body before slamming her against the nearest tree. Noni tore at Eifa's skin with her nails, tried to claw her way out of the woman's grasp, but her efforts were in vain. The iron grip that Eifa had on Noni's neck was indestructible. Noni closed her eyes. What she saw behind the dark of her lids horrified her.

It was almost like what Alex had shown her that night on the front steps. A naked, bleeding man, treading through a river of blood at his feet. His shoulders and back were covered in blood; it poured and sputtered out of his wounds. Bone, muscle, and gristle tore out from his shoulders, baring his insides to the air. Pieces of his flesh fell onto the ground as he walked, dropping into the pools of blood. Steam rose from the blood where his flesh touched. Then, slowly, his skin began to rot. Limb by limb, he began to disintegrate. He reached toward the sky, toward the stars, which spun around his head in circles. He turned, eyes wide open, as his entire body became a body of pure light. The last thing to be seen was his eyes. His eyes, solid gold eyes, glowed the brightest.

He wasn't quick enough to catch Noni before she fell.

Noni, crumpled beneath the tree and in the dirt, coughed violently as she tried to pull herself up. When she saw the body on the ground, she crawled away from it as fast as she could. Alex took a single step forward, and that was when Noni finally noticed him. Her eyes were glued to his hands, which were still glowing, electrified, clothed in orbs of light.

"Noni." He softly spoke.

She scrambled up from the ground and ran to him as if she knew it was the right thing to do, as if she'd done it one thousand times over. Sobs tore through her body, shook her to the bone. She coughed, trying to catch her breath through the tears. "Is he dead? Is Ahmed dead? Oh God," she wept. "It's my fault. It's my fault that he's dead!"

Alex held her by her arms. "The boy is fine. Ahmed is fine," he assured her. "Noni. Look at me—he's *fine*. He won't remember anything. He's headed to the edge of the woods now. He simply believes that he was intoxicated and tripped out here. Look."

Noni looked around, seeing Ahmed nowhere. She still panicked. "Where is she? The woman—where is she?'

"Gone," Alex replied calmly. "She's gone."

Together they stepped away from the body. Noni took Alex's hand; through their touch, he could feel her pain, her panic.

"—I'm gonna be sick. Move."

Jumping out of the way, Alex barely avoiding being the target of Noni's sickness. As she spilled the contents of her stomach onto the ground, Alex pulled back her twists and rubbed her back.

When Noni finished, she placed one hand against a tree and tried to catch her breath. She closed her eyes, touched her neck and flinched. Alex could see—and even smell—the raw, burned skin. Her pain reached him.

"I can fix that," he announced, "if you'd like."

"How?" Noni choked out.

"I'll heal your wound and we'll talk; there's a lot that I need to tell you."

Wrapping an arm around Noni's back, Alex helped her walk forward.

She peeled her eyes away from the body lying in the dirt and her hands hovered over her burned skin. Noni spoke as they walked, softly. "Do you always know when I'm in trouble? Is that a thing you can sense, or something?"

"Somewhat." Alex answered. "When your spirit is in danger, I sense that. Does that make sense?"

"Nothing you tell me ever makes sense, but sure. Let's go with it."

Upon reaching a quiet spot, Alex sat down on the ground and motioned for Noni to join him. She did, albeit slowly and cautiously.

"May I see your wound?" he asked. Noni nodded carefully, tilting her head back, exposing herself. The skin was pink, bleeding, and starting to blister. Anguished tears fell from Noni's eyes, and Alex swiped at them before they could reach her neck. "There's no need to cry," he told her. "You are safe now." Noni closed her eyes, breathing softly through her nose as she waited. "I'm going to touch your neck now; this shouldn't hurt."

Gingerly, Alex laid his middle and index fingers against Noni's neck. She flinched at his touch but held still. Slowly, the same, ethereal light emerged beneath his fingertips. Alex watched the cool, icy glow spread across her skin, clothing the burn in a soft radiance. Relief settled in Noni's eyes. The tension left her and her body sagged, exhausted as the pain disappeared. When the glow disappeared, Alex pulled his fingers away and watched as Noni cautiously brought her head forward and touched her neck. Feeling no pain, she heaved out a grateful sigh. "Thank you," she spoke.

Alex nodded once. "I'm sorry that I didn't get to you sooner." He paused, staring at the girl before him. She was still trembling. Her eyes darted back and forth, scrutinizing her surroundings, like a caged animal.

"It's fine," she replied, folding her arms over her chest. "Just tell me what's going on. Why are all those *things* after me, of all people to go after?"

"You're a very important girl, Noni," he began. Her eyes narrowed but he continued.

Noni's heartbeat picked up as she became frightened.

"You mean that those things, those *whatever-they-are*, are seriously after *me*? Just *me*?"

Alex nodded again. "To them, you are valuable."

Noni sat for a moment, mentally flipping through everything that had happened to her. She glanced up at Alex, afraid to ask her next question. "She told me something—" Noni closed her eyes and repeated the very words. "—*I am a celestial being. I am divine. I am a god.*" The words themselves sent shivers up and down her spine. "Is that true? Is that what she was?" She looked him dead in the eye. "Is that what *you* are?"

"She was mocking," Alex answered. "She was a Halfling, not even worthy of the title. But what I am, and what my people are, is so much more than what humans consider gods to be. You all pray to imaginary saviors in the sky, or envision spiteful gods who will strike you down and inflict death and disease if they don't receive a sacrifice every new moon. That isn't what we are. That is not *who* we are. We aren't simply gods. We are the sons and daughters of the Universe."

Alex watched Noni cradle her face in her hands, releasing a long, drawn out groan. "This *can't* be real," she whispered.

"Everything I tell you is the truth," Alex responded. "I promised you that I would tell only the truth."

Noni nodded, trusting his words. "So what do I do?" Noni finally spoke. "How do I stop this? I can't keep being attacked like this—I'll die. And you can't keep saving me either. What can I do?"

"I will help you," Alex answered. "It's why I'm here."

Noni eyed him warily. "Didn't you say you *weren't* my guardian angel?"

"I'm not," Alex said, "but I am here to help you. I will teach you how to fight them and teach you how to keep yourself safe. It will not be easy, but in order to live, you must learn. Until then, I will look after you."

"Okay," She said, with wariness behind her tone. "But what about my family? What about my friends? What's going to happen to them if things like *this* keep happening to *me*?"

"I will make sure that nothing happens to them," he told her. "Ileana will watch over your family while I watch over you."

"She's in on this too?" Noni inquired. "Does that mean she's like you?"

"Yes," Alex admitted, "she is like me."

Noni was quiet then for several moments. When she spoke again, Alex seemed to lean in, listening intently to every word.

"The night I was attacked in the alley," she recalled. "You came. And you saved me. Did you kill that man?"

"He was a Halfling as well," Alex told her. "And no, I did not take his life. I was too worried about you; I let him get away."

"I almost died then, didn't I?" Noni looked up at him, her mismatched eyes staring straight into his. "Tell me."

He told her the truth. "There was a severe injury to your skull." Alex averted her gaze. "Yes, you were near death, but I healed you, which is why you found no injury when you woke." He confessed. "I did the same thing after the car crash. I did as much as I could before the emergency personnel arrived."

"Then why didn't I wake right up? Why did I stay in a coma?"

"It was worse than what happened to you in the alley. There wasn't enough time." Alex paused, pursing his lips and breathing deeply before he spoke, "I didn't have time to completely heal you. I only had enough time to stop the internal bleeding. I left your recovery up to fate."

"So there was no guarantee that I'd live through it?"

Alex shook his head. "No."

"Wouldn't it be better if I'd have died, then? You wouldn't have to go to all this trouble."

"No, Noni," he told her. He seemed almost appalled at the question. "There is absolutely no way that I would have let you die. You are too special."

"Aside from my knack for nearly getting myself killed, there's not much special about me," Noni muttered. "But since everyone seems to think otherwise, I guess I have no choice." She sighed, "Can't let the bad guys win, I guess."

"Just remember that I'm here to help you," Alex assured her, "and so is Ileana. You will be fine and we will keep the 'bad guys' away. Trust me, alright?"

Noni didn't speak again, but she didn't need to. She only nodded. Alex's smile left reassurance in her heart.

Before he spoke again, he took Noni's hand into his and said, "I promise; I won't let you down."

Chapter Seven

"Whoa. This is unreal."

Noni, with Bianca beside her, huddled around her laptop. With the volume at its maximum, they explored the website with great interest. Upon Noni's acceptance to Oak Brooke, they allowed her to engage in a virtual tour of the college. Seeing as how it was so far from her home and she had almost no means of getting there over the summer, the virtual tour was her best shot. The intensity of the virtual tour, the detail put into it, was well appreciated. Noni was able to view the dorms, pictures of the campus itself, major-specific buildings, and there was even a snippet from a professor's lecture in one of the "virtual classrooms." It wasn't the most exciting of lectures but just watching it sparked Noni's interest in the college even more.

"Morrison College could never be this cool," Bianca laughed. "Go back to the dorms. I wanna see how much stuff you can fit in there."

Noni laughed but fulfilled her cousin's request. They discussed whether Noni would be able to fit a mini-fridge, a full futon, a TV, a microwave, and coffee machine all on one side of the room. Noni debated, saying that she may have a roommate who'd be willing to share their things, but Bianca rejected the idea.

"If your roommate's mean and doesn't want to share, you gotta have options."

"If my *options* take up too much space in these tiny rooms, I'll take my chances, thanks."

The girls continued the virtual tour, taking in as much as possible. Noni's excitement rose with every new piece of information she got. The idea of going away for college was something she'd quietly entertained all her life. However, now that she could actually go— with the help of many scholarships—the dream became reality. On her own, she could never afford college. No matter how hard Deidre worked, there was no way she could ever make enough to pay for Noni to go all the way to California. But Noni worked hard for all of the scholarships she'd received, and her efforts paid off.

"What are you two doing?"

Both girls turned to see Deidre poking her head into the living room. Bianca pointed at the computer in Noni's lap. "Look, Ma! It's literally a virtual tour of Oak Brooke, it's so cool."

The woman walked over and hung over the couch, squinting as she watched the computer. Noni showed her the features she'd already shown Bianca, went through the dorm rooms, the campus, everything.

"Looks like a beautiful place," Deidre smiled. "Can't believe you're going into nursing, Noni," she began. "Don't you think going into medical school would be better for you? Sure pays more."

Noni pursed her lips, sighing quietly, "Yeah it pays better, but I'm not really all that interested."

Deidre patted her head, kissing her hair. "Just keep thinking about it, hmm? You never know. Might change your mind."

Noni shrugged. "Yeah, I guess."

Deidre smiled again and then reached over to Bianca, kissing her forehead for good measure. Bianca groaned and dramatically wiped the lipstick-kiss from her forehead as her mother laughed and left, heading to the kitchen.

Noni closed her browser, ending the tour. "I still think it was pretty cool," she said. "Can't believe I'm actually going to be living in that place."

Bianca nodded. "I'm definitely going to have to visit as *much* as humanly possible. I mean, California? Wow. You're gonna be living the dream, girl!"

Noni laughed. "Nursing school isn't much of a dream, so far as I hear."

"Yeah but it's *your* dream," Bianca told her. "Right?"

With a quick nod, Noni agreed quietly, "Right."

Bianca shrugged. "Better come on," she said. "Almost time for work!"

Noni shut her laptop and carried it up to her bedroom. There, she changed into her work clothes: khaki pants, white shirt, ugly green vest, and even uglier shoes. She stared at herself in the full-length mirror attached to the back of her door. Sighing, she touched the blank space between her throat and collarbone. She glanced at the nightstand beside her bed. There lay the talisman. Carefully, she picked it up and placed it around her neck. She knew now that it did a lot more than just keep her dreams safe. Once it was on, Noni grabbed her knapsack and met Bianca downstairs.

At the bottom of the stairs, Bianca was still struggling to put shoes on. She cursed her brace for getting in the way. Deidre had packed their lunches for them. She handed them both to Noni, whose hands were free, and sighed.

"Be safe, you two."

"It's fine!" Bianca grinned, finally having her shoe tied. She adjusted her brace as she spoke. "I'm driving!"

Deidre shook her head, laughing, "Oh, I know."

Thankfully, it was the weekend so the girls could take the car to work with them instead of riding the city bus; they got there much faster than they usually would have.

Upon entering the store, Noni smiled when she saw Terrell. He waved at her as she got closer.

"Welcome to Michael's!" he greeted her. "All dairy items are half off today!"

Noni laughed, "Why thank you, I'll be sure to head to that aisle."

Terrell bowed to both Noni and Bianca dramatically, "Ladies."

Bianca rolled her eyes and chuckled as she took Noni's hand, dragging her into the store. "Oh my, what a man!" she teased.

"Noni, Noni!" Terrell called as they walked off. "Pizza today? My treat?"

The girl shook her head. "No," she replied. "my treat."

Bianca continued to drag her off but Noni was there long enough to watch Terrell start cheering.

A four-hour shift. That was all Noni worked. With everything on her mind, it was enough. She spent most of it restocking shelves. A large shipment came in on Friday, and it was her job to stock the shelves. Between Terrell coming to the back to chat, Bianca distracting her, and Casey asking if Noni could take her register while she went on a bathroom break, the restocking took all of four hours.

With five minutes of her shift left, Noni went to the break room to gather all of her things. Unfortunately, upon entering the break room, she was met by the very last person she wanted to see. Elijah sat at the table, watching the television as the sound and picture went in and out. Noni couldn't hear a single word of it, but he seemed to be able to hear it.

"Hi, Noni," he said, not even sparing a glance her way.

Her skin crawled just being in the same room with him. "Hey," she replied. Every time she spoke to him, every time they were in the same room together, something felt *off*. Sometimes while they worked, she felt him watching her. She didn't even need to look to know he was there.

Noni squeezed past him and into the locker room. She opened her personal locker and took out her knapsack. She grabbed her phone from the side pocket and held it tightly in her hand as she threw the sack across her back.

When she turned around, Elijah stood in front of the door.

She stood firm, eyeing him steadily. "Feeling okay?" she asked. She eyed the doorway, hoping, wishing that someone would walk through.

"Feeling fine," he replied. He stepped away from the doorway, allowing space for Noni to walk through. She went past him, careful not to let any part of her touch him. Before she could reach the door, he spoke one last time. "That's an interesting necklace."

Noni let her hand drop from the door handle. She glanced over her shoulder, staring right at him. "Thanks, it was a gift from a friend."

Elijah nodded. "Looks pretty expensive." He looked up at her. "Know where they got it from?"

Noni shrugged. She had a feeling she knew where Alex got it from, and it was probably nowhere on this side of the Universe. "Somewhere far away, I think." She noticed that he was staring directly into her face now. A prickling sensation spread across her skin. "Is there something on my face or what?"

"Your eyes have always been two different colors, right?" he asked. She nodded.

"Yeah. I mean not completely. One just has a little discoloration."

"Looks a little more discolored than before," Elijah noted.

Noni pursed her lips. "You know, creeping your coworkers out in the break room is really messed up." She faced him. "I don't know where you get off—"

"I didn't mean any harm, Noni," he held both hands in the air. "Honest."

Noni spared him no more words. She left just to get her skin to stop crawling. As she left, she pulled her phone from her pocket and opened the front camera. She stared long and hard into it, examining her right eye.

Elijah was right. The color was spreading. She blinked two, three, four times but it remained the same. Hazel leaked into her brown iris.

"Somethin' in your eye?"

Noni hadn't even realized that she'd made it out of the store. Terrell was waiting for her at the front door. Noni immediately put her phone away and shook her head. "No," she said. "everything's fine."

Together, they drove to the pizzeria. Noni worked up an appetite as best she could. Terrell, who was always hungry, had no trouble wolfing down two slices of pizza after only ten minutes of them being there. His cousin, the one who owned the place, had already begun cooking their pizza before they even arrived. Terrell probably orchestrated the whole thing, but Noni was grateful.

The pizza was as delicious as it ever was, but Noni couldn't find her hunger. She picked at her food absentmindedly, trying to forget the strange, unsettling things that happened in the break room. Tried to forget the deadness in Elijah's eyes when he'd spoken to her. It was impossible.

"You okay?" Terrell asked.

Noni couldn't find it in her to lie. "I don't know," she answered. "Terrell," she began, "What do you know about Elijah?"

"Dude from work?" he asked, with a mouth full of pepperoni.

Noni refrained from laughing but nodded.

"Eh, not a lot," he told her. "I mean he's kind of weird. Kinda quiet. Always doing scratch-offs during break. Always wins—every time. Kid's strange."

"Understatement," Noni muttered.

Terrell set down his slice of pizza. "What? Did he do something to you?"

Noni shrugged. "He just creeps me out. Every time he talks to me—I don't know. He gives me the creeps."

"I don't blame you," Terrell nodded. "I'd talk to Kris about it. If he's bothering you, he needs to stay away from you."

Noni was quiet for the rest of their meal, unable to get Elijah's face out of her memory. The knowing look in his eyes. She remained unsettled.

She ate as much as she could.

When they finished, Terrell offered to drive her home. Noni declined. She wasn't going home. She had other places to be. She thanked him for the offer of a ride and for his company. She didn't start walking until he drove off. When he did, she went straight to the bus stop

The bus came within fifteen minutes. Noni paid her fare and sat down at the very front of the bus, right behind the driver. Her destination stood only twenty minutes away. She busied herself by playing games on her cellphone, anything to pass the time and keep her mind clear.

When bus arrived at the stop, Noni got off and started walking. She reached Ileana's apartment within five minutes. She knocked at the door twice, waited for someone to answer. When it opened, Alex met her, smiling at her just as he always did.

As soon as Noni entered the apartment, Ileana swooped in. "I've prepared a meal," she announced. "Are you hungry, Noni?"

Noni shook her head. "No, I just ate." She paused. "Do you guys like, actually *have* to eat?" she questioned.

Alex laughed and Ileana just nodded. "Yes, of course." She said. "In our realm, every meal is a feast." Noni started to laugh, too, then. Ileana just smiled. "At least have something to drink?"

"Sure."

Ileana brought Noni a drink and then quickly vacating the apartment, letting Alex know that she'd be back within a few hours. When Ileana left, Alex came over to Noni and sat down. "She's been reading a lot about what you all call 'homemaking'," he confessed. "Things are a lot different where we come from."

Noni laughed even harder. "No wonder," she joked. "She'd be better off without all that stuff."

Alex shrugged. "I think she really likes it." Turning back to Noni, Alex watched her.

Noni noticed the curiosity in his eyes and shifted under his gaze.

She always felt like he was analyzing her, as if his eyes just pierced every layer of her.

"Are you alright, Noni?" he asked. "Is something troubling you?" Another question. "Your aura seems uneasy."

She sighed, refraining from rolling her eyes. There were things that he would always know, she'd gathered.

"I've just been feeling weird since my shift at work," she replied. "There's this kid I work with. And there's something off about him. I feel like he watches me." She paused. "I don't think he's a—you know—I think he's human—but he's got this weird fixation on me." She shrugged, taking a deep breath. "It's just really strange. I'm trying my best to stay away from him."

"Would you like me to look into it?" Alex questioned. "Or do you want to handle it—whatever it is—on your own?"

Noni smiled lightly, waving her hand dismissively. "I think I've got it." Settling into the couch, Noni folded her arms across her chest and took a deep breath. Exhaustion crept its way across her face and seeped into her bones. The day wasn't even half over, but enough had happened to tire her out. Noni closed her eyes, concentrating on the dark behind her eyelids, and took another deep breath.

Alex watched Noni curiously from the seat across from her. He watched her open her eyes, stare blankly at the ceiling as her breathing leveled out.

"You're very tired today," he noticed.

She shrugged, "Long day."

"Maybe today isn't the day to—"

"No," Noni began. "I can do it." She sat up, stretching her arms up in the air and her feet out in front of her. "Just gimme a sec."

"Your fatigue will only increase after this."

She scratched her head lazily, shaking her twists away from her face. "Well I guess you'll just have to carry me home then, hmm?" she joked.

"I would absolutely carry you home," Alex replied. "However, there is no need for that. I have a car."

"Sarcasm," Noni shook her head. "It's called sarcasm." She stood up from the couch, cracking her knuckles. "Okay—what do I do?"

Alex smiled at her eagerness and invited her to sit down again. "I'll show you. Watch."

Noni sat. Alex moved to the edge of his seat. He leaned forward, setting both his elbows atop his knees. Noni watched him intently. He brought both his hands together, fingertips nearly touching, and closed his eyes. Slowly, from his fingertips, needle-thin lines began traveling down his fingers and into his hand. Like cracks in the pavement, they spread farther and farther out until they overtook all of his skin, which began to take on a soft, ethereal glow. A translucent orb of light formed around his hands, gleaming and illuminating the space; electricity rippled through it, between each of his fingertips like conductors. He manipulated the orb, dimmed the light and made it brighter, so radiant that it lit up the whole room. Noni watched with awe, mouth hanging wide open as she witnessed pure magic happen before her. She could never have imagined anything like this, could never have dreamed of it. Alex noticed her astonishment, the wonder in her eyes. It was then that he reached out, took hold of Noni's hand. She pulled back immediately.

"Don't be afraid," Alex told her, holding out his hand in a nonthreatening way. "I won't hurt you."

For a moment, Noni just stared at his hand, at the glow surrounding it. Nerves weighed down her chest, but she was still brave enough to reach out. She placed her hand in his. Immediately, she was shocked by the heat. The light—the glow—was warm to the touch. It was almost like dipping her hand into a body of warm water; it soothed her skin, soothed her muscles, right down to the bone. "This is amazing," She whispered.

Alex nodded, "That it is." Holding Noni's hand, he finally looked her in the eye. "It's something I'll teach you to do."

Noni laughed, a short, high-pitched and surprised laugh. "I can't do this!" she exclaimed. "I'm—I'm a wimpy human."

Alex tried to dispute her point, but he was nowhere near human, so he wouldn't understand. Alex and Ileana were Novaens. Alex spoke extensively of their origins, telling Noni as much as he could without overwhelming her. He told her about their realm, Nova, about the country and the kingdom they came from. Just like Earth, the realm had a rich history. Alex spoke about multiple universes, where vastly different realities existed. His universe was the farthest from hers and there, they lived like gods—they *were* gods, as far as Noni was concerned. As unbelievable as it sounded, it was all real.

"You're special," Alex responded. "You're a very special girl, Noni. More connected to this universe and its power than most humans. There's power inside of you. Untapped power that you will soon learn to use. If you plan to protect yourself, and your family, you'll learn," he smiled. "I believe in you. You will succeed."

Noni folded her hands together in her lap as she sighed, twirled her thumbs forward and backward. Alex watched her stare down at them, unblinking. She looked away from her hands, at the walls, away from the hazel eyes that seemed to penetrate her very being. He had the most intense eyes, and his stares always seemed to reach her core. He didn't know how to just *look* like a normal person would. Then again, he wasn't a normal person at all.

"I just don't get this," she said. "Are there any others like me? Who have this hidden power, or whatever?"

"Many," Alex replied. "It isn't as strange as you think." He motioned for her hand. "Here."

Timidly, Noni reached out once more. A strange tingle passed between her palms and his, sending a shiver along her skin. Alex took her right hand into his and silently requested her left. His skin was soft, still warm to the touch. Noni curled her fingers around his brown hands, finally meeting his eyes.

"Now," Alex started, "close your eyes. Clear your mind as best you can."

"I'm holding hands with a celestial being in an apartment, trying to make light shoot out from my fingertips, and you expect me to clear my mind?"

"Noni, your humor and human sarcasm will not help you here."

She refrained from letting out a sigh. "Okay. Clearing my mind."

"Take as much time as you need to remove all that you can. Think of nothing but blank space. Empty space."

With her eyes shut tightly, Noni nodded. Iron-willed, she tried her best to concentrate on Alex's words. "Just focus on the sound of my voice. No other sounds. See nothing but the empty space around you. See yourself there. Breathe in. You should see nothing but the empty space, now. Let it take over; let it envelop you. It is endless. It is limitless. Breathe out. Focus on the push and pull of your lungs, the rise and fall of your chest. Focus on the pulsation of your heart, the steady beating. The space grows with every breath ..."

Noni opened her eyes. She saw nothing. Endless darkness surrounded her. "Hello?" she called out. Her voice echoed in the dark, loud at first, then slowly dying out. She was left in silence. "Alex?!" The echoes came again; her voice distorted and reverberated through the space. Noni's breathing quickened. She could feel her chest tightening, could feel her throat closing. She clasped her hands together desperately. "Come on, come on." She hoped, begged for some sort of spark, a spark to illuminate the dark. But there was nothing. No orb of light, no electricity between her fingertips. Nothing. She cursed under her breath, wrapped her arms around herself, and shuddered. "Wake up, wake up," she whispered to herself. "How the hell do I wake up?"

"Noni."

A child's voice startled her; the sound of her own name nearly made her jump out of her skin. One hand stretched out from the darkness. It was covered in dirt, ashes, and soot. "Come on," said the voice. "We're going to my house!"

Noni grabbed the hand without a second's hesitation.

When she opened her eyes, this time, she found herself in the front lawn of her old home. She whipped around, searching for whoever had brought her there, but she was alone once again.

The air was still, stale and stagnant. Not a single bird flew through the sky, nor did the wind blow through the trees. Everything was silent there. Noni wanted to turn back, to walk away from the home she barely remembered, but something compelled her to move forward. Her feet carried her through the unkempt grass, through the unruly weeds that whipped at her legs, and up to the red brick house. She grasped the handle of the metal storm door and found it to be unlocked.

She opened the door and stepped inside. "Hello?" Noni called out to the seemingly empty house. Abruptly, she heard a shuffling sound coming from the kitchen to her right. Turning immediately, Noni saw them. Just as she remembered them.

"Mom...Dad?"

The two sat together at the small wooden table. Her mother wore a plain gray dress, and her father wore his old blue scrubs. Both of them stared down at their clasped hands atop the little table. Noni called out to them again. They didn't move, didn't react to the sound of her voice. She raced toward them, rushed to her mother's side and shouted her name. Nothing. She reached out to touch her, but Noni's hand slipped right through her. Staggering backward, Noni fell into the doorway, bewildered.

"David, I know what the doctor said," her mother spoke. She looked up, pushed her long black hair behind her ear, chin jutted out defiantly. "I know what she said."

"Then why aren't you listening?" her father bit. "Theresa, you know what this is. You know what could happen—to you, to the baby, to this family—"

"I know the risks," Theresa spoke calmly. Her arms wrapped around her flat stomach protectively. "David, I've wanted a child for so long…I would risk everything."

"You could die!"

"I know that!"

The argument continued, both of them shouting across the table. The sound of their voices faded out, and Noni's vision began to blur. Slowly, black smoke crept across the kitchen tiles. It billowed in from the windows, shot out from the air vents. Suddenly, her parents were shrouded in it, covered, and became invisible to her. Noni called out to them but the smoke choked her, filled her lungs, and smothered her. A violent coughing fit shook her, forcing her onto her knees. She tried to scream, but no sound came. The smoke poured out from her mouth in waves. She shut her eyes. Everything was on fire again.

When she opened them again, she was back in Alex's living room.

Shaken, Noni shuddered. "It wasn't real," she whispered. Tears welled up in her eyes and she snatched her hands away from Alex. "It wasn't real," she repeated the phrase over and over.

Tentatively, Alex moved to the couch and sat beside her. He offered her a hand. Noni took it without hesitation, even went so far as to let him embrace her. Carefully and quietly, he spoke to her.

"Often times, within the recesses of one's mind, we see things that ought to remain unseen."

Noni breathed deeply, tried to shake off what she had seen. "I don't understand," She choked out. "What I saw—it didn't make sense. I thought I was just supposed to make my stupid hands glow, not—" she shook her head. "You could've warned me."

"It's different for everyone," Alex admitted. "Whatever you saw is specific to you. Eventually, it will help you get to where you need to be."

Noni nodded slowly, even though she truly didn't understand. She wanted to be brave, and she wanted to be strong, but there were so many things that she couldn't understand. She didn't understand what she'd seen. She was shaken most by the feelings that lingered afterward. Her throat was raw, and the taste of smoke lingered in her mouth. She could almost feel the heat from the fire that had swallowed her family whole. Noni shut her eyes, trying to fight back the fear and the guilt that always followed these memories. She would never understand why she had been the only one to survive.

Alex, seeming to notice her discontent, loosened his hold on her and craned his neck to look into her face. "What can I do to help you?" he asked.

Noni hesitated, staring down at her hands again. "I'm just lost," she finally confessed. "I feel like there's something I'm missing here, something I don't know. I mean, there's a lot I don't know, clearly. But I'm just—I don't know." She pinched the bridge of her nose between her thumb and forefinger. "I don't know how you can help."

"I could tell you more," Alex began. "About the power you're trying to manifest. Maybe that will help?"

Noni simply nodded. "Sure," she turned toward Alex on the couch, pulling her knees up to her chest, "That might help."

Alex turned to Noni, folding one leg underneath himself before he started speaking. "Well, to start off, these powers manifest themselves in a spiritual realm. Every person born to this earth has a spirit, a soul. Some spirits are telluric: they are grounded, worldlier. Some spirits are more connected to the Universe. These spirits, these people, are able manifest such powers. Four powers, or manifestations, exist. Most only awaken one or two of them. I myself have already awakened two, and I have lived for quite some time."

Noni opened her mouth to interrupt, but thought against it. She motioned for Alex to continue.

"The first manifestation is Light. It's what I've shown you, what you're trying to learn. Light is…warmth, it is protection; it is a guiding force. It shows truth to those who possess it. It's something that comes naturally to beings like Ileana and myself. Manifested at birth, it seemed."

Noni rested her head against the couch, letting her eyes fall shut as she listened to Alex. The cadence of his voice was calming.

"The second manifestation is Healing. Like Light, it brings warmth, but it brings relief to those who are in pain. The manifestation of Healing draws out the Light from within and transfers it to another entity, curing them of whatever ails them. It leaves the user feeling drained if performed too often. It can be used on oneself but does greater good when helping others."

"So that's what you did for me?" Noni asked him, opening her eyes and sitting up. "When you found me, when the crash happened—that was it? The manifestation of Healing."

Alex nodded. The corners of his mouth pulled downward, as if he was pained by the very memory of it. "It was," he told her. "It was the best that I could do. When I found you, I used every bit of power inside me to heal you. But you did the rest, Noni. You brought yourself back." He grinned.

Noni returned the gesture, laying her head against the couch again. "You know, I never asked you this, but how did you know exactly where I was?" she questioned. "How did you find me?"

Alex just smiled. "That's simple; I will always find you, Noni." He spoke. "No matter what happens, I will watch over you until you no longer require my presence."

She drew her legs in further, biting back a fierce grin. "I think you're pretty cool, so, you know, I'll let you stick around."

Abruptly, the apartment door burst open. Both Noni and Alex turned to watch Ileana charge through the door, with her jacket bundled up in her arms. She had the wildest, most cheerful expression on her face as she sat down on the couch across from them, beaming expectantly. "While I was out," she began. "You will never believe what I found!"

"More books?" Alex guessed.

Ileana shook her head. "Even better!" She quickly, though carefully, unraveled the bundle in her arms. Beneath the fabric, two black ears popped up and a pair of green eyes stared directly at Alex and Noni. "It is a very small cat!" Ileana exclaimed. "A kitten!"

Noni cautiously reached toward the animal. "Where'd you find this little one?" she asked. It swiped at her hand and she pulled back. "Kinda feisty, huh?"

"This one was roaming around a parking lot, lost, with no one to care for it." She smiled down at the kitten, scratching its head with her finger. "He is feeble and young; I couldn't leave it all alone!" She picked the kitten out from the bundle and cradled it in the crook of her arm. "I've never had a pet before."

"Do you like animals?" Noni asked.

Ileana nodded. "It's rare that any of us get to interact with any worldly beings. Whenever we're here, on Earth, it's usually a very serious matter, and there is no time to explore. However, this is a different occasion." She smiled at Noni and then looked back down to the kitten. "This one is very cute. I'm going to keep it during our time here." Ileana then glanced up at Noni again. "Will you name it?"

"Me?" Noni peeped. "Why me?"

"I'm assuming you're better at naming animals than I am. You've experienced this, yes?"

"I mean, my parents had a dog when I was a kid but I just named it Spot. Not creative," she replied.

Ileana watched her expectantly, waiting for her to bestow a name upon the kitten.

Noni sighed, "Why not," she said. "Let's name him…Ash. How's that sound?"

"Perfect!" Ileana stood with the kitten in her arms. "This will be fun!"

Alex watched the kitten warily. "What do we feed it? How will we take care of it? We have many other things to attend to—"

"—Cats eat cat food, isn't that right, Noni?" Ileana looked to her for an answer.

Noni just nodded, trying her best not to laugh.

"I catalogued an array of information about felines on my way back home."

"You catalogued?" Noni questioned, eyebrow raised.

Ileana nodded. She pulled a strand of her long black hair away from the kitten's paw before she spoke. "I can access any information existing on the earth's surface. It's readily available to me."

"Alex, can you do that?"

Alex shook his head. "Unfortunately, no," he admitted. "Ileana has Sight, something I haven't been able to manifest."

"So that's one of the four powers, then?" Noni asked.

Ileana's eyes widened at her comment. "Ah! You're learning!" she cheered. "You'll be an expert in no time!"

Noni shrugged, embarrassed. "I only know what Alex just explained to me," she admitted. Getting back on topic, she asked, "What else can you do with Sight?"

Ileana immediately took her seat again. She settled the squirming kitten into her jacket. "I can see people's truths," she began. "No matter what one may hide, I can see right through it. Sight allows me to experience the past. It allows me to predict future events to an extent. It resembles the power of what you all would call a 'prophet'— depending on what decisions one makes, I can see the outcome."

"That's pretty awesome," Noni marveled with wide eyes.

Ileana nodded. "It can become troublesome. Hesitation and indecision cloud visions. Some larger truths are hard to behold—it is a power that I use sparingly."

Noni, awed by all that she'd heard, laid her head against the couch again and breathed deeply. "This is a lot to take in," she confessed.

Alex touched her shoulder gently, reassuringly. "Don't try to absorb it all at once." He told her.

"I want to know more," Noni announced. "But it's all so new and strange, and I'm not even sure if I believe this is real," she disclosed. "I hear myself talking about this stuff and I just can't believe it." She shook her head. "But then I remember all that's happened to me, all that I've learned, and I just know. I know this is all too real."

"You're one of the few humans to know just how real it is," Ileana revealed. "Many believe in angels and messengers. Many believe in gods and deities, in heaven and hell, in aliens and mythical creatures even, but would not believe it if you told them that we are among them." She gently tugged at the kitten's tiny ear. "I've found that humans are very strange. They believe in celestial beings but don't believe that the divine may live and walk this earth. It's all very peculiar." She shrugged. "And then there's you, Noni. The true believer!"

Noni laughed. "Listen, if Alex wouldn't have saved me, if he didn't tell me everything, then I don't think I would've believed at all. I've never been the existentially speculative type."

"There's so much to know, Noni. So much to learn. There's so much out there!"

Noni stared at the two before her; Ileana, fascinated by the climbing kitten that clung to the arm of the couch, and Alex, who was always fascinated by Noni. They were Gods, on Earth.

She took a deep breath and managed to smile.

"I bet there is."

Hunger struck her the minute she entered her home and dragged her to the fridge where she began tearing leftovers from the shelves. As she spooned yesterday's mashed potatoes and gravy onto a plate, she sensed someone at the doorway. Turning, she found Bianca smiling at her as she absentmindedly chewed at a piece of beef jerky. Still dressed in her uniform, Noni deduced that she must've just returned from work.

"Noni," she began, batting her eyes sweetly. "Will you make some for me too? Please?" She dragged out the last word for so long that Noni didn't even protest; she just grabbed another plate with a sigh and a roll of her eyes. Bianca clapped cheerfully and kissed Noni's cheek with a loud smacking sound. "You're the best!"

"Yeah, right." Noni pulled leftover roast and creamed-corn from the refrigerator and added them to their plates.

Bianca sat down at the small kitchen table. So where'd you go after work?" She asked. Her voice was muffled by the jerky that she tore her way through.

Noni put Bianca's plate of food into the microwave. She set it for one minute and thirty seconds. "I hung out with Alex for a while."

"Really?" Bianca asked incredulously. Her eyes widened at the very mention of him. "So, what? Y'all are friends again now?"

Friends? Noni shrugged. "Yeah, I guess," she answered. "He's cool. I hung out with his sister too. She's pretty nice." She smiled to herself. "Really likes cats, too."

"So you hang out with a really attractive guy and do what?" Bianca probed. "Really, what do you guys do?"

Noni watched the timer on the microwave. This had to be the longest minute of her life. "I don't know; we just talk. We talk a lot about where he's from, and I tell him stuff." She drummed her fingers against the countertop. "We talk about college. Sometimes we just hang out and watch TV." The microwave finally beeped and she hurriedly opened the door, grabbing the plate and getting a fork for Bianca. "He's really chill."

"Oh, I'm sure." Noni handed Bianca the plate and fork. "You know, if you're dating the guy, you can just say so." Bianca started eating, grinning at Noni. "I mean, I wouldn't be surprised at this point."

"Bianca, quit it." Noni scolded. "Alex isn't—we are not interested in each other like that, okay? We're friends. It's all one-hundred percent platonic." She put her own plate into the microwave. "You know, you can be friends with someone of a different gender without wanting to date them."

The other girl shrugged and shoveled food into her mouth. "You're

right," she said. "Sue me for being concerned about your dating life—
or lack thereof."

Noni laughed. "I don't have time to date," she said. "Literally
leaving for school in the next few months—there'd be no point," she
added. Not to mention she was too busy discovering the fact that
gods existed and that she had strange, extraordinary powers that no
one but Alex and Ileana could explain. That, too, was enough to keep
her busy.

Bianca nodded. "Makes sense."

Once Noni's food was hot enough, she sat down at the tiny table
with her cousin. They ate together and Bianca talked about some
party she planned to go to that night with Charli and a few friends
from their high school. She laid out her plans for the week, told Noni
about all the other parties she was invited to. She invited Noni, told
her it'd be fun to get out of the house and not think about work or
college for a while. Unfortunately, Noni had far more on her mind
than simply school and her job. Since meeting Alex, since learning
about everything, life's normalcy had escaped her. Every day, she felt
like she was living in a dream where no one was awake but her.

"Suit yourself!" Bianca stood from the table after she finished
eating. She set her plate into the sink. "But tonight, if you're not doing
anything, I'm going to the lake. I invited Charli and a couple of other
people. No pressure though."

Noni smiled. "I'll think about it."

After cleaning the kitchen, the two girls parted ways. Bianca went
for a run, and Noni went to take a nap. After eating, fatigue set in.
She slept for a short time, restlessly, twisting and turning, but never
able to find a comfortable spot. After a while, she woke up, realizing
that she couldn't rest because her mind was still racing. Now that
she was alone, she was forced to face her thoughts. Behind her closed
eyes, she could only see flashes of Alex and Ileana, of Alex's hands as
they glowed and illuminated the entire room. She couldn't push the
memories from the forefront of her mind.

She sat up, folded her arms in her lap and sighed. Noni stared down at her hands. Brown skin. Short, stubby nails that needed cleaning. How could these hands do what Alex's had done? She shook her hands, wiggled her fingers, and stared at all the creases in her skin and veins beneath the surface.

"Normal hands," she said. "normal girl, right?"

However, there was nothing normal about her, nothing normal about what she'd been dragged into. She was afraid. But the strangest part about her fear was that it did not come from the fact that she had come in contact with otherworldly creatures. Her fear stemmed from the fact that *she did not fear them*. What scared her was how natural it felt to be in their presence, how natural it felt to learn about the supernatural. Noni knew that they weren't human—she had seen what Alex could do.

Now, faced with the unusual truth about the power that lived inside her, Noni was forced to try to bring forth a power from within that she never knew existed. She was no god, but simply a human faced with inexplicable purpose.

She shook her hands again, her normal trembling hands. She remembered Alex's words.

There's power inside of you. Untapped power that you will soon learn to use. If you plan to protect yourself, and your family, you'll learn ... I believe in you. You will succeed.

Power. Noni sat cross-legged on her bed. She closed her eyes, clasped her hands together in her lap. She wondered if she could awaken that power on her own.

Taking a deep breath, she called to mind the calming words that Alex had spoken earlier that day. She tried to remember the peace, the quiet, the stillness that she'd felt. She began her own silent mantra, listened to the sound of the wind blowing outside her window, birds chirping as they flew past. The sounds lulled her into a trance; the darkness behind her eyes wrapped around her like a blanket, shrouding her in a dream. Her heartbeat slowed. Time ticked away.

Noni opened her eyes.

No longer was she in her bedroom. She sat cross-legged in the middle of the street, in front of the redbrick house she once called home. The air felt the same as it did the last time she was here: stale.

Noni stood up, stared down at her hands in front of her. "How can this be real?" she whispered to herself. She looked up and her eyes locked on the house before her. The brick and mortar called to her.

Swallowing her fear, Noni stepped forward through the unkempt grass and cracked pathway, she trudged. She knew the door would be unlocked, so she walked right in.

There they were. Theresa and David Grace. Seated at the kitchen table staring down at their hands, unmoving. She didn't even bother calling out to them, for she knew that her cries would fall upon deaf ears. Noni walked into the kitchen and leaned against the countertops, watching her parents like a hawk.

The conversation began. It was the same as before, and like a child she hung onto their every word. She watched her mother. Watched the curl of her lips as she cursed her father, yelled and fought through her words. Even in her anger, she was beautiful. Noni wished that she'd have noticed her beauty when she was still alive, but she had been too young to recognize the value of loving one's parents while they were still around.

They fought on. Noni braced herself, brought the collar of her shirt up to shield her mouth and nose from the smoke. Noni waited and waited, watched the vents and the windows, but the smoke never came. She released her collar. She looked back to her parents. Her father had walked to her mother and was now begging, pleading in front of her.

"Theresa, listen," he huffed. "I want a family just as much as you do, but I am not willing to risk your life for this."

"Coward," Theresa spat. "I'm willing to risk everything. I want her, David. I want this baby."

Noni's world came to a halt. She seized up, fists clenched against the countertops. "It's me," she shuddered. "They're talking about *me*."

Just as she spoke, a shadow entered the room.

Her parent's voices grew quieter and quieter until she could no longer hear them; she could only watch the way their lips moved as they yelled.

Through the doorway, the shadow came. A dark figure without a face. It stalked into the kitchen, swept its way to where her parents were. It stood between them, hovering amid their silent screams. From its black shadow of a frame, two arms emerged. The shadow reached forward, placed its hands on either side of Theresa's belly.

"No," Noni spoke. The word left her mouth before she was even aware of it. "No! Get away from her!" She shouted.

The shadow turned. It had no face, no eyes, but Noni knew that it was looking right at her. She stumbled backward. It crept toward her.

"Wake up." She hit her arm, smacked it as hard as she could. "Wake up!" She pinched herself and twisted her skin until the pain was unbearable. The shadow slithered toward her, no arms, just a body and a head, a dark abyss that looked as if it would swallow her whole. Noni shut her eyes and screamed. "*Wake up, wake up, wake up!*"

The room was still. Noni opened her eyes.

She sat on her bed, cross-legged. Her hand trembled violently, so much that she couldn't even flex the fingers. Instinctively, Noni reached up and grabbed the talisman around her neck. She clutched it tightly as her hand shook. All of a sudden, the shaking began to slow. She held onto the talisman until her hand grew completely still. When she released it, she slowly flexed her fingers, drawing a fist and then letting it go. No tremors.

It was black outside. The birds chirped no more.

"How long have I been like this …?" Noni reached deep into her jeans' pocket and pulled out her cellphone. It was well after nine.

A knock at the door roused her. "Noni!" Bianca's voice rang out. "You awake? Unlock the door!"

Noni hopped out of bed, unlocking the door that she didn't even remember locking. Bianca stood, drawstring bag in hand, dressed in a thin sweatshirt and shorts.

"You coming or what?"

Noni kept staring at Bianca and her confused expression must have made sense to Bianca because she replied.

"The lake, remember?"

"Oh," Noni could kick herself for forgetting. "Right, right." She searched around her dark room. Bianca flipped the light switch for her. "Yeah, just let me...let me find some shorts or something." She walked over to her dresser, rummaged through the drawers until she found her bathing suit, a pair of shorts, and an old sweatshirt.

"Charli's picking us up," Bianca announced. "Be ready in five?"

Noni silently nodded. Bianca closed the door and left so Noni could dress. Hurriedly, she pulled off her day clothes, slipped into the bathing suit, and threw on the sweatshirt and shorts. She pulled her puff of hair back into a tight bun and took a deep breath, held her face between her hands. "Act normal," she whispered. With a heavy sigh, Noni dragged her hand down her face and walked towards the door. "Nothing's ever going to be normal."

Bianca waited downstairs at the front door. Noni grabbed a jacket from the coat rack beside the staircase. "Are we sneaking out right now or does Auntie know about this?"

Bianca choked out a laugh. "I told her earlier," she answered. "I promised we'd be back by midnight."

Noni nodded. She slipped on a pair of flip-flops—she wasn't sure if they were hers or Bianca's—and then they left.

As Bianca said, Charli awaited them outside. Noni instinctively climbed into the back seat of her car. The ride to the lake was filled with chatter. Noni tried her best to keep talking. It kept her mind occupied. Her words ate up the thoughts in her head, shrouded them for a time. Once they got to the lake, Noni surrounded herself with as many people as possible. She was thankful, for once, to be in a crowd.

To her surprise, Terrell was there. When he saw her, he rushed over to her, smiling wildly. "Noni!" he shouted. "Didn't think you'd come!"

Noni shrugged. "I could say the same for you." She rolled up her sleeves as she spoke. "What brought you out?"

"Bianca invited me while we were working. Said I should do something other than spend all my time at the store," he laughed. "I guess I don't relax enough."

"Don't feel bad; Bianca says the same thing to me all the time."

At least ten people showed up. They started a bonfire in one of the fire pits on the shore. Noni sat in between Terrell and Bianca. She made a great effort to talk to keep the conversation alive within the group. Being in a group with people her age, with *humans*, made her feel normal. It made her feel real. She wrung her hands together just to make sure they were the same—nothing felt the same. Since meeting Alex, Noni's world was spinning, and she felt like she was relearning everything she thought she knew. Was she still the same girl? Or was she something different now? She couldn't say. She didn't know.

Noni kept her eyes on the faces of her friends. She didn't even want to blink.

"You wanna swim?"

Noni looked up, hearing Terrell's question. "In the water?"

"No, Noni, in the sand," he laughed. "I'm dying next to this fire. How are you still wearing that thing?" He motioned to her sweatshirt. "Swim?"

She stood, pulling off her sweatshirt. "I don't know how to swim," she confessed, "but I'll get in the water with you."

"You can't swim?" His eyes widened in surprise. "Nobody ever taught you?"

Noni shrugged her shoulders. She stepped out of the circle, slipped out of her shorts and shoes. "It's not that." She answered. "Bad experience as a kid. Almost drowned. After that, I never really wanted to learn."

"Damn." Terrell stepped closer to her. "We don't have to go if you're not comfortable."

She shook her head. "I'll be fine."

Terrell nodded. They headed toward the water. There were already a few people there, splashing and fooling around. Noni sat cross-legged in the water, making sure that it only reached a few inches above her waist. The water cooled her down, and she breathed deep, letting the waves lap at her stomach. A few feet from her, Terrell floated through the water, eyes closed. The moon shone down on him, making the water around him shimmer and shine. Noni stared up at the sky, letting her head hang back. The moon illuminated the whole sky. She didn't know how long she stared like that, counting the stars and watching the moon.

"You look really pretty." She looked over to find that Terrell was watching her. "With your hair pulled back, I mean. You never wear it like this." He shrugged. "It's nice."

Noni could feel her face heating up. A nervous laugh left her lips. "Thanks," she said. "Didn't put too much time into it."

Terrell came up and out of the water. "You don't need to." He shook water out of his ears, ran his fingers through his hair to get rid of the moisture. He sat down next to Noni, hands in his lap as he watched her. "Something's different about you."

"Besides my hair?" Noni joked, easing her own tension.

Terrell laughed. "Besides that," he said. "I don't know. You just seem different. Also, you've had this stressed look on your face all night, so I mean, something's gotta be up."

"That obvious?" Noni asked. She swallowed hard, ignored the heat building in her stomach. "It's been a rough day," she replied. "a weird day."

"Stressed about stuff with school?" he questioned.

Noni nodded. "Yeah," she lied through her teeth. What else could she say? School was the least of her worries, but the truth was unbelievable. "Just a little overwhelmed."

"I get that." Terrell splashed the water back and forth with his hand. "In the same boat. Getting everything worked out—it's pretty stressful stuff."

"Absolutely," Noni echoed. The waves of water came in heavier, slapping against her, even pushing her back. She inched back from the water.

Terrell stood up, extended a hand to her. "Water's only gonna come in harder," he cautioned. "Wanna walk?"

Noni took his hand and let him pull her to her feet. She stared down at his hands. Normal hands. Normal boy. She nodded. "Yeah."

Noni felt almost ordinary again. She knew it wouldn't last but she still walked along the edge of the water with Terrell, the ordinary boy of whom she'd become fond. She kept her eyes wide open, kept them on the moon while they walked. The lake was too dark for her to feel safe. She'd begun to fear the absence of light, to fear whatever was hiding within it. She could still see the shadow; she could still paint its picture in her mind. If she closed her eyes, she feared it would be waiting for her.

Silently, she reached for Terrell's hand. He grasped hers and kept talking as if nothing had happened. Noni was grateful.

"You know," Terrell spoke, lacing his fingers with Noni's, "I used to walk along this lake with my mom all the time when I was little." He smiled sadly at the ground. "She used to walk on the side of the water because she said she didn't want the water to come take me away."

Noni shouldered him gently. "Is that what you're doing? Protecting me from the water?"

"Exactly." Terrell grinned.

Noni kicked sand as she walked. "Your parents live around here?"

"Nah," Terrell stared at the ground again. "Never knew my dad. Mom died when I was fourteen. So," his voice trailed off.

Noni glanced at Terrell. "Me too." She squeezed his hand. "I'm in the dead parent's club too."

"How'd it happen?"

"Electrical fire. On Thanksgiving, nonetheless. The whole house was gone." She took a deep breath, shaking the memory from her mind. "I was seven. It was a long time ago."

"Remembering is hard." Terrell spoke a soft, calming voice. Noni closed her eyes momentarily, just trying to find peace. "I try remembering all the good stuff, if I can help it. It still hurts but, you know, it's a good hurt."

Noni nodded. She remembered the good things sometimes. She remembered painting with her father. She remembered the first canvas he ever bought her, how he helped her paint portraits of her favorite stuffed animals. She'd never been more proud of herself.

She remembered reading with her mother. Every night, they would read a book right before she put Noni to sleep. Theresa would curl up in Noni's tiny canopy bed, get underneath the blankets with her, and read with her until Noni finally fell asleep.

There was always good to be remembered.

"My mom was always really big on school, you know," Terrell began again. "She was really smart. Had two master's degrees and a Ph.D. Dunno how she did that while being a single mom, but she did. And you're smart like her—she would've liked you." He grinned at Noni, taking a deep breath. "That's why I decided to go back to school. I know it'd make her proud."

"I understand that," Noni replied. "That's why I want to go into medicine. If I could ever make my parents proud, I'm sure this would be the way to do it."

Terrell nodded. He wrapped one arm around Noni's shoulders as they walked. "Dead Parents Club sucks."

Noni forced back the tears in her eyes as she laughed. "Yeah, yeah it does."

CHAPTER EIGHT

The following week was a whirlwind. Noni found herself spending less and less time at home and work, and more time with Alex and Ileana. She wasn't able to tell her family or friends about what Alex and Ileana were or about what she was learning. Because of this, Noni thought it best not to spend too much time around Bianca and her Aunt. Noni only saw her cousin and Aunt a handful of times. Bianca continuously tried to get Noni to come out or stay home and spend time, but Noni continuously declined, always creating some excuse as to why she couldn't make it. She couldn't tell the truth.

Terrell, too, had been contacting Noni nonstop. Ever since the lake, he'd been texting her, trying to see her outside of work. As much as Noni liked him, she couldn't do it. She was a horrible liar, Terrell was her friend, and she couldn't risk spilling secrets. So she stayed away. She avoided him at work, and when she left *Michael's*, she was MIA.

Noni went to visit Ileana and Alex. Upon entering Ileana's apartment—and almost tripping over Ash, who tried desperately to capture her shoelaces—Noni found Alex, sitting straight up on the couch, unmoving, captivated by the television. Noni recognized the movie he was watching, as it was one of hers and Bianca's favorites.

Ileana came up behind her and closed the door. "He is absolutely mesmerized by this film," she noted.

Noni started taking off her shoes. "*Titanic*," she said. "It's a pretty good movie." Noni picked up the kitten at her feet, cradled him in the crook of her arm to calm him. She and Ileana headed into the living room, and upon hearing the approach of their footsteps, Alex turned. Noni smiled at him before she spoke. "So this is what you do when I'm not around?"

"Have you seen this film before?" Alex questioned. "This is incredible!"

"It's a great movie."

"The way these two gravitate toward one another—they have such a profound bond." He shook his head, eyes wide, mouth curled up into an incredulous grin. "Remarkable."

Noni held back a laugh. She had to remind herself that they weren't human and were not used to things she'd experienced her entire life. "Well they love each other," she shrugged. "That's the whole idea of the movie. Love transcends time, or whatever." She leaned over the edge of the couch and saw at least eight movies spread across the short coffee table. She recognized most of the titles. "How many of these have you watched?"

"Only four," Alex responded.

"*Only?*"

"We can watch one together, if you'd like."

"Maybe later." She edged around the couch and plopped down beside him. "There's something I need to ask you," she began. She looked up at Ileana. "Both of you." Ileana hurried over and sat on the couch opposite Alex and Noni. Alex paused the movie and turned to Noni. She started speaking again. "I should've told you sooner, but things have just been so busy I—it slipped my mind." Noni confessed, "A few days ago, I was practicing using that power. I tried to do what you showed me."

"Did it work?" Alex eagerly asked.

Noni shook her head. "No, it didn't," she replied. "I went back to the same place—saw the same thing I saw the first time. But, it was different somehow." She sighed, reached up and began twisting at a strand of her hair. "The first time, I was in a room with my parents. They were arguing. Before they could finish the argument, this dark smoke filled the room, suffocating me, and then I woke up." She took a deep breath. "When I did it alone, it was almost the same except there was no smoke. But this figure—this shadow—came in and was sort of lurking near my mom. Then it tried to—well it looked like it was trying to get *inside* her. Then I shouted at it and it turned and looked right at me—"

"What?" Ileana interrupted. "It looked at you? At *you*? Are you sure? Was there no one else there?"

She shook her head again. "Aside from my parents, it was just me. It heard me. I know it did." She glanced between Ileana and Alex. "I have a feeling that's not supposed to happen."

Between the two of them, a glance was shared, one that Noni could not immediately understand. Ileana pursed her lips and looked to Noni.

"A Shadow. A Halfling," she revealed. "They sometimes prey on profound memories. Memories hold power, you know."

"I wasn't exactly *alive* at the time," Noni pointed out. "How is that a profound moment in my life?" She heaved a heavy sigh, cradling her face in her hands.

"You were also in a very vulnerable position," Ileana admitted. "Until you're able to master the power of Light, there's really no way to protect yourself." She paused. "Unless Alex or myself is there, of course."

"But you can't always be there," Noni pointed out. She looked at Ileana, and then at Alex. "There've been times where you've barely made it to me. I don't want to keep risking my life. If I have this power inside me, that means I can protect myself. I *will* protect myself, and my family too."

It wasn't long before Noni asked Alex if they could try again. This time, Ileana joined them, taking Alex's hand into her left, and Noni's into her right. She smiled at Noni before they began.

"Remember, we're here," Ileana said. "You'll come back when the time is right."

Noni watched as their hands begin to glow. Their skin was warm to the touch. She closed her eyes. Alex began his soothing mantra, guiding Noni's mind into a calmer place. The last thing that Noni felt was Ileana's hand squeezing hers in silent reassurance.

When Noni opened her eyes, she was standing in the middle of the street. She scrambled up from the ground, marched toward the house, took a deep breath before going inside. She shut the door behind her and then pressed her back against it, closing her eyes and silently waiting. She listened to the argument she knew all too well, listened to the rising, angry voices. She couldn't bear to watch it again, to see them shouting at one another for a third time. Noni didn't know what else she would find lurking in that room with them; she wouldn't enter again.

Suddenly, her mother came rushing out of the kitchen in a fit of rage. She raced up the stairs in front of Noni. Noni watched her father come to the bottom of the stairs. He thought about following Theresa, thought about calling out to her, but he didn't. She never looked back. David, face contorted into a deep scowl, fists clenched, turned towards the door. Noni leaped out of the way, watched him throw the door open and leave. The door slammed behind him. Noni gripped the knob and tried to open the door to follow him out, but it wouldn't turn and the door would not budge. She pushed the blinds to the side, tried to look for her father out the window, but there was nothing beyond the glass. Nothing.

Noni let the blinds fall shut. Her eyes lifted, stared up at the staircase before her. She clenched her fists; she wiped her sweat on the front of her denim shorts. Noni went forward, grabbed the banister and stepped up onto the first stair. A weight set in her stomach, a hollow heaviness, spreading through her body. Her arms hung weakly at her sides, numb. Noni's body grew heavier with every step; her feet were cinderblocks, dragging her down every time she tried to rise. Once she was at the top of the stairs, she grabbed at her own chest, trying to find air to breathe, or some sort of peace. Finding none, she walked on. Her parent's room was just at the end of the hall. From where she stood, she could see her mother's back, could see her kneeling at the foot of the bed. Noni took a step forward but stopped when she realized where she was standing.

To her right was her own bedroom. The blue walls, covered in paintings of castles and dragons, called to her. She remembered when her father painted those pictures. For her sixth birthday, he asked her what she wanted the decorations for her room to look like. They sat together on her canopy bed. He looked at her and said, "What do you want me to paint, Noni? You could have Cinderella, Rapunzel, or Snow White—" Noni shook her head and spoke. "No Daddy. I want you to paint dragons. I'll be the princess! I'll fight the dragons and live in a big castle!" she grinned. The next day, and for two weeks thereafter, her father painted. Three dragons soaring through the sky, castles beneath them, and he'd even painted Noni as a princess, standing at a castle, sword in hand. An ache rose in her chest; she gripped the doorway with her shaking hands. The memories of this room had been untouched for years.

She stepped back from the door. This house burned down a long time ago.

Noni was steadfast as she walked into her parent's room. Her mother was still there, still on her knees. Noni could hear her; she was praying. She was shaking.

"Please." Her voice trembled, "Please, take care of my baby." She brought her hands together, clasping them desperately. "Please just let me live long enough to bring her into this world. That's all I want. That's all." She couldn't continue the prayer. She wrapped her arms around her abdomen and wept. Noni stood against the doorframe, one hand over her mouth and the other clenched at her side. She knew there was nothing she could do to comfort her mother; she could neither touch her nor let her know she was there; she could do nothing but stand and listen to her cries. There was no one listening to her.

Noni slid down the wall, sat and closed her eyes. "Why am I here?" she whispered to herself. She opened her eyes, stared down at her hands. "Why don't I just wake up—"

From the ceiling, something small landed in her hand. A tiny spark, smaller than a dime, danced in her palm. Noni closed her hands around it, looked up, and witnessed the smallest of sparks falling all around her. The source of them spiraled downward, an orb of light no larger than her hand. It was brighter than anything she had ever seen, even brighter than Alex's hands had been. It landed next to Noni's mother, trailed around her as she cried, leaving flickering sparks in its wake.

When it started to grow, Noni stood up.

It expanded, growing taller, thinner, no longer the small sphere it had been. It extended into five parts, into arms, legs, and a head. It stood, now a body of celestial light, hovering over Theresa, shedding light onto her and around her. It reached out and touched her shoulder. Light began to overtake the room but it wasn't the light from the figure; it was the spark from Noni's hands, shooting out from between her fingertips. Noni opened her hands. Light poured through, shining so much that it blinded Noni to the scene before her. Her hands shook with its power, pulsated as it grew and grew. She shut her eyes, shielded them from the brilliance of it.

She kept her eyes shut until the light died out.

When she opened them, she was sitting on the couch in Ileana's living room. Alex and Ileana stood before her, no longer holding her hands, but smiling.

"Oh Noni," Ileana spoke, clasping her hands together at her breast. "You've done it."

Noni looked to Alex then. He held up his hands, looked down at them, and motioned for Noni to do the same.

She did.

They were glowing.

"Holy—"

Noni nearly jumped out of her own skin. She threw her hands out in front of her, turning them over repeatedly. Lines broke across her skin; a soft white light emerged from the cracks. Trembling, she traced one of the lines on her right hand from fingertip to wrist. It felt no different, except her skin was warmer there than the rest of her body. The light was much dimmer than anything Alex or Ileana had shown her, but it was there. It was real.

"How do I make it go away?" she inquired.

Alex answered her softly, "You must simply will it so."

She nodded once. She stared at her hands for a moment before closing her eyes and breathing deeply. When she opened her eyes, the glow was gone. Her hands were back to normal. "I can't believe that just happened." She muttered. Suddenly, Ash climbed onto the couch beside her. The black kitten pawed at her hand, tiny claws catching her skin. She barely felt it.

"You may feel fatigued soon," Alex informed. "Your body won't be used to this."

Noni had already begun to feel the effects of her feat. Her body seemed heavier than before. She was thirsty, hungry, and exhausted; all urges simultaneously attacked her body at once. She brought a hand up to her forehead, pushing her hair back to touch her skin. She was scorching. Groaning, she lay back against the couch.

"Would you like some water?" Ileana asked. "Food, perhaps?"

"Anything would be great," Noni replied. "Thank you," she paused, looking between both Alex and Ileana, "for everything. I mean it."

Ileana went to the kitchen to get Noni a glass of water. Once Noni had it in her hands, she gulped down every drop, as if her life depended on it. The last time she felt that intense of a thirst was when she had awakened from the coma. Water had never tasted so refreshing.

"Better?" Alex asked. Noni nodded, setting the glass down. "You'll be much safer now."

"What can I do with this power?" Noni wondered. "I've never actually seen you use it against one of the others." She paused, clasping her hands together in her lap. "What is it that I'm supposed to do now?"

"We use this power for protection against all things," Alex revealed. "Once touched by Light, a Halfling cannot return to this part of the Universe, at least not by the same means. It's almost like branding them to keep them away from Earth." he explained. "If one of them ever comes after you, you only need to use the Light, grab hold of them with purpose, and it's done. It will expel them."

"It's like poison to them," Ileana chimed in. She set down a plate of sandwiches before Noni. "Like setting fire to them from the inside."

Noni picked up one of the sandwiches and began eating. "What about the stronger ones?" she could barely chew through her exhaustion. Her mouth wouldn't cooperate, wouldn't chew fast enough.

Alex shook his head. "Another time. Eat," He encouraged.

She bit into the sandwich again. Chewing slowly, she closed her eyes and focused on eating. Food had never tasted as good as it did in that moment. She finished the sandwich within minutes, reaching for the next one with tired hands.

"Would you like to stay for a while?" Alex asked. "You look like you're ready to fall asleep."

Noni laughed. "You're right, I'm exhausted," she admitted. She'd taken a bus to the apartment. She was too tired to wait at the bus stop and, although she knew Alex would take her home if she asked, she was too tired to leave the couch. Staying there, with Alex and Ileana, wouldn't be too bad. She at least felt safe with them around.

"We should watch a movie," she declared. "Something boring to balance out what just happened."

A smile lit up Alex's face. "Excellent!" He picked up four of the DVDs from the coffee table. "Which one would you like to watch?"

She chose a movie, one that she hadn't ever seen. Noni brought her legs up to her chest and cozied up on the couch. Alex sat down next to her again, and eventually Ileana joined them, sitting on the floor with Ash in her lap. For the first few minutes, Noni tried to pay attention to the flick, but after a while, her mind began to stray.

Her hands still tingled from wrist to fingertip. She was in awe at what she had accomplished. Nothing in the world could compare to this moment.

Glancing up at Alex, she smiled; his eyes were glued to the TV and he didn't notice her watching him. Here, next to him, she felt safe, secure. Things had changed drastically since they'd met. She knew what he was, saw what he could do, and finally learned the truth. She trusted him; he had shown her more than she ever thought she'd see in her life. Noni felt a certain closeness with Alex, one that she couldn't rightfully explain or understand. From the moment she'd met him, she'd felt it. There with him, she'd never felt more at ease. Perhaps it was because, through the power that lay within Noni, they were connected; perhaps it was because Alex had saved her life on more than one occasion and that her safety was always his utmost concern.

Noni wasn't sure. She did believe, however, that he truly was something like her guardian angel, no matter if he denied it.

Later on that afternoon, after indulging in the old movies, Alex offered to take Noni home. She was tired, but she was reluctant to leave Alex. She could've watched movies on the couch with him for the whole day if he'd let her. However, he seemed to know better, and suggested that she go home to rest. Noni dozed off on the short ride back. She was so tired that Alex offered to walk her to her front door just to make sure she got inside without falling over.

Upon reaching the door, she turned to him and smiled. "Thanks again," she spoke, yawning lightly. "I couldn't have done any of this stuff without you."

Alex smiled. "You could've," he said, "but I'm glad I could help—"

Abruptly, he was cut off as Noni leaned into him and hugged him. She wrapped her arms around him and yawned again. "Thank you for keeping me safe."

Alex's skin seemed cool against Noni's. He smelled of nature, a sweet earthy scent, like the scent of the soil after it rains. As they embraced, Noni could swear that she felt warmth building in his chest. The same static tingle jumped between their skin, giving her goosebumps.

"I'll always do my best to keep you out of harm's way."

CHApTER NINE

Noni resigned herself to the couch as soon as she walked inside. No one was home, so she knew her nap would be uninterrupted. Though she'd dozed off at Ileana's apartment and even in the car, she was still exhausted. Her whole body felt like it was buzzing, but she attributed that to the fact that she'd done something she assumed was impossible. As soon as she lay down, her necklace tangled around her neck. Instead of untangling it, Noni took it off and laid it aside on the coffee table. She buried her face in the pillows and sighed.

You're special, Alex had said to her. Noni wondered what else she'd learn to do; she wondered how far she could go, and what more she could learn. It was terrifyingly exciting. Still, with the ever-present buzzing in her chest, her hands, and even her head, Noni closed her eyes and prepared to sleep.

She would have slept peacefully if not for the abrupt knocking at the front door. Startled (and mildly annoyed) she pulled herself away from the couch and went toward the front door. The knocking never ceased or slowed down.

"Coming!" she called irritably. When she finally opened the door, she nearly jumped out of her own skin. Noni narrowed her eyes and clutched the doorknob tightly. "What are you doing here? And how do you know where I live?"

Elijah, dressed in jeans and a gray hoodie despite it being the dead of summer, held his hands up in surrender as he spoke. "I know this is weird," he began. "and I know you probably think that I'm crazy, but I'm not. I thought I was, but I'm really not." Hands in the air as if to brace Noni for his words or to show her that he wasn't dangerous, Elijah spoke again, "I know." He paused, staring down at the ground. "I know about Alex. I *know*."

Noni tried her best to hold her face together to hide her emotions, but she had already pressed her lips into a thin line and her breathing quickened. "What—what are you talking about?"

"You know what I'm talking about." Elijah's eyes were tired. Noni couldn't pick him apart. "I'm not trying to scare you; I know this is hard to believe. But I've seen things. I *know* things, and you need to know what I know." He let his hands fall to his sides and glanced back and forth. "Would you mind letting me inside? It's not safe." His dark brown eyes seemed to grow darker.

Although she didn't trust him, Noni understood. "Come inside."

Elijah stepped in, and Noni quickly shut the door behind him, leaving it unlocked. He turned to face her. She quickly stepped back.

Elijah shook his head again. "I'm sorry," he apologized. "You don't have to be afraid of me. I just want to help."

"How do you know about Alex?" she interrogated. "Do you know him? Have you been following him? Following me?"

"In a sense. This is going to sound ridiculous." Elijah ran his hands over his fade, dragging them down his face.

"I'm sure I can handle it." Noni folded her arms over her chest.

Elijah mirrored the gesture and took a deep breath. He touched his forehead, touched his mouth, and then spoke.

"I have nightmares," he confessed. "I can't sleep at night because all I see in them is him—and the girl. His sister? I don't know." He wrung his hands together, shaking his head. "And you, Noni." His hands shook and he tried his best to keep them still. "I know about the things that follow you, you know. The shadows. Or Halflings—that's what *they* call them, right?"

"I don't understand how you can possibly know about any of this," Noni's voice trembled. "You need to leave. You need to get out of my house or I'm calling the—"

"—I've seen terrible things. Things that are going to happen to you."

Breath left Noni's lungs. She couldn't speak. She could only stare wildly at Elijah, whose terror was her own.

"I know more than I want to. Ever since you got in that crash I—I don't know, I just started seeing things. Dreaming things. I didn't believe that any of it could be real. I saw doctors, psychologists—my mother thought I was losing my mind. Put me on all these meds, and for a minute I thought she was right." He took a deep breath, still wringing his hands together. "But then I saw him in person. That day at the park."

She knew exactly what day he meant. "You were there?" Her voice was soft, breathless.

"I wasn't following you. I was taking a walk to clear my mind. I hadn't slept very well the night before. And that day, I saw you run from him and I saw him fighting the shadow. That's when I knew it was all real. I kept seeing things—glimpses of the two of you. Weird things, like orbs of light flying around. I saw the shadows so many times." He breathed deeply. "So many times."

"Have you told anyone else?" Noni asked.

Elijah shook his head. "My doctor, but she just thinks I've lost it." He shook his head again. "Everyone thinks I'm mentally unstable—you did, too."

"I'm sorry," Noni apologized. "I couldn't have known."

"You couldn't have," he agreed. "but I didn't come here to talk about that. I came here to try to help you. To warn you."

"Warn me?" she questioned. "Don't you think I know what's going on here?"

"No," Elijah answered, "no, I don't think you do." Noni was taken aback. "I think you think you're safer than you actually are. Last night, what I dreamt…it's why I'm here now. I would've stayed quiet, would've waited this all out—hell, I'd rather drug myself up until I can't talk than be here. But here I am."

"What did you see?" she asked. "Last night—what did you dream about?"

"I saw you fighting a shadow. I watched one of them attack you, and I saw it kill you—I watched you die."

They were silent after he spoke. Noni sat down at the foot of the stairs, gripping the banister. Elijah leaned against the front door, staring at the ground. Noni cupped her face in her hands. "That can't be true," she whispered. "It just can't be true—I don't know anything about fighting, about killing. I couldn't. I can't!"

"But you know how to use those powers. That light. You know how to use it," He told her. "And you will. And then you'll get yourself killed."

"I'm not going to let anyone kill me." As terrified as she was, Noni was defiant. "Why are you telling me all this—really?"

"To warn you. To help you. To make you more aware of what's going on around you. There's something bigger happening and even I don't know what that is. But if you're not careful, you'll die." He watched her and took a deep breath. "You're not invincible, and neither are your friends. No one is."

"When are they coming?" Noni asked.

Elijah shook his head. "I don't know."

"How many of them will there be?"

"I don't know."

"What *do* you know?"

"I only know what I see in my dreams. And it's never a lot—just glimpses." Elijah sighed heavily, folding his arms across his chest again. "I think there's more to this than I know," he spoke softly, eyeing Noni from where he stood. "I think there's more to this than either of us knows."

Noni sat silently, at a loss for words. She stared at her hands, turning them over, her eyes tracing the lines in her palms. "Don't you think it's dangerous that you know all this?" she asked Elijah.

He laughed mockingly. "I think that being anywhere near you or knowing anything about you is absolutely dangerous. Yet here I am."

Noni rolled her eyes. "No one asked you to come."

"I'm trying to help save your life here."

"I didn't ask for your help!" she suddenly exclaimed. "In fact, I didn't ask for any of this! I was living a simple life, okay. A *normal* life up until all this stuff started. I never asked for any of it!" she yelled. The volume of her voice seemed to shake the room. A heat built up in her chest, and when she closed her mouth, Noni realized that she'd barely been breathing. Pushing out a defeated sigh, she hung her head.

Elijah's hands went up in the air again, a gesture of surrender. Noni's sudden anger sent him back into retreat. "I'm sorry," he apologized. "I didn't mean to upset you, I just," he sighed, shaking his head. "After everything I've seen? All the things I've dreamt? I really thought I'd be helping you."

Noni paced. "I get it." She wrung her hands together, ignoring the awful tremor in her hand. "I'm sorry for yelling. I'm usually not like that. It's just—this is a lot."

Elijah nodded, "I get it." He extended his hand to her. "Let's try this again. I think I can help you. I *want* to help you, even if it might be dangerous. So...peace?"

Noni nodded and tried to smile. "Yeah," she spoke. "Peace." She took his hand. The moment their palms touched, a tremendous heat exploded across Noni's skin. A prickling, like explosions of lightning, broke across her hand and crawled past her wrist and up her forearm. She saw it, then. Sapphire lines splintered through her skin and Elijah's too. He froze as he watched the light overtake his hand.

A sphere began to grow from their hands, light engulfing them. Electricity crackled around the orb, loud and bright. Then, with no warning, the light grew and grew, and it exploded, swallowing them—swallowing everything.

Everything was dark, silent and unmoving.

Noni, lying on the ground, felt a steady pulsation against her spine, a warm rhythmic beat.

She opened her eyes, and the first thing she saw was Elijah lying next to her. Still clasping his hand, she tugged at his arm lightly until he began to stir. He awoke, startled, and turned to face her. When she looked at him, she immediately noticed the difference.

His eyes were different, a honey color. Almost golden.

"This is the place," he whispered.

"What place?" Noni questioned. He finally released her hand and motioned for her to look around. She did, and that's when she finally noticed where they lay. In a field of grass, red grass, that grew higher than she had ever seen before. She quickly climbed to her feet, fighting back the overgrown blades. Once she sat up, she could finally see it all, and she was in awe.

It was like nothing she could have ever imagined.

The sky, cloudless, was the color of a sunset; the hundred shades of red and orange were endless ribbons. The sky was filled with stars shining far off, twinkling brighter than any star on earth. They all seemed to be flying, twisting and turning in the air. In the distance, the land seemed to stretch on forever, and the red grass grew over hills as far as they could see. It swayed in the wind, which carried the sweetest, thickest scent like fresh, warm honey. Noni breathed as deeply as she could, taking it all in.

"This is the place I always see in my dreams," Elijah spoke. His voice, barely above a whisper, seemed to tremble. He whipped around and took Noni's hand again. "Look." he pointed.

Noni turned and finally she saw what he saw. "That's it," she said. She remembered the name that Alex had used. "The Tree of Life."

"I knew this was all real," Elijah laughed. "I knew I wasn't making this all up!"

There it stood, a tree taller than any measurement could meet. It reached so far into the sky that Noni couldn't even see its branches. Its roots, the size of average trees, were high above the ground, forming a cavern of roots. Even from where they stood, Noni could feel the same pulsating from before. It was in her chest, infiltrating her muscles, her nervous system, her entire being. The tree seemed to call to her. It was alive.

"Do you feel that?" Elijah asked.

Noni didn't look at him; she only nodded. She never let go of his hand. "Come on," She spoke as she began walking toward the tree. He followed suit.

Their eyes were fixed upon it, never blinking. They walked in unison, stepped in time, seeming to match the pulse they both felt in their chests. The ground, too, seemed to shake with their every move. Without warning, they both began sprinting, racing as fast as their feet could carry them. The faster they ran, the heavier the pulse became; it was then a deep thudding in the land. The wind whipped at their faces, cut at their eyes, but nothing slowed them.

In a matter of seconds, they reached it. The pair stood together, marveling at its beauty and size. Its trunk seemed to throb; like a heart, it beat.

"Look!" Elijah shouted excitedly, pointing into the sky.

Noni looked. Thousands, millions of lights lit up the red sky. They were like stars, except they carried much more life. They seemed to fly, soaring around one another, buzzing and crackling like balls of pure energy. "This is crazy. This can't be real," Noni whispered to herself.

Elijah gripped her hand. "But we both know it is."

He was right. They knew all too well.

Suddenly, Elijah grabbed hold of the tree. It was too late for Noni to stop him. With that, the tree began to glow, an enormous all-encompassing light. It engulfed Elijah first, swallowing him completely before it spread to her. For once, Noni wasn't afraid. She placed a hand on the tree, breathed deeply, and closed her eyes.

"Noni—NO!!"

The scream woke her. Ileana's voice rang loud and clear in her head. Noni heard the sound of Ileana's feet beating the pavement. She seemed to be running toward her, but looking right through her. Noni reached out and began to walk toward her, but Ileana ran right past her.

She found Alex, then. Lying face down in the middle of the street, and he didn't seem to be breathing.

Another shriek.

Noni turned again to follow Ileana's path, and that was when she saw herself. Hair flowing—flying—in every direction, with an azure, ethereal glow surrounding her. Her hands carried a deep red glow and she seemed to be walking toward someone. Fighting someone.

A Halfling.

Noni ran forward, behind Ileana, who was racing toward her counterpart. However, before Ileana could even reach her, Noni heard herself let loose a sound that she had never heard herself utter, something akin to a battle cry. The earth shook with it. The red glow built and suddenly, red orbs left her hands, energy balls shooting out, aimed for the enemy. It fought hard, dodging the attacks as they came. Noni knew that she couldn't fight as fiercely as this. What she was seeing was inhuman, unnatural—she did not possess these skills. But there she was, fighting as if this came naturally to her. She grabbed the Halfling by the throat, raising it high above the ground before slamming it into the pavement. The ground splintered and cracked, sending rocks flying out in all directions. Ileana reached her, tried to stop the fighting, but when she touched Noni, she was repelled and sent flying across the street. Noni herself began to run toward the fight, feet carrying her before she even knew she was moving. She watched herself slam the Halfling into the ground over and over, forming a deep crater in the earth. The red glow of her hands only grew. Somehow, the Halfling managed to break free of her hold in a split second. Noni could see her own face then. Light poured out from her eye sockets, her mouth was a wide grimace, and she barely recognized herself. Terrified of what she had become, she looked away. In that moment, everything stopped.

Ileana's shriek echoed in the streets.

Noni looked up, and saw that the light surrounding her counterpart was dying out, a slow fade to black. Blood stained her shirt. It began to pour out of her in waves, pooling beneath her. Noni screamed.

Gasping for air and catching the scream in her throat, Noni shot straight up. Elijah lay on the floor, sprawled out as Noni had been. She released his hand, crawled closer to him and began shaking him wildly. She called his name frantically, her voice trembling as she cried out. Seconds later, Elijah's eyes flew open and he inhaled, taking in a deep breath. He was calm, not frantic as Noni had been, and lay still, staring up at her, right into her eyes.

"What was that?" She asked desperately. "What *was* that?"

"That was what I saw in my dream," Elijah confessed. He sat up slowly, pushing himself up on his elbows. "In my vision."

"I died," she shuffled away from him, kneeled and brought her hands up to her face. "Oh my God, I died."

"That's just what I saw before—you fighting, with the light all around you," Elijah recalled. He was staring off now and his voice lowered as he continued, "and then it kills you. And all the lights just die out."

Noni covered her mouth with one hand, biting back the bile that rose in her throat. The vision shook her to her core; she couldn't erase what she'd seen, couldn't expunge the memory from her mind. It was in her body. She could almost remember what it felt like. The gaping hole in her chest.

Elijah touched his head. "Everything's all mixed up," he said. "I don't know why I'm seeing these things. But now I know that it's all connected to you, for sure. This stuff isn't natural."

"It isn't," Noni agreed. "You're like me, I think. Special. You have these powers. It's hard to explain."

"Can you at least try? I'd really like to feel sane again."

Noni could hear the exhaustion in his voice. She nodded,

continuing, "It's called Sight. I learned about it from Alex. It's a special power that some of his people have. And sometimes, normal people like you and me are able to tap into it." She sighed. "He's been helping me tap into mine—Light—and learn how to control it. Once the attacks started, he started helping me learn so I could protect myself."

"Why were you being attacked in the first place?" Elijah questioned.

Noni inhaled deeply. "The Halflings. They need what's inside me. The Light. It's one of the powers I have. It's like my life-force, almost."

"Like your spirit," Elijah gathered. Noni nodded. "This is wild." He turned to her again. "How can you be so calm about all this?"

"Do I seem calm? I'm absolutely not. I'm still waiting on someone to tell me vampires and werewolves exist next."

"Still got a sense of humor. That's a good sign." Elijah began to stand up from the floor. Noni followed suit, standing beside him. She took a step closer and spoke again. "I think you should talk to Alex," she blurted out. "Or maybe Ileana. I think they could help you sleep."

"I'm doing a fine job without sleeping. No need to convene with your super friends."

"I don't think it's safe for you," she admitted. "After what's happened to me, all the times they've come after me—it's only a matter of time before you're on their list. I think Alex and Ileana can help you."

"The way they've helped you? Dragged you into something you can barely explain?" he laughed. "Listen. I'm having a hard time digesting all this. And to be real, I'm scared shitless. So forgive me for not wanting to meet them." He ran his hands across his short hair, dragging one down the side of his face. "It's all too...much. It's good enough to know I'm not losing my mind. I think I can sleep knowing that." He started towards the door, but Noni touched his shoulder, stopping him. She could feel the electricity jump from his skin to hers and she snatched her hand away immediately.

"Let's at least exchange numbers," she spoke quickly. "In case something happens."

After a few seconds of staring at her, Elijah agreed, albeit begrudgingly. He put his number under the name "Eli" and handed her phone back to her. He went toward the door again and Noni stopped him, speaking one last time. "Look, I know you're scared," she told him. "I am too. Terrified, actually. But I just think it would be a good idea for us to stick together. Considering."

"Considering." Eli repeated.

"I'm pretty much alone in this. I think it might be better, safer, if we watched out for each other."

"Feeling a bit friendlier now, eh?" He asked, shaking his head as he laughed. "I get it. I do. I'll keep in contact. I just need a few days. A few days to mull over all this. I'm still having a hard time believing I'm not dreaming." He admitted. "I hope I did some good, coming here."

"You did. And if I didn't say it before, thank you for trying to help me. I think the vision was something I really needed to see." She looked him in the eye then. "And I hope it's something you never have to see again."

Eli nodded once. "Me too."

She watched him leave. She didn't take her eyes off him until he was in his car and driving down the street. When Noni closed the door, she considered calling Alex.

She didn't.

Chapter Ten

There was no light.

The only sound she heard was the clicking of her soles against the ground. Her eyes darted around in the dark, but she could still see nothing. Outstretching her arms in front of her, she felt nothing. However, when she reached to her sides, she felt cool, rutted stone. She followed it with her fingers, trying to find patterns in the stone. Soon, she realized that she was traveling down a long, empty corridor. The sound of her footsteps ricocheted off the walls. She quickened her pace, hoping for an end, a door, or a way out. Suddenly, her foot collided with something hard and immovable. She used the tip of her shoe to feel the shape of the object. It was short, stone, and when she lifted her foot higher, it seemed to end just before she felt another object on the higher level.

Stairs, she thought.

Cautiously, she climbed the stairs. She kept her hands against the wall, using touch to see in the dark. The staircase seemed to wind, twisting and turning, as she climbed higher. Still, no light or sound broke from the bottom or from the top, which she wasn't sure she'd ever reach. The darkness was harrowing, and the silence—despite the sound of her own footsteps—was distressing. She breathed slowly, calming the fear and anxiety bundled in her chest. Beads of sweat gathered at her brow. Her heartbeat quickened. Her hands shook as they grazed the stone.

All of a sudden, she saw it. A lone beam of light shooting through the darkness.

Quickly, she raced up the staircase, careful not to trip over the gown trailing at her feet. She gathered bundles of it in her hands as she sprinted. She could see a door, and between the cracks in its wood, more light shone through. Swiftly, she scaled the last few steps. She reached the door, grabbed the handle and threw it open.

Bright light spilled in from every direction. Blinded by the intensity, she threw her arm up to shield her eyes. She squinted, using her fingers as a filter and walked out into the light.

She could see everything from where she stood. She found herself standing on a balcony that overlooked vast flatlands of scarlet ground. She raced to the edge, gripping the stone railing as she peered over the edge. From the top, she could see a mass of people, heading out together in a crowd of carts and tools. Horse-like creatures led the carts on which the people rode. Brown-skinned children trailed behind them, skipping and laughing as they raced hand in hand. They parted the thick sea of red blades as they headed farther into the glade. She looked out and saw an enormous sun on the horizon. Farther out, another already sat high in the sky, surrounded by bright lights. Stars.

"It's beautiful, isn't it?"

The sudden voice broke her reverie. She swung around to find a man standing in the doorway from which she had just exited. His smile was just as warm as it had always been.

"Alex," she spoke, taking a deep breath and allowing a smile to grace her lips as well. "Yes," she replied. "Yes, it is beautiful. What is this? Where is this?"

"Nova." He came toward her, meeting her at the edge of the balcony and standing beside her. "This is Nova."

"This can't be real," she whispered to herself. She looked up at him and found that his eyes were on her. "This is real?"

"It's as real as you make it."

As she watched him, taking him in, she finally saw *him. From his neck hung a gold medallion. He wore golden wristlets, rings, and even a golden headdress over his long black hair. Bathed in gold, even his brown skin seemed to glisten underneath the light. She reached out and touched his arm, bringing it closer so that she could examine the wristlet he wore. But just as she touched him, an electric shock shot through her hands and straight up her arm, sending painful spasms through the limb.*

"Ow!" She cried out, jumping almost a foot away from him. Her fingers moved of their own accord as the shock tore through her. "What was that?" she shrieked.

"I'm sorry—I'm so sorry the—the current is unbalanced." He tried to come closer but she jumped back again. "It's just the current," he paused. He watched her. "Where's your talisman?"

She touched her neck.

It was bare.

"It's the current, Noni, it's the current."

She woke up, tangled in wet, sweat stained sheets, with glowing hands and a loud buzzing in her head. Noni squinted at her hands, blinded by the white light that illuminated her bedroom.

"Oh crap—crap." She shook her hands rapidly, waving them back and forth in the air. "Stop. Power down. Shoo!" she hissed at herself. Nothing changed. Noni huffed heavily, groaning as she stared at her hands. She tried to remember what Ileana and Alex had taught her.

Taking a deep breath, she closed her eyes and tried to steady her heartbeat. She breathed slowly for a while, drawing in calm and pushing out her anxieties. She imagined the light from her hands fading slowly. By the time she opened her eyes, there was nothing left besides a glimmer at her fingertips. She turned her hands over, watching the glow recede through her veins. After it dulled and finally disappeared, Noni heaved out a heavy sigh and fell backward onto her mess of sheets.

"Was that a dream?" she whispered to herself in the dark. Silence was her only answer. She rolled over onto her back and stared at the ceiling above her, pondering her own question. Her alarm clock glowed red in the dark. It read 4:37 am. Noni rolled over, facing the window and turning her back to the clock. Her heart was still racing, and her skin still tingled.

"There's no way I'm getting back to sleep," She groaned, yanking the blanket up to her chin. But after lying there for an hour, Noni became restless. She threw her blankets off, climbed out of bed, grabbed a jacket and her cellphone. Before she left her room, she touched her neck. It was bare. Her talisman.

She rushed downstairs. Thankfully, she found it right where she'd left it. On the coffee table in the living room. *What a place for it,* she told herself. Noni slipped it around her neck, and instantly she felt a bit calmer.

The sky grew brighter. Noni left the house only to go outside and into the back yard. She found a dry patch of grass and sat cross-legged on the ground. Light broke across the horizon. Noni sat alone, chin in her hands, watching the sun make its ascension. The sunrise brought warmth across the city and Noni closed her eyes, letting its rays wash across her skin. The calm of the morning brought her peace. The still in the air helped her breathe. Her skin had finally stopped tingling, her heart no longer bounced around in her chest, and she felt normal again. Noni did her best to put the strange dream behind her as she absorbed the morning rays.

The neighborhood had yet to stir. Noni lay on her back, legs bent at the knee, as she watched orange and yellow spread across the dark blue sky. The colors spilled into one another, and for a moment Noni was reminded of something. The memory skirted around the edges of her mind but she couldn't quite grasp it. A feeling of nostalgia settled in her stomach. She closed her eyes, reached for the memory as best she could, but nothing came. Just the feeling.

The grass was soft beneath her, and she found herself drifting off, calmed by the quiet of the morning. She didn't dream, but behind her closed eyes, she saw images of the orange and yellow sky mixing with the dark.

Noni didn't know how long she'd been asleep in the grass, but when she awoke, it was to the sound of tires screeching and metal colliding with a loud *CRASH*. She shot up from the ground, climbing to her feet in a panic.

Terrified cries could be heard from the street. Noni bolted from the backyard to the front of the house and to the street. The sight before her was gruesome.

Two cars, a red Honda civic and a silver pickup, had collided head-on in the middle of the street, right in front of her home. People were pouring out of their houses, all staring aghast at the wreck. Someone screamed to call 911. The driver from the pickup had managed to climb out of his truck. Covered in gashes and blood, he lay on the pavement underneath his open door. He was alive, breathing, leaning up against the truck and cradling an arm that was bent at an unnatural angle.

The driver in the Honda had yet to stir. The front of the car was completely compressed, smashed into itself and twisted up.

Everything that happened next was a blur. Noni was running before her brain could register the movement. Her heart pounded in her chest as she raced to the driver's side. There was a Latina woman inside, slumped against a bloody steering wheel. She didn't seem to be moving. Noni tore off her jacket, wrapped it around her hand and, with strength she had never possessed, punched a hole clear through the glass window. She unlocked the door from the inside and ripped the door open. Noni gently took the woman's head into her hand and laid her back against the seat. Her eyes were closed and her chest wasn't moving.

"Don't be dead," Noni whispered, grasping the woman's shoulder. "*Please* don't be dead." She unbuckled the woman's seat belt and took her into her arms. Noni wasn't sure how she could support the weight of a grown woman, but she didn't stop to think. She lifted her from the seat and cradled her on the ground, steadily repeating her mantra.

Then it happened.

A white aura began swirling around the base of Noni's feet. It picked up speed, strength, and wind. It whirled around Noni and the woman in her arms, and their hair began to flow in the air. Noni's eyes darted around; she didn't understand what was happening. But her thoughts were immediately cut off when the woman's eyes shot open. She arched her back and her mouth opened, inhaling all of the white light that surrounded them.

The wind ceased.

The woman's eyes locked on Noni, staring wildly at her.

"I was..." she started to speak. Tears pooled in the creases of her eyes. "I swear I was...dead. I was *dead*." She wept, tightly clutching Noni as she buried her face in the girl's shoulder, smearing blood all over her shirt. "*Dios santo*, thank you."

"I didn't...I didn't do anything." Noni shook her head. "I—"

Before she could say another word, the paramedics arrived. They pulled her away from the wreck and immediately saw to her.

"Miss? Are you injured?!" A paramedic shouted at her. Noni could only shake her head. He walked her back to her side of the street, where Bianca and Deidre frantically waved her over. But before she reached them, her knees buckled beneath her.

The paramedic caught her before she hit the ground.

They told her she'd gone into shock after the crash. The scene had been too gruesome for her to handle, and she'd seen a heavily injured woman up close. The sight had been too much, her body had gone into shock, and she passed out.

That's what they told her. But she knew better.

The victims of the car crash had already been taken to the hospital and the wreck was currently being dealt with. One of the many paramedics had stayed behind with Noni, checking her vitals and making sure that she was alright. Before the paramedic left, she told Noni that she had simply gone into shock. Noni now sat on the couch with Bianca at her side and Deidre in the armchair across from them, slowly shaking her head.

"A tragedy," Deidre said. "Such a shame."

"At least they both lived," Bianca noted. "Could've been much worse." She sighed. "We've seen enough crashes for a lifetime though."

"Noni?" Deidre spoke. "Are you sure you're okay? I really think you should go lie down."

Noni shook her head, mustering up the courage to finally speak. "I'm fine," she answered. "I...I was just shocked, like the paramedic said. I'll be okay."

Deidre watched her intently.

Noni hadn't had any fainting spells since the crash. But she remembered what that had felt like, and what she felt like when she passed out on the front lawn; the two were completely different. Her body had completely given up on her out there. It felt like she had been drained of energy from head to toe; her limbs were bricks and not a single drop of life had been left in her body.

But what was that light? she wondered. *What had been the aura that swirled around her like a tornado?* It felt so *powerful,* like nothing she had ever felt before. *And what had it done to that woman?* She saw the aura leap straight into her body. And when her eyes opened, it was as if she wasn't even hurt.

Noni stood from the couch.

"Where are you going?" Deidre and Bianca interrogated in unison.

"I just need some fresh air," she lied. "I'll be back in a few."

"I should go with you," Bianca announced, "to make sure you don't faint again or get hurt—"

"—No," Noni interrupted. "I'll be okay, I feel fine. I'll be back soon."

She rushed out the door before either of them could say another word. Once outside, she pulled her phone out of her pajama pocket to call Alex. However, she saw that she had two text messages from Eli just then, both from well over two hours ago.

Msg: Noni are you alright? Had another dream. Something weird happened right? Just let me know if you're ok.

Msg: theee comingf you hav t

She couldn't decipher the second message at all. But the first was most troubling. Had he known what was going to happen to her?

There wasn't enough time to decide. She dialed Alex's number.

"Noni." His voice sounded almost relieved.

"Something happened," she forced out the words. "I need you to come pick me up. We have to talk."

"I am not within range. I will have Ileana come for you. I'll meet you at the apartment. Deal?"

"Deal." She hung up the phone and went back inside the house. Bianca and Deidre were still in the living room talking. When they saw Noni walk in, their voices ceased. Deidre gave a half-hearted smile, but Bianca just looked sad. Noni took a deep breath and headed up the stairs.

After only a few seconds of thought, she concluded that they must be worried about her. If she were one of them, she'd be worried, too. But there was no way she could explain this to them. There was no way they could understand the strangeness that had infiltrated her life.

She took the fastest shower in the history of showers. Throwing on a pair of jean shorts and a ratty t-shirt, Noni gathered her things and bolted down the stairs. Thankfully, the peanut gallery wasn't there to stare her down this time. Just as she opened the door, Ileana pulled up in Alex's car. She had her hair pulled back into a tight, serious bun and her eyes were grave. Noni didn't like the look on her face.

"Are you alright, Noni?" she asked once the girl reached the silver car.

"I am—I think."

Ileana watched her carefully, narrowing her eyes as she scrutinized

Noni's appearance. "We will talk more with my brother." That was last thing she said until they reached the apartment.

Noni and Ileana only had to wait ten minutes before Alex arrived. The first thing he asked when he walked in was "What happened?"

Noni explained the whole thing, from the moment she fell asleep in the grass to the moment she collapsed in the arms of a paramedic. Every detail. Every single one.

A look passed between Alex and Ileana as if they knew something they weren't telling her. Noni hated when they did that.

"What is it?" she asked almost frantically. Alex opened his mouth to speak, but just then Noni's phone began to ring. She looked at the caller ID and saw that it was Eli, again. She picked up. "Hello?"

There was nothing but static on the other line. Occasionally, she heard a whisper of his voice but she couldn't make out any of the words he spoke.

After about ten seconds, she was about to hang up the phone. That was until she heard a chilling, frantic scream on the other end that made her hair stand on end.

"Eli?!" she shouted, pressing the phone to her ear. The line clicked. Dead silence.

"What in the world was that?" Ileana questioned.

"My friend, I mean—this guy, Elijah. From work."

"The one who was bothering you before?" Alex asked.

Noni didn't know how to answer. "I mean he wasn't exactly bothering me. He was weird, but considering everything that happened—" Then she realized— she hadn't told them *anything* about what had happened. She looked both Alex and Ileana in the face and took a deep breath. "Guys, I think you should sit down."

Again, Noni was forced to spill everything. She told them about every strange thing that had happened between Eli and herself before going into the events of the previous day. She was sure to describe in detail just what had occurred. What they saw, what he'd told her, how she'd felt—everything. Anything to get answers. She even showed them the confusing text messages he'd sent her early that morning.

Ileana's face turned grim. "I should have foreseen this." she spoke. "Your friend Elijah is in great danger."

"You said he touched you." Alex looked to Noni. "He touched you and there was a spark?"

Noni nodded. "Yes," she said. "It's like I could feel it in my veins. In my whole body. It was like a—" just then, she remembered her dream. "Like the current." The words came out of her mouth as if she'd said them all her life.

She couldn't read Alex's face. His mouth was pressed into a hard line and his eyes looked cold. He took her hand and pressed his thumb to the middle of her palm. In a flash, her veins lit up like a Christmas tree.

"What are you doing?" Noni questioned.

"Searching for his energy signature."

She wasn't sure what that meant but somehow, she knew that it was important. Eli was in trouble. She didn't know what had happened to him but it wasn't good.

One vein in her arm turned bright, neon green, showing through her skin. Just as it did, the color slowly spread up into Alex's hand, past his wrist and into his forearm where it glowed underneath his skin as it did Noni's.

When Alex finally released her hand, her arm went back to its normal brown, but his veins still glowed. As he watched the color pulsate, his eyes grew even colder.

"Your friend is gone."

"Gone?" Noni repeated. "Gone as in dead?"

"No," Ileana responded. "Gone as in no longer in this realm." She took a deep breath. "We can find him and bring him back," she looked right into Noni's eyes. "But you must stay here. It's too dangerous."

"But who would do something like this? And how?" After less

than a second, she answered her own question. "The Halflings. They took him."

"From what you've told us," Alex began. "Your friend has the gift of Sight. And he knows too much."

"You have to help him. We can't let them hurt him. Eli might not be the most normal guy, but he tried to help me and we just can't let him get hurt."

"We won't," Alex responded, "but you need to go home and rest. After everything you've experienced today, it's a wonder that you're still on your feet."

"Why not stay and rest here?" Ileana offered. She glanced at Alex. "We will be back in no time."

Noni wasn't sure she believed that, but she didn't argue. When they left, with dark eyes and ashen faces, Noni wondered just what it was that they hadn't told her.

She didn't stay at the apartment.

As much as she knew she should've, Noni couldn't just sit still. There was too much on her mind, too much going on. She chose to walk home instead. The walk wasn't terribly long, but she decided to walk through downtown instead. The bustle of people and activity kept her mind calmer. She could concentrate on something other than her own confusing life.

Noni stopped at her favorite smoothie bar. The owner knew her by name and was excited to see her, commenting on how it'd been so long since he'd seen her. Noni bought a strawberry banana smoothie. She sipped it halfheartedly.

It was noon and the streets were busy. Most people were on their lunch breaks and were scrambling around to find something to eat within thirty minutes. The sky was cloudless, and the sun beat down on the town and its people. Noni was boiling hot and the smoothie in her hand was melting. Condensation on the cup made it hard to grip.

She considered sitting down to finish the smoothie, but all of the seats and tables outside of the smoothie bar were occupied. It was unfortunate because those tables had umbrellas above them, shielding people from the sun's rays. Noni sighed and started to walk on.

"Just a moment, Miss."

At the sound of a man's voice, she looked back. At the table directly in the middle of the group sat a man that could have been no older than forty. His skin was dark, but it glowed in the sunlight. His smile was warm, almost inviting. The one thing that threw Noni off about his appearance was his eyes. His eyes were golden. Nostalgia tugged at her conscience. "Who are you?" she asked. "Do I know you?"

"Who I am is not important," he spoke. His voice was smooth, calming even. "Please, sit."

Noni was compelled to sit down. It was almost as if her body made the choice before her mind did. She sat at the table across from him, never taking her eyes off his. He was grinning, she could tell from the creases at the corner of his eyes, but she couldn't break his stare.

"Miss Noni, it is so lovely to finally see you again."

Noni struggled to break free from his gaze, but she couldn't. Her voice was almost monotone as she spoke. "How do you know my name?"

"We all know your name."

Golden. Noni thought. *His eyes are completely golden.*

"You're very brave, talking to a stranger," he began again, "though I suppose I'm not a complete stranger."

"I don't know you."

"You did, once," he told her, "and you will again." He glanced around, breaking the stare for once as he surveyed the area. Noni quickly shook her head and batted her eyes, trying to clear the fog around her mind. But she was too slow. He had already caught her eye again. "Where are your companions?"

"Gone," Noni answered.

He grinned again. "Such a pity. I was hoping to see them." The man reached out and grabbed Noni's hand. She wanted to resist, but found that she couldn't. He pressed his thumb in the middle of her palm, just as Alex had before. Her arm lit up again, in a rainbow of colors. But the man singled out two, violet and deep blue. He grinned again, a devilish smile. He released Noni's hand, leaving it on the table and he dusted off his hands, ignoring the violet and blue glow in his veins.

"Well, sweet Noni," he began, reaching toward her. She wanted to pull away but his influence was too strong. Instead, she was still, unblinking and unmoving. "We'll meet again." He pressed two fingers to the center of her forehead, just above her brow line. Suddenly, a warm, calming wave washed over her entire body, making her limbs go numb along with her mind. For a brief moment, her eyes closed. When she opened them, she picked up her watery, melted smoothie, put the straw to her mouth, and tried to remember just why she'd sat down at the table in the first place.

CHAPTER ELEVEN

"Where'd you go?" Bianca stood in the doorway, staring down at Noni who sat on the front steps, staring out into the street. There were still tire marks on the asphalt.

Noni pinched the bridge of her nose, trying to dispel the sudden haziness in her head. "I just went for a walk," she lied, "and then I walked through town." Her mind seemed to blank. She remembered getting her smoothie, and she remembered coming home. She stared at the empty cup in her hand. "Got a smoothie, then came right back."

"Mom was worried sick. You can't go all beast mode on a car window, faint, and then disappear for hours and expect her not to worry," Bianca insisted. "What's been going on with you? You disappear all the time, you're never home, you're distant, and suddenly you can punch through car windows? The Noni I know can't even run a quarter of a mile without having an asthma attack."

Finally, Noni turned to face Bianca. Bianca's brow furrowed and the edges of her mouth pointed downward. Noni sighed.

"I know you're worried—"

"—Worried doesn't even cover it, Noni," Bianca cut in. "You've never been like this. What the heck's going on?"

"I just need some space, okay?" Noni announced, annoyed with her cousin's tone and approach. "I've got a lot on my mind and a lot on my plate."

"Then talk to me about it!" Bianca exclaimed. "We used to talk about everything! Ever since this summer started, getting you to come around has been like pulling teeth!"

Noni desperately wished that she could just talk about it. She wished that she could just spill all her secrets to Bianca, tell her everything about Alex, Ileana, and even Eli. Tell her about what she was learning, what she'd seen, and what was to come. However, all of that was unrealistic. There was no way she could tell Bianca the truth. She could lie, tell her it was college and work, but Bianca would be able to tell that she was lying. Instead, Noni simply grew silent.

"You wouldn't understand, Bee. Just let it go," she replied, seconds later. "I'm okay. If it was anything serious, I'd tell you. I'll work it out."

Bianca's mouth was pressed into a thin line. Her eyes were stony. "Fine," she bit. She said nothing more. Bianca returned to the house but made sure to slam the door behind her as she went.

Noni buried her head in her hands.

Her cell phone began to ring in her pocket. Hoping that it was Alex or Ileana, she quickly pulled it from the pocket of her jean shorts. Surprisingly, it was a call from her boss.

"Hello?"

"Noni," the woman spoke from the other line. "It's Friday; you were supposed to be here about fifteen minutes ago."

Noni grit her teeth, cursing herself. "I'm sorry, Kris," she apologized. "I'll be there soon. I am *so* sorry."

"It's fine, Noni. Get here when you can. And if you don't mind," Kris added, "could you stay two extra hours? Elijah was supposed to be here, too, but he hasn't turned up either."

Noni's stomach dropped. She closed her eyes and took a deep breath. "Sure, I can do that." Kris thanked her and hung up. Noni hoped with every fiber of her being that they'd find Eli.

Against her better judgement, Noni borrowed the car in order to make it to work on time. Bianca was still smoldering when she handed over the keys. She pretended not to notice.

When she got to work, they put her on register, which she didn't mind. The store was packed that Friday afternoon, and so Noni kept busy for her whole shift. Once her shift ended, she took over Eli's shift. Kris had her clean for an hour and let her go to her normal position as a greeter.

Terrell was there, smiling as he invited customers into the store and handed them free coupon books. When he saw Noni, his eyes lit up.

"Fancy meetin' you here," he grinned, handing her a stack of books. Noni strained her face to smile. "Heard you almost missed your shift."

"Overslept," she told him. "Took a nap and missed my alarm."

"Late night?" he asked.

"Um yeah, something like that."

Terrell kept talking, and Noni tried to keep up with the conversation. Her body was there with him, but her mind was worlds away. She kept hoping, praying that a call would come, but she received nothing.

Noni worked relentlessly. She went above and beyond her duties just to keep herself occupied. When she left for the day, her boss congratulated her for working so hard. Noni couldn't wholeheartedly accept the praise.

As she was gathering her things in the employee locker room, Terrell walked in to grab his bag.

"Need a ride home?" he asked.

"Not today," she replied. "I drove."

"You actually drove here? Without freaking out?"

Noni shrugged. She'd been in a panic before she even got in the car. Nevertheless, it was strange, she noted, that when she was behind the wheel, she hadn't felt the slightest anxiety about driving.

"Yeah. I guess things are getting better," she replied. She hurriedly threw her knapsack over her shoulder and was about to rush out the door, but Terrell was still standing there. She looked at him head on, trying to examine the look on his face. He looked like he wanted to say something to her, with his eyebrows pinched together and his mouth pulled tight to one side. Noni thought about the last time they'd had an actual conversation. It had been the night that they had walked across the beach, holding hands underneath the moon. It seemed like so long ago, when it reality it couldn't have been more than two weeks. So much had happened since then that Noni had almost forgotten. Terrell, however, had not. Noni's shoulders sagged as she exhaled deeply, trying to be still for once.

"Listen," she began, "I know we haven't talked much since the lake."

"Understatement," he said. "I text you all the time, you know."

She cringed. She'd gotten every text. But every time he'd texted her, she'd been in the middle of things—in the middle of things she definitely could not explain to him. "I know, and I'm sorry for not answering," she replied. "It's just that I've been...busy." Even as she said it, the words didn't feel right. "There's just a lot going on right now. I can't really concentrate on anything else. I'm sorry."

Terrell just nodded. "Cool, cool. I understand," he said. "I really like you, Noni. Can we, you know, still hang out or whatever? If you have time?"

"Of course!" she exclaimed, relieved that he wasn't upset. "And don't get me wrong. I like you, too. It's just...the things I'm dealing with, I—"

"—I get it. You don't have to explain to me."

She smiled and thanked him. He was a great person, and Noni felt guilty for shutting him down, but it just wasn't the time.

"Maybe in another lifetime," she muttered as she left the store. The sun was setting, slowly making its descent. Noni headed home, for lack of a better place to go. She drove in silence, trying to cage her thoughts and concentrate on something other than her kidnapped coworker.

When she got home, Bianca was still upset. She sat in the living room, reading a book. She didn't even look up when Noni closed the door.

Now or never. Noni thought to herself as she walked into the living room. "Bee, can we talk?" The words tumbled out of her mouth like rocks.

Bianca's eyes were daggers. "Oh. Now you want to talk." It was more of a statement than a question. Noni let it slide.

"I don't want to fight with you," she stated earnestly. "I didn't mean to shut you out earlier." What could she say? What could she possibly say to make her cousin understand?

Bianca closed her book and set it down beside her on the couch. Noni took that as a peace offering. She stepped into the living room and sat down in the arm chair across from the couch.

"Just tell me what's going on," Bianca spoke. "I'm not trying to get all up in your business, but you're basically my sister, and I want to help you if I can."

Noni considered the truth. She chose a half-truth instead. "I'm not so sure about my future right now." She exhaled, digging deeper into this truth than she ever had before. "Nursing school—California—I just don't know if it's right for me. And I'm struggling. I just don't know what I'm going to do with my life. I don't know what's in store for me," she explained. At least that much was true. Noni had no idea what would come next for her. She barely knew what would be happening in the next half hour. Ever since the crash, ever since Alex saved her life, the future she'd imagined had been wiped away, replaced with uncertainty and doubt.

"Noni," Bianca began, "we could've talked about this. I mean, you seemed so sure before."

"I know," Noni replied, "but now, I'm not. All this time, I've been thinking that it would be great to follow in my mom's footsteps. You know? I want to help people like she did. I always have. But I just don't think it's what I want to do. Or what I should be doing." She didn't know what she should be doing. "I feel like I don't know who I am right now."

Bianca's eyes were softer now, not hardened with anger as they were before. "Noni, I had no idea," she spoke gently. "But honestly, you shouldn't worry about school so much. There's always time. You can always change your major and find something that you love."

Noni forced a smile. She felt sick, completely ill. "Yeah," she nodded mechanically, "you're right."

Bianca got up from the couch to hug her. "You don't even have to go to California! You're so smart you could go to any school you want! You're such a perfectionist, Noni. Don't stress over this kind of thing." There was so much concern and care in her voice. "Don't let this stuff get to you. Your mom would be proud of you no matter what."

Noni's throat was full. Hugging Bianca, she fought back tears. She wondered just what her mother would think if she knew.

Ileana didn't text Noni until well after midnight. It was a simple message.

We found him.

Noni knew it would be in her best interest to stay at home. She had to work at 8 a.m. and she had barely slept as it was. Nevertheless, she knew that she wouldn't be able to sleep if she didn't *see* Eli. She knew he was safe now that he was with Alex and Ileana, but she still needed to see him for herself.

She snuck out. She'd learned enough tricks from Bianca over the years to know how to leave without being caught. Noni didn't take the car because that would be too obvious. She tiptoed out of her room, leaving the door slightly ajar. She softly treaded down the stairs and left through the back door, which tended to creak less than the front. She bounded through the backyard, through the fence, and down the street. It was late, and the buses in their area had stopped running at least an hour ago. The walk from her house to their apartment wasn't long. However, her heart still beat just a bit faster as she hastened her steps.

When she reached the apartment, Noni rushed up the stairs and burst through the door. She saw Eli lying on the couch, completely still. Ileana's fingers were at his temples and there was a blue glow surrounding his head. Noni rushed toward him but before she could get close, Alex came forward, grabbed her by the shoulders, and shuffled her back toward the door.

"Is he okay?!" She was frantic, craning her neck to look past Alex. "Is he? Alex, Is he—"

"—He's alive," Alex assured her. "Speak softly. Ileana needs to concentrate on healing him."

Noni stood still, finally taking a deep breath. She looked up at Alex, whose hands were still on her shoulders. "How bad is it?"

"Physically, he's fine," Alex informed. "But his mind—" Alex's eyes grew darker. "Ileana is working very hard."

As they stood there under the light of the hallway, Noni finally got a good look at Alex. His skin glistened with sweat. There were rips and tears along his white shirt, which barely covered anything because of the damage. There were scratches and cuts along his chest, but his face was the worst of it. There was a deep gash above his brow and blood still seeped from it, streaming down the side of his face.

Instinctively, Noni reached up and brushed his hair away from the wound, tucking it behind his ear. The gesture felt almost automatic. "Why haven't you healed?" she asked. She realized that her hands were still in his hair and so she pulled her hand away, and her face immediately grew hot. Alex smiled—she wasn't sure why.

"The weapon that was used on me wasn't a mortal weapon. It'll take longer to heal, but I'll be fine." He gave her the once-over and frowned. "You haven't slept, have you?"

Noni shrugged. "I've been worried all day. I couldn't sleep."

"Noni you must rest. You're human." As he said this, his frown seemed to grow even deeper, as if her mortality was something that displeased him. "You need rest."

"Listen, I'll sleep once I know that Eli is okay." She folded her arms over her chest, as if to solidify her act of defiance.

Alex didn't protest. "Come into the kitchen, then. We need to give Ileana some space."

When they walked through the living room, Noni couldn't help but glance at Eli and Ileana. He lay across the couch, one arm over his chest and one dangling off the edge. His eyes were closed, but they moved behind his eyelids. He was sweating profusely. Ileana was deep in concentration, unmoving with closed eyes. Noni wondered just what she was seeing inside his head, and just what she had to fix in order to put him back together.

They sat in the kitchen at the island. Noni drank a cool glass of water and Alex just sat. Something was off about him, but Noni couldn't pinpoint the cause. But sitting in silence made her skin crawl.

"So, where did you go?" she asked.

"Another realm," he answered, wincing. The cut on his face had to be painful, Noni could only imagine. "Elijah was in another realm."

"How did you get there?"

"There's only one way to travel between realms," Alex told her. "And that is through the Yggdrasil."

Noni remembered the Yggdrasil. She'd seen it in her dreams, more than once, and in more than one form. She remembered the humongous tree, stretching hundreds of feet into the air, with orbs of light being born from its branches. She remembered the pulsations that the tree sent through the ground, through her whole body. It was a living, breathing organ.

"How do you get to the tree; I mean how's that possible?"

"Portals exist in every realm," Alex informed. "You just have to follow its roots, and it can take you anywhere."

Before Noni could ask another question, she and Alex were jarred by a sharp shriek. Alex was up before Noni. He raced into the living room and found Ileana kneeling beside the couch, where Eli was finally awake, sitting straight up with wide, frightened eyes.

Quickly, Alex helped Ileana to the armchair across from the couch, checking to make sure she was still with them. Noni noticed then that Ileana, too, was covered in gashes and cuts. Her clothes were torn to shreds, hair singed, and her brown skin seemed to have lost its glow.

Eli turned to Noni, blinking slowly as he eyed her.

"Eli?" she spoke softly as she inched toward him.

"Noni," He spoke her name. "didn't think I'd see you again." His voice was dazed, as if he wasn't all there. "Didn't think I'd see anyone, or anything, again."

"Eli—what did they do to you?"

He dropped his head, his eyes no longer meeting Noni's. Eli was silent for several moments. Noni's eyes darted over to Alex and Ileana for a split second. Ileana's eyes were closed and Alex stroked her hair carefully with a solemn expression on his face.

"I saw things, Noni." Eli's voice trembled as he spoke. "I saw everything that has happened. They made me watch it all. They forced me to have vision after vision after vision." His voice cracked. He reached up, cradling his head in his hands. "It felt like my skull was splitting. I saw so many things that I don't even know what I know now. It's all so scrambled…and scattered. And none of it makes sense." He shook his head, as if to try to make the memories disappear, but they wouldn't. "They brought me to this tree—"

"—the Yggdrasil."

Eli nodded slowly. "Yes, the Yggdrasil. They tried to drain my blood. All of it. They were going to let me bleed out. And they just sat there. They just sat there and watched the whole time. Smiling. Laughing. And I screamed and screamed for them to let me go, but they wouldn't, Noni, they wouldn't." His voice broke then, and Noni watched his eyes gloss over, watched tears pooling in the corner of his eyes.

"They weren't trying to kill me. They wanted to…they wanted to *use* me. And they kept saying, *Blood holds power, and he will come for you.* Over and over again. *He'll come for all of you.*"

"He?" Noni spoke. "Who is he?"

Eli's entire body seemed to shudder. "Negus…his name is Negus."

Chapter Twelve

"Negus." The name felt familiar on her tongue. Noni's brow furrowed. She looked to Ileana and Alex. Ileana's eyes were open and sharp. Alex was staring right at Noni, as if he were expecting something to happen. "Who…who is Negus? Who is that?" Noni questioned. *And why does that name sound so familiar to me?* She left the second part of her question out, but she needed to know.

"Negus, King of Kings," Eli recited. "Death. Destroyer of Realms." His voice was monotone, emotionless. He looked up at Noni again. "He is a very bad man, Noni."

"There are things that you need to know about the history of our realm," Alex spoke directly to Noni. "About every realm." His eyes were deep, grave.

Noni could tell that this was something he did not want to speak on, but she knew it was necessary and so did he. There was so much she didn't know. Maybe this would be her chance to figure it all out.

Ileana stood from the armchair then. She went straight over to Eli and took his face between her hands. "You've seen so much," she whispered to him. In that moment, Ileana looked older than she ever had. She pressed her lips to his forehead and immediately, his eyes closed. "Rest," she told him. He was asleep before the words even left her mouth. She propped up his head with a pillow and folded his arms across his chest comfortably. She returned to the armchair, wiping the sweat from her brow and taking a deep breath.

"In the beginning," Ileana's eyes closed again as she spoke. "there was Ruuxa, and there was Jidh. Together, they created everything..."

Noni sat down on the floor beside the couch where Eli lay. She watched Ileana and listened closely as her story unfolded like an ancient tapestry.

...Jidh was the first God, ruler of the land, and Ruuxa was the sky. Jidh wandered the land for eternities and Ruuxa always cared for him. When he thirsted, she gave him water. When he hungered, she gave him sustenance. When he tired, she gave him a safe place to lay his head. She always watched over him, ensuring that all of his needs were met. Jidh loved Ruuxa for all she had done and for all she had given him. He knew that Ruuxa had always been there watching over him and that his happiness was important to her. However, he knew that she deserved happiness too. Ruuxa deserved to feel the happiness that Jidh felt every day. He knew that she loved him, and that she desired to be with him. He knew that she wanted to roam the land with him, to touch him, and to live. She wanted something tangible. She deserved a true existence.

"Come to me. We can exist here!" *Jidh shouted to the sky.* "We can be together!"

Ruuxa's only response was a crack of thunder across the sky. The skies turned gray, clouds rolled in from all directions. They crowded around a single tree that stood in the middle of the field where Jidh had made his home. Lightning struck the tree, sending power through all of its branches and roots. The tree glowed with divine light, almost blinding Jidh. When he opened his eyes, the glow of the tree had died down. But its branches were lit up with sparks, and out from the trunk walked a woman he had never seen before. Bare-skinned, she stepped out onto the grass and looked at him. Her golden eyes matched his. An ethereal glow surrounded her and that was when Jidh knew that Ruuxa was like him—she was a goddess.

They were together for quite some time before they began to change.

Though they loved one another, they craved more. They needed more. Therefore, Ruuxa decided that they should have children. Together, using the tree from which Ruuxa herself had been created, and a fraction of light from each of them, they brought forth two children. Their first child was Malika, whose name meant queen. Their second and final child was Negus, whose name meant king. Their children were beautiful, powerful, and they were the second generation of gods and goddesses. Malika was the more powerful of the two and she was the oldest. Her powers began to manifest when she was just a girl. Negus, however, did not receive his powers until he was well into his adolescent years. Their parents focused on Malika for much of their life. Jidh and Ruuxa helped her to grow with her powers, focused on her strength. Negus grew envious of his sister and jealousy boiled under his skin like poison. A darkness began to grow in his heart, eating away at the light that Ruuxa and Jidh had given him. Out of violent jealousy, Negus plotted to kill his sister, Malika. But she was powerful, and she knew of his plans. Before he could go through with his plot to kill her, she banished him into the darkness, making it so that he would never see the light again. Unfortunately, doing this drained almost all of Malika's power. With the last of the power she had, she went to the tree and asked it to divide her light equally, twelve ways. The tree absorbed her and from its branches, twelve children were born, six boys and six girls.

Stricken with grief, Ruuxa returned to the sky. Jidh remained landlocked, raising their daughter's twelve children. Ruuxa provided all that they would need, just as she had in the beginning. Jidh missed Malika terribly, but he knew that he must raise her children, just as he and Ruuxa had raised their own. He did not make the mistake of favoring any child. In fact, when the children were fully grown, he offered a gift to them. Jidh was old, and he was tired. He wished to retire to the sky, with Ruuxa, but he knew he needed to give Malika's children one last gift before his departure. To the tree, he sacrificed all of the light that was left in him. The tree offered six realms; Viumbe, the realm where everything started, had been split into six. One male and one female would be the designated protectors of one realm of their choosing. Using the tree, two by two, they were transported to the new realms. Through the power of the tree, the Yggdrasil, they were always connected...

"...But Negus was not to be forgotten. Because his sister split her power into so many pieces, the chains that bound him to the darkness weakened. And now he's back."

Noni was torn from the story as the tone of Ileana's voice changed. She noticed that the woman's eyes had grown hard and cold.

"After eons of imprisonment, he returned. He and his Halflings have been waging war on every realm."

Noni grew silent. She tried to process Ileana's story as best she could, but it was too much for her to take in. She pulled her legs to her chest and rested her chin on her knees.

"He's here to destroy the Earth," Alex stated firmly. "He has already overthrown several realms. Thrown them into darkness."

"Why didn't you tell me this sooner?" Noni's voice was barely above a whisper when she spoke. "All of this is *terrifying*. I've been in the dark this whole time."

Alex shook his head. "Noni, the time wasn't right," he admitted. "The time still isn't right."

"What do you mean *the time wasn't right?*" She sardonically imitated his voice. "What were you waiting for? *Why* would you wait? People could die! Eli could've died! Hell, I could've died countless times but you waited until now to tell me about some crazy god who's trying to destroy the earth?" She stood up angrily, blood boiling underneath her skin.

"Noni—"

"—*No!*" she exclaimed. "All this time, I've been willing to do whatever I had to do to keep everybody safe. Half the time I don't know what's going on, or what any of this means, and I'm tired of being in the dark!"

"I'm trying to protect you!" Alex shouted, rising from his seat on the floor. He had never raised his voice like this. The power of it seemed to shake foundation of the entire apartment building. "I have *always* tried to protect you, even if you don't remember—" He stopped himself. Whatever he'd been about to say was left unsaid. Ileana gripped the arms of the chair, and Noni could tell that the wood had cracked underneath her grip. Alex's hands were glowing bright blue. And when she looked down, she realized that hers were glowing too.

An overwhelming sadness seemed to wash over Alex's face. Immediately, the glow around his hands died down. He turned away from both Noni and Ileana. He was silent as he left the apartment, not even bothering to look back. Noni was left there, trying desperately not to cry as she shook her hands, wishing away the glow.

"Oh, Noni." Ileana was up and out of her seat. She wrapped her hands around Noni and pressed the teen's head against her shoulder.

Noni tried to fight the tears, but she was so riled up, so angry and overwhelmed, that she couldn't. "I just don't understand," she wept. "This is all just too much. Ileana rubbed her back gently, trying to comfort her. "None of this makes sense! And—And what did he mean?" Noni pulled back from Ileana, shaking her head. "What did he mean, *even if you don't remember?*" she repeated his words. "What am I supposed to remember?"

"He's just upset, Noni. Don't take it personally," Ileana assured her. "The journey took a lot out of us. The more power we expend, the more *human* we become." She took Noni's hand and took her to the armchair. Noni sat and Ileana spoke more. "That's why he let his emotions get the best of him. He can be very intimidating, but he really didn't mean any harm." Ileana knelt down at the chair, taking Noni's hand into hers. "I know you're frightened, and I know all of this is confusing, but everything will make sense soon. I promise this."

Ileana hugged her one last time after she stood. "Please excuse me for a moment. I need to change out of these clothes."

She left Noni in the living room with Eli, who was snoring loudly and sleeping blissfully. Noni cleaned her face, wiping the angry tears with the back of her hand. Her mind was still racing. Nostalgia skirted around the edges of her mind again, and she knew there was something she was forgetting. There *was* something she should remember—she could feel it.

Noni pushed herself up from the armchair, despite her limbs crying for her to stay. She quietly left the apartment, not wanting to disturb Eli or alert Ileana, and headed down the stairs. To her surprise, she found Alex standing at the edge of the sidewalk, staring up at the sky. He had his back turned to her. From where she stood, he looked like a statue, cold and unmoving. Even so, there seemed to be a glow about him, some ethereal radiance. From where she stood, he looked like a god. She was quiet, slow to approach him, stepping carefully as she walked forward.

Nevertheless, he knew she was there. "I'm sorry that I raised my voice." He didn't turn as he spoke. He kept staring off. "I wasn't upset with you, just overwhelmed."

"It's okay," Noni spoke softly. "I'm sorry that I yelled too. I got a little carried away." She walked closer to him and stood beside him. When she looked up at him, she saw that the wound on his face had finally stopped bleeding, even though it didn't look any better. Noni resisted the urge to reach out to him. "Alex, what did you mean upstairs when you said—when you said I didn't remember?" she asked. "Is there something I'm forgetting?"

He stared at her for a long time. Noni could not explain the expression on his face, but she knew that somewhere, underneath, he was hurting. And she couldn't explain why.

"Many things are forgotten with the passage of time," he told her. "Everything will happen as it should."

Noni didn't ask again. She stared down at the ground, down at her torn up Nikes. She was more exhausted than she could explain. "Alex, I'm scared," she whispered. Her voice trembled. "I'm *really* scared."

Surprisingly, Alex turned to her and wrapped his arms around her shoulders. She didn't fight it. She didn't want to. Noni leaned in and pressed her face against his chest, ignoring the tatters of his shirt that tickled her cheek. His chest was hard, but his skin was soft and smelled of summer rain.

"I know," Alex said.

They stayed that way, with Alex's arms wrapped protectively around Noni and her face pressed to his chest. She closed her eyes and listened to his steady heartbeat as it thudded behind his ribcage. She felt like she was melting underneath his warm touch. His arms were so tight around her, so secure, and she couldn't think of a place where she felt safer than she felt then. For a moment, Noni almost felt self-conscious for being so comfortable in his embrace, but when his arms tightened, pulling her even closer, the thought left her mind. She felt at peace. She felt like she belonged there, as if she had always belonged there. But suddenly, she was shocked out of the trance when a spark of electricity ignited between their skin. Noni instinctively jumped back, patting her clothes as if she was on fire. Alex, however, didn't look surprised at all.

Noni looked up at him. "It was like my dream," she said.

"Your dream?"

"Yeah," she replied, "in my dream, you were—" Noni was immediately aware that she was about to tell Alex that she'd had a dream about him, and her stomach did a flip. But it was too late; she was already in too deep. "In my dream I saw Nova from the top of this tower. I could see everything for miles. And then you came along and you were dressed really weird, but I knew it was you. And you touched me and there was a spark, just like that. And you called it the current." She looked up. "That's what it is, right? Like an electrical current?"

"Yes."

Suddenly, Noni realized how cold she was, now that he wasn't holding her. She then realized how mortified she was that she'd let it happen in the first place. Her face grew hot with embarrassment.

"Is it always gonna be like that?" She asked, staring at the ground. "When we, uh—you know, touch?" she stammered. She realized then that she'd noticed this before—this spark when they touched. It hadn't been this strong before—it'd been nothing more than a tiny spark, like static when pulling laundry apart. Barely noticeable. But now, it was so strong that it almost *hurt*.

"It's always been that way," Alex confessed. "You're just starting to notice it now."

"So it's always like that for you?" she inquired. "Doesn't it like, hurt? It hurt me a little."

"It's a constant. I barely even notice it anymore, if I'm being honest."

"Oh." Noni nodded, breathing deeply.

Without warning, Alex went towards Noni. With a soft smile on his face, he placed one hand behind her head, curled his fingers in her hair, and leaned down to press one, slow gentle kiss to her forehead. It was so soft, so innocent, and Noni barely even felt it. For once in her life, she was speechless.

"You need to rest," he told her.

He was right. She didn't argue.

Alex took her home. He knew that she was too exhausted to walk home on her own. He dropped her off a few houses down at her request because it was well after two in the morning, and if her Aunt found out she'd snuck out, there'd be hell to pay.

She went in through the back door, locking it quickly.

"You know if you're going to sneak out, you could at *least* close your bedroom door."

Noni nearly jumped out of her skin.

Bianca stood behind her with a glass of water in one hand. She was in her pajamas, her hair was tied up, and it looked like she had just woken up.

"What are you *doing*?" Noni hissed.

Bianca shrugged. "Getting water. What are *you* doing?" She calmly sipped her water. "Oh don't worry, Mom's conked. Sleeping pills, you know."

Noni released the longest sigh. "Thank goodness." She leaned against the fridge, breathing deeply.

"So where'd you go? You never sneak out. Like, ever."

Noni shrugged. "I was—well, I was with Alex."

"*Really.*" Bianca spoke. She arched one curious eyebrow. "Haven't seen him in a while. You two been spending a lot of time together, hmm?"

"I mean, I guess you could say that," Noni replied "but it's not what you think, really." As the words left her mouth, she was reminded of the soft brush of Alex's lips across her forehead, and her face began to heat up all over again.

Bianca grinned. "You were always such a horrible liar, Noni."

"Wait, I swear. Listen, I'm not lying. We are really just friends."

"Friends who hang out until 2 AM when *one* of them has to work in the morning? Sounds real convincing Nons. Anyway," Bianca laughed before finishing her glass of water and placing the empty cup in the sink, "bedtime, right?"

Noni gave up on defending herself. She was too tired to try to get Bianca to believe her. Quietly, they headed up to their respective bedrooms. Noni closed her bedroom door for good measure. When she slipped out of her clothes and into her pajamas, she nearly toppled into bed.

She was asleep within minutes, and for once, she didn't dream.

Alex showed up at Noni's doorstep at noon the next day.

Bianca answered the door with a look of feigned surprise on her face. "Well, well, the long, lost savior returns," she joked. "Whisking my cousin away again, I see."

"I've been monopolizing her time; I apologize," Alex spoke, smiling bashfully. "I just—it's complicated."

Bianca rolled her eyes. "It's not complicated. You have a crush on my cousin. It's really simple, actually," she grinned. Alex glanced down at the ground anxiously, sweeping his wavy hair behind his ear.

"So I'm right?"

"I don't know if 'crush' is the right word," he laughed nervously, "But I think you're on the right track."

Bianca grinned and opened the door, allowing Alex inside. "Well, I'm always right." She closed the door behind him and skipped into the house. "Noni! You got company!" she called up the stairs. Bianca turned to Alex and smiled politely. "Try to get her back at a decent hour, will ya?"

Noni came bounding down the stairs without a second's lapse. Bianca headed up as she came down. When Noni saw Alex, however, her face hardened.

"Did something happen? Is everything okay?"

Alex quickly shook his head. "No, everything's fine. I'm here to—well, I'm here to do normal things. I'm here to do normal things with you." He timidly admitted, "I know that a lot has happened and that you're overwhelmed, and so I wanted to do something to make up for that."

Noni stood at the foot of the stairs, clutching the end of the banister. She watched him carefully and exhaled all of the anxiety in her body. "You want to do normal things," she repeated.

Alex breathed out, chest deflating slowly as he did. "I want to do normal things." He smiled. "I heard that there was a carnival going on near the city. I thought you might like that."

Noni bit back her smile and nodded once. "I think I might like that."

"Good, I think I'll like it too."

It took less than a minute for Noni to get ready. Though she tried to hide her eagerness, it was almost impossible. Despite the fact that Noni was still apprehensive toward Alex, it was always hard to hide her excitement when she was near him. Everything about him was warm and welcoming, and after last night, Noni felt strangely connected to him. In the car on their way to the carnival, she felt like she was buzzing, tingling all over. She knew now that it was the current and that she felt like this because, in some roundabout way, she and Alex were on the same wavelength. It wasn't rocket science. It was just weird, like everything else about her life.

The day was unusually cool for the summer. The sun was low in the sky, covered by clouds, and a breeze was blowing through. The sound of the trees rustling in the wind left little room for quiet conversation. Alex parked his car far enough away from the carnival congestion. He and Noni walked, silent and side by side, until they reached the fairgrounds.

When they arrived, Alex stood at the entrance, gazing at all of the hustle and bustle before him. A light grin graced his face. "This is very interesting," he marveled.

Noni laughed, admiring his awe. "Humanity at its finest."

"It sort of reminds me of home," he whispered thoughtfully.

They walked together, swimming through the crowds of people. Noni thought of taking Alex's hand just to keep track of him, but the thought of touching him again was too much for her. She wasn't sure if she'd get sparked by the current. She didn't want to risk total embarrassment in public. This was the first time they'd done 'normal things' in public since they got ice cream together at the beginning of the summer. Noni wanted this to be simple, to be easy and ordinary.

"So tell me more about it," she began. "You know, about Nova. I feel like there's so much I don't know. I mean, what's it like there? What do you do?"

Alex grinned, shrugging. "We have festivals like these. Though, there aren't any of these screaming metal contraptions." He motioned toward the roller coasters in the distance, just as a group went down, screaming. Noni couldn't help but laugh. "There are castles and towers that reach higher than your tallest buildings. The suns always shine, even during the rain. It's peaceful, for the most part. There, we all take care of each other. We are all family. It's—it's really nothing like here. Well, it's remarkable. It's alive, it's…home. It's home." He walked beside her, arms swinging at his sides. "There, I do what I can to protect my homeland and my people."

"Must be amazing," Noni mused, twisting a bit of hair between her fingers. "Do you miss it?"

Alex shrugged. "I do. But it's nice to visit other realms, to see what else is out there."

"I wish I could see what it looks like," Noni sighed. "You know, I saw it in a dream. But I'll bet it's nothing like the real thing. I just wish I could see it someday."

Alex nodded, smiling softly. "Anything's possible."

"Do you really think so?" Noni asked, glancing up at him eagerly. "I mean—I know I'm not like you or anything but do you really think so?"

Alex gingerly touched her forearm. Noni felt a slight spark across her skin, but she didn't jump away. "Anything is possible, Noni."

They hiked on, finding themselves going toward the food stands. A small cotton candy booth immediately caught Noni's eye. A woman stood with her partner, pulling a piece of her blue treat from the fluff and pushing it into his mouth. The man laughed and stole another piece.

"Cotton candy?" Alex questioned.

Noni's eyes lit up. "You've never had cotton candy!" she exclaimed. She took Alex's hand and led him to the booth. "He's never had cotton candy!" she announced to the girl behind the booth, who chuckled at her enthusiasm.

Noni bought one extra-large, blue-raspberry flavored cotton candy puff on a stick. She pulled off a piece and ate it. "It melts in your mouth, see." She showed him her blue tongue and Alex laughed. "Try it."

Alex pulled one fluffy piece from the bundle. He stuffed it in his mouth without hesitation, closing his eyes momentarily. He pursed his lips and when he opened his eyes, he smiled. "It's good!"

"Yes!" Noni happily cheered. She quickly handed him the stick. "It's yours, have at it." Alex took a huge bite out of the sweet treat and kept grinning.

Noni continued leading him through the carnival. They stopped at almost every booth. Noni taught Alex how to throw rings, play darts, and how to play many of the other carnival games. She even got him to go into the petting zoo to feed animals with her. Noni fed one of the small baby goats. Its black and white fur was covered in hay, but she thought it was the cutest goat she'd ever seen. Noni allowed the goat to eat the snacks from her hand. Without warning, her hand began to shake. All of the food spilled from her hand, onto the ground, and the goat bleated, frustrated.

"What was that?" Alex questioned, grasping Noni's hand and turning it over in his own. "What was it?"

The current shot through her muscles, causing her fingers to break out in even more spasms. She snatched her arm away from his, gripping her talisman immediately.

"I don't know," Noni admitted. "It's been happening since the crash. Since I woke up. I don't know what it is but, every time I grab my talisman it all goes away, like it was never there. And my hand calms down again."

Alex seemed to stop moving. He watched Noni carefully, his eyes meeting hers, traveling down to her talisman, and then meeting her eyes again. "It brings you peace." Alex smiled, almost sadly.

Noni nodded, confused. "Isn't that what it's supposed to do?" She asked. "I know you told me that the inscription on it meant 'Peace' so...?"

"Yes. Yes, exactly," Alex quietly agreed.

Noni didn't say anymore. She picked up the food from the ground and hand-fed it to the baby goat, who was shy to return. "So much for normal," she muttered under her breath.

They spent the rest of the evening traveling through the carnival together, eating bad food and playing cheap games. Alex didn't bring up Noni's tremor, Noni didn't ask any more questions about Nova, and Alex certainly didn't touch her again.

Chapter Thirteen

The next week was like a dream. Noni spent most of her time working. Eli hadn't come back to work yet, but Noni understood his reasons. He was still pulling himself back together. She didn't blame him for taking a few days to himself. She wasn't sure what he'd told their manager, but she allowed him the days off and let him keep his job. She made much more money than she'd made weeks before, but none of it really mattered. Even if her plans for school were murky, Noni still figured that saving her money was a wise choice.

Aside from the time she'd spent with Alex, she didn't see much of him and Ileana. After everything that happened, after everything that Ileana had told her, Noni just needed a break from it all. Alex had tried to lessen the blow from the new information, but it was useless. The whole world was in danger, and Noni was more terrified than she'd ever been. Maybe being with them might have been safer for her, but she just couldn't face them again.

Noni spent more time with Bianca. Her relationship with her cousin had been deteriorating all summer. Both she and Bianca knew that they didn't spend as much time together, and so Noni made it a point to at least try. Although she couldn't exactly tell Bianca the truth of what was happening, Noni could still enjoy her company. There were so many things going on in Bianca's life that Noni hadn't known—she and Charli had officially started dating; Bianca was already taking online classes at the community college; she'd even been offered an on-campus job, so she was thinking about quitting the grocery store. While she spoke, telling Noni everything, Bianca seemed happy. Just that made Noni happy and thankful that her cousin was so blissfully ignorant to everything happening in Noni's life. It was nice to be able to talk to someone who knew nothing. The pressure was off—Noni could finally be ordinary, if only just for a few hours.

Deidre was thankful for her presence, too. Noni knew that her Aunt had noticed her absence for the last few months, but she hadn't said much about it. For that, Noni was grateful. As much as she had tried to keep her family safe from harm, she'd almost forgotten to spend time showing them that she cared about them. It was so easy to get wrapped up in the whirlwind that was her life. Stopping to take a breath of fresh air, however, was something that she desperately needed.

She did things that she'd neglected. She went shopping with her Aunt and Bianca, which was something that they used to do together all the time. Bianca was the one who usually walked away with armfuls, when Noni and Deidre maybe walked away with a shirt or two. They ate together—breakfast, lunch, *and* dinner. Deidre always valued family meals, and her cooking was delicious so Noni couldn't complain. They watched movies together in the living room, old 80s movies, which were the girls' favorites. Noni was just beginning to feel normal again.

But, there was always a tingling in the back of her mind, an itch that she could never scratch, constantly telling her that this wasn't real—telling her that nothing lasts forever, especially not this. Noni ignored her instincts. She was very good at that.

Friday evening, the end of the week, Noni and Bianca were walking downtown, enjoying the coolness of the night while they sipped fruit smoothies. They'd seen a movie together at Bianca's request—an action film, of course—and afterward, just meandered around town.

"Come on Nons, you can't tell me you didn't like the movie at all!" Bianca exclaimed.

Noni sipped her smoothie calmly. "All the guns and explosions and muscles don't really do it for me, Bee. I'm not sayin' it was bad! It was just *so* unrealistic."

"You've gotta be kidding me. What was unrealistic about it? Dude's family got massacred and he was out for revenge! You can't tell me if something happened to me, you wouldn't avenge me!"

"I think my form of revenge would be a lot subtler than blowing up the White House, Bee."

"You need more imagination, more fire, more vengeance!" Bianca laughed with the straw between her teeth. "Well even though you didn't like it, thanks for coming anyway. This was nice."

"It was—it really was," Noni agreed.

Just then, her cell phone began to ring. Noni reached deep into her purse to pull it out. When she saw the caller ID, her mood instantly plummeted.

"Hey, Eli," she answered. "Please, please be good news."

"You know, Noni. I don't think that Seers ever have good news. I think it's in the job description—*make sure you ruin someone's day.*"

Noni refrained from rolling her eyes. "Ha-ha-ha," She dryly replied. "Listen. Can this wait? I'm kind of out, with Bianca. Trying to, you know—"

"—Be normal? Yeah. Tried it. Didn't work," Eli replied. "I just need to talk to you for two seconds. It's about that vision I had. You know, the one where you...didn't make it." Noni didn't need reminding. She remembered watching the same vision. She knew every detail, even though she wished she didn't. "I've just been having that vision a lot lately. I'm dreaming about it every night and it's worrying me. I just want you to be safe. Ileana's been helping me a lot. And I'm starting to understand a lot about this...power. And if there's one thing I do know, it's that repeatedly having the same dream-vision is never a good sign." He sighed on the other line. "Just be careful, Noni."

"Yeah," she replied. "I will. Thank you. I hope you can get some sleep. You sound tired," she pointed out.

Eli laughed. "Tired doesn't even explain what I am. But thank you. I think once this is all over, I'll finally be able to rest."

Noni didn't know what he meant by 'once this is all over', and she wasn't sure that she wanted to know. "Thanks again, Eli." She silenced her ringer before throwing the phone back into her purse.

"What's up with that?" Bianca asked.

Noni shrugged. "Eli needed another shift covered so I told him I'd take it for him."

"Oh! Well that's nice of you. I thought you didn't even like that guy." Bianca noted, slurping her smoothie through the side of her mouth as she spoke. "What happened?"

Noni drank her smoothie slowly, eyeing the ground as they walked.

"We have a lot in common."

Together, the two girls sat outside the smoothie shop, chatting aimlessly as they finished their drinks. Noni did her best to push Eli's phone call to the back of her mind. She sat with Bianca and enjoyed the evening, as it was one of the most beautiful she'd experienced in a while. The sun had almost ended its descent in the cloudless sky. Rays of orange, red, and yellow shot out in all directions, painting the sky like a canvas. The wind was calm; a simple breeze blew in the air, carrying scents of summer. People walked back and forth, mostly teens around Bianca and Noni's age. They even saw a few people from their graduating class. Some of them were off to school, some were leaving for the army, and some were just staying home to work. Noni was thankful that no one asked her about her actual plans because she knew that she'd never be able to give a straight answer. They took off after an hour or so, leaving Noni and Bianca alone again.

"It's getting dark," Noni noted. "We should probably get home soon, before Auntie starts worrying."

Bianca groaned. "Come on Noni, it's *Friday*. Ma will be fine," she said. Noni didn't seem convinced. "Fine, do this—call her and let her know we're going to be out a little later if you're so worried."

Noni rolled her eyes, pulling her phone out of her purse to call her Aunt. She noticed that she'd missed two calls, one from Alex and one from Ileana. She didn't call them back. Instead, she called her Aunt as Bianca had suggested.

The streets emptied as they roamed. Shops began to close and the only things left open were two small diners, but they were both pretty empty. They stopped at their favorite diner, Rhonda's, and ordered dessert—peach cobbler with a glass of milk, of course.

They laughed, talked, and ate. *This feels right*, Noni thought to herself. With Bianca smiling across from her, mouth full of dessert, she felt refreshed.

"So I was telling Charli," Bianca talked with a full mouth, "I was telling her that there's no way..." Her voice trailed off. Her eyes seemed to stare right past Noni, straight to the front of the restaurant. "Well, would ya look at this," she grinned devilishly.

Noni quickly turned and when she saw who was coming, her heart sank.

"Bianca," Alex regarded the girl with a tight smile.

She smiled back. "Nice to see you again." She curiously eyed the woman beside him.

"I'm Ileana," she smiled at Bianca, "Alex's sister."

"Oh, that makes sense," Bianca replied. "Noni's talked about you before."

"What are you guys doing here?" Noni questioned, breaking apart the friendly greetings.

She could tell that neither Alex nor Ileana was in a very good mood. Their stiff shoulders and hard eyes told it all.

"We called." They spoke simultaneously. Both of them glanced at Bianca, who cautiously watched them both.

Suddenly, Eli came bursting through the door of the diner, causing the bells above the door to jingle frantically.

"Eli?" Bianca and Noni exclaimed in unison.

He saluted them both. "Noni, we have got to get out of here."

Ileana nodded, looking to Noni. "He's right."

Noni glanced at Bianca with wide eyes, then to Ileana, to Eli, and finally to Alex. Her chest was so tight with anxiety that she felt like she was going to have a heart attack. Ileana was the first to understand Noni's obvious unease. She knelt down beside Bianca and took her hand, looking directly into her eyes. Bianca started to protest but when she looked into Ileana's eyes, her whole body seemed to relax. From where Noni sat, she could see Ileana's eyes. They were illuminated. They were golden.

"Bianca," Ileana spoke in a soft, calming voice. "You are going to leave this place and you are going to go straight home. You're not going to stop anywhere. You are going to get in your car and go straight home."

"I'm going to get in my car and go straight home." Bianca repeated in a dazed voice, head tilted to the side, as she listened.

"And if anyone asks where Noni is, you will tell them that she's working late."

"Noni is working late." Bianca nodded.

"You won't remember any of this," Ileana told her. "When I let go of your hand, I want you to get to your car as fast as you can, okay?"

Bianca nodded with a lazy smile. "Okay."

Ileana released her hand. Bianca stood up from the table, unblinking, and didn't even spare Noni a second glance. Her eyes were completely blank. She pushed past the group, walking briskly, leaving the diner and rushing down the street. Ileana stood up, blinking once. Her eyes returned to their normal brown and she suddenly looked exhausted. Those golden eyes reminded Noni of something, but she couldn't bring forth the memory quick enough.

"How did you do that?" Noni asked, looking up at Ileana. "How can you just control people like that?"

"I'll explain another time," she spoke quickly. "Right now, we must leave."

Noni stood from the table. She pulled a balled up ten-dollar bill out of her purse and left it on the table. Alex led the group outside. The sky was black, completely dark. There were no stars tonight.

"Someone, please tell me what's going on," Noni begged.

Just as she spoke, thunder rolled across the sky. The force of it seemed to shake the very ground they walked on. Suddenly, Alex walked in front of Noni, guarding her with his body. Ileana did the same for Eli. She watched her tear off the necklace she'd been wearing. It was a talisman that resembled the one that Alex had given Noni. However, when Ileana held it in her hand, it began to glow. It grew in size in her hand; it grew into the shape of a dagger. The blade was almost as long as her forearm, and she held it firmly in one hand.

"Stay behind us," Alex warned.

Thunder rumbled once more. Noni took a step forward, clutching the back of Alex's shirt as she spoke. She knew something terrible was about to happen; she could feel it in the pit of her stomach. "Please be careful," she whispered.

Lightning struck the earth. Sparks flew. The power of the lightning tore apart the black asphalt, forming deep cracks in the ground. It forced the street apart, creating a deep crater in the earth, so deep that it forced the ground to shake again. Jagged edges shot up from the ground, blowing gravel and dirt into their faces. As the light died down, Noni saw smoke rising from the crater. And fire. She could smell it burning deep below. Smoke rose.

The smell of burning flesh filled the air.

Hands grappled at the edge of the pit. They clawed their way to the surface, covered in ashes and dirt. The sickening scent intensified. The smoke kept rising and they kept climbing.

The first Halfling that crawled out of the pit had long, black hair. Her features were sharp, like crystal. Her skin was gray, colorless, and her mouth was blood red. Noni remembered her.

The skin of her arms was charred black, but as she stood and straightened her spine, the burns began to heal. She looked up at Noni and her eyes flashed silver.

"Hello again, darling Noni." Eifa's silver eyes landed on Alex next and she grinned. "It's nice to see you again, Alex."

At least twenty of the Halflings gathered behind her. There was no way that Alex and Ileana could defeat them alone. There was no way that they would make it out alive. Alex ripped off the talisman he wore. In his hands, a golden sword materialized. "Don't move."

That was all Alex said before he charged. Noni had never seen someone move so fast. He was glowing all over, every inch of his skin. He illuminated the night. Alex zipped through the streets like a flash of lightning. Ileana was right behind him, just as bright, and brandishing her dagger as she raced. He attacked Eifa first, slicing at her with his sword. She was just as fast as him, and dodged every blow. She laughed as they fought. Her hands were like claws as she slashed at him. They glowed red and the sight of it made Noni feel sick. She didn't want to know what would happen if she touched Alex with those hands.

Ileana cut down Halflings like it was easy. With just a dagger, she brought them down, one after another, moving as swiftly as the wind. They bled black, and Ileana was covered in it.

Eli grabbed Noni's arm, pulling her back. "We need to get out of here and hide."

"I can't leave them," Noni told him. Something held her to that spot. She wasn't sure if it was fear or stupidity, but she couldn't move. "I can't."

"They can handle themselves!" He exclaimed. "We're not like

them, we can't fight. We'll die if one of those *things* comes at us." He grabbed her by the shoulders, shaking her. "Noni. I know you care about them. But we need to go."

She couldn't. "You go," she told him. "I'll be fine."

"I'm not going to leave you."

Noni nodded. She took a deep breath and closed her eyes. *I have to do something*, she told herself. She could feel the warmth building deep in her stomach. It traveled through her veins, her skin, and her entire nervous system. When she opened her eyes, her hands were glowing brighter than they ever had before. She followed her gut instinct. She grabbed hold of the talisman at her neck and pulled, breaking the chain. As her hands glowed around the necklace, it began to transform. It grew and grew, and finally, in her hands, Noni held a golden bow and a quiver filled with arrows. She looked at Eli and he looked at her.

"Do you have any idea how to use that thing?" he asked.

She slung the quiver over her shoulder and drew an arrow. "Not a clue." She set the arrow against the string, pulling back as far as she could before releasing it. But just as she tried to steady it, her faulty hand began to tremble. The arrow flew up into the air, completely missing any target she might have had. Noni cursed under her breath.

Come on, she thought. *You have this for a reason. He gave this to you for a reason.* Noni drew another arrow. She took a deep breath, closing her eyes as she concentrated. She tried to find peace in all of the chaos. She steadied her breathing and prayed that she could do something worthwhile. Then suddenly, something in her mind cracked and sparked. The shock was physical, shooting through her entire body. Her hand was still, unshaking. Suddenly, her shoulders straightened and her body was as rigid as the bow in her hands. Eli gasped and Noni opened her eyes.

She was glowing all over. Everything, even the bow and arrow, illuminated the darkness. Noni aimed her arrow straight for Eifa. She let it fly.

The arrow hit Eifa, embedded itself deep in her shoulder. The Halfling released the most awful screech that had ever touched Noni's ears.

Alex turned, eyes wide, as he stared at Noni. She could see her light reflected in his golden eyes. In the midst of this all, he smiled at her. She had never seen him smile like this before. He mouthed her name but she couldn't hear him because she was screaming.

Noni saw Eifa coming before Alex did. He should have never turned his back on her.

Eifa's red claw tore through his chest. Blood began to spread across his white shirt. His eyes were still on Noni when he fell, and she watched the gold color drain right out of them.

Ileana screamed.

Noni's vision went black.

When Alex fell, Noni fell, dropping her bow to the ground as she hit head first. Eli knelt at her side, turning her over as he tried to shake her awake, but Ileana knew what was to come, and so did Eli. Ileana knew that she couldn't get to the pair of them. Halflings, all of them with hungry silver eyes, surrounded her. Every time she went for one, more of them came at her. There was no way she could make it to Noni in time.

Alex lay face down in the middle of the street, bleeding out.

Ileana fought her way through the Halflings, trying to get through before Eifa got to Noni.

Neither of those things happened.

A terrified scream tore through Eli's body.

Noni, without a word, had begun to rise. She almost hovered above the ground, standing firm. Her hair was flowing, flying as the glow of light pulsed around her. When she opened her eyes, they were glowing. Golden. Dead set on Eifa.

The Halfling cackled, tearing the arrow from her flesh.

"Ah, *Aisha*. Free at last." She spoke. "Did you miss me, sister?"

"I have never been your sister, filthy Half breed." The voice that rose from Noni's mouth wasn't hers. It was too hard, too filled with rage. Nothing about Noni was hers.

"Blood calls to blood, Aisha. And you are finally your old self again. You can thank me later."

Noni charged, leaving the bow and arrow behind. The glow around her hands wasn't white anymore. A deep, angry red surrounded them. When she screamed, the earth seemed to shake.

Ileana broke through the crowd of Halflings, slashing left and right as she tried to get to Noni before it was too late. She had seen Eli's vision. She had watched Noni die before and she wasn't going to let it happen again.

Steam rose off Noni's skin as if she were burning alive. She attacked Eifa, landing blow after blow after blow. She fought like she had never fought before, demolishing the woman before her. Noni landed a solid kick to Eifa's stomach and Eifa doubled over in pain, spitting blood. Noni grabbed her by the throat and raised her above the ground, right before slamming her into the asphalt. The ground splintered. Noni raised her up again, only to bring her body crashing down, over and over. She never stopped screaming.

"Noni—NO!" Ileana shouted as she took the life of one last Halfling. He fell to her feet with a thud and she leapt over his body as she raced toward Noni and Eifa. Noni's hand was still wrapped around Eifa's windpipe when Ileana reached her. But she made the same mistake she'd made in Eli's vision. She grabbed Noni, touched her without even thinking, and the current surged through her body. She was repelled, sent flying backward and into the smoking pit from which the Halflings had crawled.

"No! It can't end like this!" she shrieked. With every bit of power in her body, Ileana dragged herself out of the pit. Hands bloodied, she pulled herself over the edge.

She went toward them again; Noni had Eifa by the throat, and was dangling her high above the ground. But Eifa was smiling. Through blood and dirt, she smiled. Ileana knew what she had to do. Instead of going for Noni again, she sent her dagger flying, straight for Eifa's head. It was a shooting star, a glowing double-edged blade, heading straight for her. It lodged itself in her temple before she could even scream out in pain. Her body went limp in Noni's grip.

When Ileana reached them, she stayed several feet back from Noni. Although the girl stood deathly still, gripping the Halfling's throat, there were tears streaming from her eyes. Ileana inched toward her.

"Aisha," she whispered, "please. It's over. Put her down."

"*She hurt him,*" the girl cried, still squeezing the Halfling's windpipe. "*I watched the light leave his eyes. I saw it.*"

"He'll be fine, my lady. I swear it," Ileana reassured, "but you have to give her back." She pleaded, "You have to give Noni back to us."

For a long time, the girl didn't move. Seconds felt like minutes. The air was still, frozen.

"The humans will wake soon. Please."

The Halfling's body fell to the dirt with a heavy thud. Golden eyes looked upon Ileana with high regard. "*Save him.*"

Ileana caught Noni's body as she fell. She picked her up and carried her over to Eli, who had pressed himself against a brick wall, eyes wide with terror. She gave him one command: "Don't let her out of your sight."

She turned back to her brother, who lay bleeding in the street. She knew he was alive, she just wasn't sure how she would carry the both of them.

Chapter Fourteen

When Noni opened her eyes, she found herself sitting in a dark room, cross-legged on the floor. Across from her sat a woman who couldn't have been much older than she was. Her hair was much longer, a curly crown that made her face appear small in measure. She was dressed in a long white gown that pooled around her. She looked like she was sleeping, but the grimace on her face told Noni that she couldn't have been. Slowly, Noni crawled toward her on all fours. She stared intently, watching every twitch of her eye and tic of her brow.

Suddenly, the woman began to cry. Tears spilled down her cheeks in waves and they didn't stop. Noni backed away from her quickly, returning to her spot on the ground. When she sat back down, the woman's eyes opened with a flash of light. She inhaled deeply, and her eyes lost their glow, only to be replaced by golden pupils. Immediately, those eyes focused on Noni. The woman smiled softly, almost sadly. Noni stared at her for several moments, and something stirred inside her. Somehow, she knew this woman.

"Who—who are you?" Noni questioned.

The woman's smile remained, but Noni could see the pity in her expression.

"I am Aisha. I am you."

All of a sudden, the ground began to shake. Terrified, Noni shuffled across the floor, but there was nowhere to go—nothing but darkness surrounded her. She looked to the woman across from her and saw that she was calm and unmoved.

"It's okay to return," she spoke, pressing her hands together before bowing her head in Noni's direction. "You will remember everything—it will all make sense soon."

The ground caved in.

The memories came rushing back.

When Noni woke up, she woke up crying, and she wasn't sure why. She was not surprised, however, to find herself lying down on the couch in Alex's living room.

The first person she saw was Ileana. The woman immediately threw her arms around Noni, hugging her with tears in her eyes. Noni didn't return the gesture. She sat there, eyes wide, staring blankly.

"You're okay." Ileana squeezed. She released Noni only to grab her by the shoulders. "What were you thinking? Attacking Eifa like that? That was foolish Noni, you could've been seriously hurt—"

"—Ileana," Noni whispered, staring at her. Before she could speak, tears began to well up in her eyes. "Why didn't anyone tell me?" she asked, voice cracking as she spoke.

Realization dawned in Ileana's eyes. "Oh, Noni," she said, with pity and sadness behind every word. "How much do you remember?"

Noni didn't answer. It didn't matter. She stood up and pushed past Ileana, ignoring the spinning in her head and her churning stomach. Ileana didn't even try to stop her. Noni rushed out the front door, down the stairs, and out of the complex.

She started running. She didn't know where she was going, but she had to get as far away as possible. She couldn't stay there. She knew she couldn't go home, so she kept running, racing through the empty streets. Her heart thudded in her chest and with every step came a deep pounding in her head. Memories swirled around her consciousness, making her dizzy, making her feel sick. She tried to hold them back, but they hit harder.

In her mind, memories of Nova rolled in. She could see the entire kingdom. Red grass covered the ground, growing up towards the sky, swaying in the wind. Noni could see the enormous stone castle in the middle of the land, surrounded by small stone houses and buildings. She knew this castle. She knew just how many steps it took to get to the very top of the tower. She could almost taste the sweetness in the air. She could almost feel the peace, the calm, and the quiet of the realm. It felt like home.

Noni recalled faces of people she'd never met before. They were all smiling at her, smiling and waving as they passed. She could feel the happiness well up inside her, but it wasn't *hers*. These memories weren't hers. They belonged to someone else. They belonged to Aisha. She tried to fight back; she tried to recall memories from her own life. Memories of her parents, memories from high school, and memories from all the time she'd spent with the people she loved—but everything was cloudy and jumbled. She couldn't split the memories; she couldn't separate them. Everything was hers and it wasn't. There was no chronology—everything was scrambled. Noni couldn't rid herself of Aisha's memories.

No, Noni thought, *they're my memories.*

She kept running, trying to outrun the thoughts, but they caught up to her effortlessly.

She saw glimpses of Ileana. She was dressed in armor and wore her hair in two long braids down her back. Her golden dagger was in a sheath at her waist, but resting on her shoulder was a stainless battle-axe. She called out commands to the mass of female warriors that flanked her, all armor clad. They marched in unison, following her lead.

The memory faded, seeming to blur out of vision. The scene began to reform— only this time, it was Alex. Noni's heart jumped when she saw him. He was dressed almost identically to the way she'd seen in her dream. He was bathed in golden jewelry. His gilded wristlets matched the golden staff he carried with him. His sword was sheathed against his waist, and he wore armor just as Ileana had. But his eyes were still soft. He stood atop the tower of the castle, in the doorway, watching a girl who stared over the edge. He watched her and a slow, loving smile began to spread across his face. When she noticed his presence, she turned and grinned back at him—that was when Noni saw her face.

That's me, she thought to herself. *No, that's not. That's not me... that's her.*

They were identical. The only thing that separated Noni from Aisha was the clothes they wore. Otherwise, it was impossible to tell them apart. Noni could feel a chill breaking out across her skin. *This* was what Aisha had meant when she said, *I am you.* Noni knew now that, somehow, they were one and the same. But it didn't make sense. All the conflicting memories and conflicting emotions were too overwhelming.

When Noni's body finally gave up, she found herself in the middle the city park. She didn't know how long she'd been running or even how she'd managed to make it this far, but her legs couldn't take anymore. She dragged herself to the nearest bench and collapsed. It didn't help that the sun was beating down on her, making her even more tired. Her vision was hazy and her breath was short and uneven. It felt like her whole body wanted to shut down.

Noni felt sick. She didn't know what was hers and what wasn't. She tried to steady her breathing and calm her rabbit heart. Through her exhaustion, she tried to rationalize everything that was happening, but there was just too much to sift through.

She heard quickened footsteps coming toward her. When she looked up, she wasn't surprised to see Ileana running her way. She didn't look hard and cold like she did in Noni's memory; she was warm and she looked concerned. When she stopped in front of Noni, she hadn't even broken a sweat and didn't show a single sign of exhaustion. Carefully, she walked to one side of the bench and sat, leaving at least a foot of space between herself and Noni. Noni didn't make eye contact. She just stared down at the ground and continued to stabilize her breathing.

Ileana watched her, a solemn expression on her face. It took her quite some time to speak. "I know you're scared and confused," she began. "This is exactly what my brother and I wanted to avoid. We knew that your memory was lost, but…in order to help you, we knew it had to come back." She shook her head, closing her eyes. "But not like this—we never wanted it to happen like this."

"Ileana, I don't know who I am," Noni whispered. "It's beyond being scared, beyond being confused. I don't know who I *am*." She could already feel her eyes swelling with tears. "I have all these memories, I don't know if they're hers or mine, and I just can't do this."

"Noni, they're *your* memories." Ileana said. "I know it's hard to understand, but you and Aisha—you're the same. Her spirit is your spirit. Her light is your light. Your names may be different, your lives may be different, but your spirit is one, and spirits are forever. It's… it's reincarnation."

Noni wished that she could argue. She wished that Ileana was wrong, but she wasn't.

"Think about it," Ileana pressed. "Haven't you always felt like something was missing?"

Ileana was right, much to Noni's dismay. There had always been bits and pieces of her life that she couldn't seem to remember. There had always been things that she felt like she was constantly forgetting, but she could never pinpoint them. Maybe this was it—maybe *this* was what she had been forgetting.

"I don't know why you lost your memory, but you did. And maybe you'll figure it out on your own one day," Ileana reached out and touched Noni's forearm, gripping it. "But what's important, right now, is that you're safe and you're alive. Everything will make sense soon," she assured her.

Noni nodded, remaining silent.

Ileana took her hand. "How about I take you home?"

They walked back to the apartment in silence. When they got into the car, Noni brought her knees up to her chest and held them there. She stared out the window the whole drive home. When they reached Deidre's house, Ileana told Noni to call if anything happened. Noni didn't speak. She nodded once and left the car, closing the door behind her.

She avoided both her Aunt and Bianca when she entered the house. She went straight into her bedroom and locked the door. In bed, alone and closed off from everyone, Noni wept. Her whole body shook with sobs. She muffled them with her pillow so no one would hear her, but she sobbing wracked her frame. She bit down on the pillow as she rocked back and forth, but she couldn't contain the overwhelming emotions that she felt. She felt like the weight of the world was crushing her.

Everything she had ever known about herself felt like a lie, like a dream. Why did those old memories feel realer than all of the memories from her normal life? No matter what anyone else said, Noni had to deal with this on her own. No one could fix this for her.

Eventually, exhaustion took over. No more tears would fall. Noni fell asleep with a pillow tucked underneath her chin. She stayed that way in a dreamless sleep until a rapid knocking at her door woke her.

She shot straight up in bed, wiping her face even though it was dry. She dropped the pillow and went to the door, opening it before she asked who it was. Surprisingly, the person standing on the other side of the door was Eli.

"Um, hi," he waved awkwardly. "Bianca let me in. I didn't know you were sleeping—I can leave, I'll just come back another time."

"No, it's fine," Noni told him. She flipped the switch on the wall to illuminate her bedroom. "Just come in I guess." She stepped back and motioned toward the only chair she had in her room, a green net chair. "Sit if you want."

Eli sat quickly. Noni climbed back onto her bed, grabbing the pillow and holding it against her chest. She didn't speak and neither did Eli for a while. A heavy silence hung above them for quite a time. They didn't make eye contact. Noni stared down at her bedsheets, and Eli stared at his hands as he twiddled his thumbs. After a while, however, Eli broke the silence.

"I'm sorry about the other day," he apologized. "I was pretty useless back there."

Noni didn't respond. She could barely even recall what happened. Bits and pieces came back to her, but she didn't want to remember it anyway.

"But I didn't come over to talk about that," Eli said. "I just thought you could use a friend, or something."

"We're not friends," Noni bit harshly. "The only reason we ever spoke is because you knew something was weird about me. About the both of us. That's the only thing we have in common. It doesn't make us friends."

Eli didn't even bat an eye. "We could have a lot more in common, you know," he replied. "I know you're having a hard time. Hell, if I found out I had a secret godly past, I'd be having a hard time too. So," he looked up at her, "we could try being friends. I could definitely use a friend."

Noni immediately regretted her words. She lowered her eyes shamefully, shaking her head. "I'm sorry, I didn't mean that."

"No, you did. And that's okay," Eli said. "You've been through a lot." He sat back in the chair, leaning it against the wall. He took a deep breath before he spoke. "Let's try it—my favorite color is green. I have a cat at home, and his name is PB, short for Peanut Butter. I'm an only child, but I've got a load of older cousins. I really love video games, I own every game system there is, and I'm really into Japanese anime." He smiled at Noni. "Your turn."

She eyed him suspiciously. "You're not serious," she said.

Eli shrugged. "Friends, right?"

Noni sighed. "Fine. I…my favorite color is purple. I'm an only child too. I like…art and stuff."

"Art and stuff?" Eli repeated.

Noni rolled her eyes. "I'm not good at this, okay? You started this."

His hands went up in surrender. "You're right," he replied. "Continue."

The girl clutched the pillow. "I've never had any pets. I like 80s movies a lot. And—I don't know. What else am I supposed to say?"

Eli shrugged again. "Whatever you want," he told her. "Here, I'll go again."

He started talking, telling Noni facts about himself. For the rest of the evening, they traded details about their lives, going back and forth. Noni even laughed a few times. After hearing a wild story about how Eli had accidentally ate his cat's food, mistaking it for tuna salad, she couldn't hold back the laughter. Somehow, they both ended up on the floor, Eli sitting cross-legged and Noni on her back with her knees bent. He was full of stories, she noticed, and he was a great storyteller. She'd never known that about him, but she was glad she found out. Eli was funny too—the good kind of funny, the expressive kind, the talks-with-his-hands kind of funny. He didn't miss a beat. He kept the conversation alive and kept a smile on Noni's face. She wasn't sure how long they sat there together, talking and laughing, but the sun was gone before they knew it.

"It's getting late," she told him. "You don't have to stay if you have to get home or something—"

"—I'm having a good time," He said. "Are you having a good time?"

Noni smiled and nodded once. "Yeah, I am," she admitted. "And thank you for coming over. And doing all this," she said, waving her hands in the air.

Eli laughed, shaking his head. "It's not a problem." He stood up from the floor, stretching his limbs. "Wanna show me some of those 80s movies you love so much?"

They watched *Pretty Woman* together.

Bianca even joined them, though she was perplexed as to why Eli was still there. However, she didn't ask. She popped popcorn, they passed it around, and everything was good. Nevertheless, Noni never let her guard completely fall, and neither did Eli. She knew this much because of what he said to her when he left.

"I hope you'll be safe tonight," Eli told her, standing in the doorway. "I know I'm not much help, but if something happens, call me." He nodded.

Noni returned the gesture. "I think I'll be alright." After taking a deep breath, she looked straight at him. "What's going to happen now?" she asked. Noni knew that there was a lot that Eli knew now.

"I feel like there's some unspoken rule about influencing the future too much." He laughed softly. "But in all honesty ... I can only really make out bits of pieces of what I was shown. It's all fragmented, like glimpses—you know?"

Noni nodded. She knew.

"I just have a feeling that things are gonna end up okay. What's the saying—*everything's okay in the end. If it's not okay, then it's not the end,*" he recited.

The girl rolled her eyes. "You're pretty optimistic for a guy that got kidnapped."

"The bright side is the only side left in this situation. I figured I might as well see what it's like over there," he joked, shrugging.

Noni cracked a smile, for Eli's sake. "Thanks, Eli," Noni replied. "It was really nice of you to come here, even though being around me usually gets you into a lot of trouble."

Eli chuckled lightly. "I think we're going to be getting into a lot of trouble together for a while, Noni. Might as well get used to it."

Noni wasn't sure what was in store for her, but she had a feeling Eli was right.

Chapter Fifteen

Three days went by. Things were calm, calmer than normal. The quiet of the days left Noni feeling uneasy and on edge. She couldn't sleep through an entire night. It wasn't the dreams that kept her awake; it was anxiety. She was constantly anticipating an attack. With her memory came an onslaught of heightened senses. She was far more in-tune with her surroundings than she would have liked. Her vision was sharper, and she found that she could see farther than ever before. Her hearing, too, had become so hypersensitive that sometimes it was painful to be around too many sounds at once—her hearing was so sharp that every night, she could hear Bianca's heartbeat, beating rhythmically from the other room.

From the memories, Noni gleaned that there was a lot of fighting in Aisha's past—in *her* past. She wasn't sure how she felt about that, about any of this.

She didn't think she'd ever get used to this—thinking of herself as the person she remembered. Noni knew the truth now, but that didn't make accepting it any easier. She wasn't sure if she would ever fully come to terms with it.

Ileana tried to help Noni with the memories and to help her make sense of things, but it only frustrated Noni more. Surprisingly, Alex was nowhere to be found. Noni hadn't seen him since the night of the attack downtown. Ileana said that she hadn't seen him since she'd healed him. That night, he'd taken off and hadn't come back.

Noni could admit to herself that not seeing him made her uneasy. She would not admit the reasons for that. She didn't ask Ileana where he'd gone—only accepted that he was gone and hoped that he'd be back before more terrible things started happening.

She'd talked with Eli every day. Noni began to realize that the two of them were in this together, whether she liked it or not. He wasn't exactly what she was, but they were similar enough that they had to stick together. They had to keep each other safe, and alive.

On the third night, Noni tried her best to ignore her senses. They kept her awake at night. She swore she could feel the world moving; she could feel the animals scurrying outside in her backyard. She could feel the warm wind moving through the trees; she could feel the clouds overhead, crowding in the dark, preparing for rain. That night, she could sense all this, and more.

An extraordinary power surrounded her house. It was everywhere, cloaking her home in warm light. She could tell it wasn't an enemy. The aura that surrounded Halflings was always harsh, always cold and sharp. What she sensed now was warm and inviting. She calmly rose from bed and dressed under moonlight, pulling on a tank top, a pair of denim shorts, and her sandals. Noni quietly left her bedroom, leaving the door open, as she glided down the stairs. She followed the aura. As she grew closer, a tingle spread over her skin—the hairs on her forearms stood straight up, as if she'd introduced them to static. Noni unlocked the front door, opened it, and boldly stepped outside.

She couldn't restrain her tired smile.

"I knew it was you," she confessed. "I could feel you."

Alex stood at the sidewalk. An ethereal glow seemed to surround him. Noni wasn't sure if it was the glow from the moon or if she was seeing something that had always been there. The tingling sensation on her skin grew stronger; she could feel the hairs on the back of her neck standing at attention.

He came toward her slowly, tentatively, like a wounded animal. She couldn't fully decipher his expression, but in his face she saw pain.

Noni felt the overwhelming urge to touch him. To embrace him and lock her arms around him. It was strong and terribly difficult to resist, but she wouldn't let herself fall victim to instincts she couldn't explain. Instead, Noni sat down on the concrete steps and clasped her hands in her lap. Alex sat down beside her, holding on to the metal railing.

"I'm sorry." That was the first thing he said to her. He didn't make eye contact; he stared directly at the ground. "For everything."

Noni couldn't look at him either. She looked down at her hands. "You didn't tell me the truth," she accused. "You said you would always tell me the truth. And that you would never lie to me again." Noni tightened her hold on her own hand. "Why did you have to lie, Alex?"

She felt the shift in his energy almost immediately. For an instant, everything felt sharp and cold. Alex shut his eyes, as if his response would cause him pain.

"I thought I'd lost you," he admitted. "I know you don't remember, but we were—" he cut himself off, shaking his head. "Things were different before. After you disappeared, I thought I would never be able to find you again. And when I did…when I realized that you had lost your memory, I wanted to do everything in my power to bring it back. At first, I wanted to tell you everything." He glanced up, catching her eye for a split second before looking away again.

"I wouldn't have believed you."

He nodded. "You wouldn't have. Nevertheless, Ileana wouldn't let me tell you. She knew that it would scare you off. Or worse—you *would* remember, and you would go into shock. And it would have been worse than before. Instead of destroying Halflings, you…it could have been much worse for you, not knowing how to control that power." He held onto the railing tighter. "So I kept the truth from you as long as I could. I wanted you to be able to control your powers, if only just a bit, before you remembered everything. Getting your memory back was inevitable. We just wanted to reduce the…damage."

Noni let the words soak in. She allowed a silence to settle between them. The sound of the cicadas crying out filled the space.

"Am I human at all?" she quietly asked.

Alex responded slowly. "In a way. Your body is mortal; your spirit is not of this realm. Your spirit is Novaen."

Noni nodded solemnly. She brought her knees up to her chest. She didn't know what to say to him.

"I'm sorry for what I've done. I shouldn't have kept so much of the truth from you," he apologized. He released the railing only to link his own fingers in his lap. "I just—I wanted things to be different. I wanted—"

"You wanted me to be her," Noni finished. She finally looked at him full on, meeting his eyes. "I'm not her, you know. I have all of those memories back now, and I'm starting to accept that that's who I used to be. But that's not me anymore. I'm different—everything is different."

Alex held her gaze for as long as he could before looking away. "I know that, Noni." He stood from the steps quickly, and he looked to be wiping his face. "I don't wish for you to be anything more than what you are. I hope you know that." He didn't look at her again. "I'll go; I don't want to keep you up all night."

Noni remembered what it felt like to love him. She remembered it vividly, but she couldn't say that. She couldn't own it. "I remember a lot of things now," she confessed. "I *know* what things were like. And I don't think I'll forget again." Noni thought back to the first day that she met Alex. She couldn't explain the feeling then, but she knew now. *And I don't think my spirit ever forgot,* she thought.

Alex smiled despite himself. He didn't hug her, and he spared her a second kiss to her forehead, but he did smile. "Goodnight, Noni."

He left without another word.

Alone, Noni sat on the cold concrete landing. The tingling on her skin began to subside. She closed her eyes and wished for an escape from her own mind.

Minutes later, she got her wish. Bianca bounded out of the back yard, dressed in a white t-shirt and denim shorts, almost identical to Noni.

"Bee?"

The other teen yelped and turned toward her cousin, scared out of her wits. "Jeez, Noni—what are you *doing* out here?" she questioned.

"I would ask what you're doing out here, but it's clear that you're sneaking out."

Bianca rolled her eyes. "You avoided my question, but I'll let it slide. I'm going with Charli. There's a glow party tonight in the Edge. You should come!"

Noni knew about the Edge. The place was far from their small town, closer to the bigger city, on the shore of Lake Erie. Long before they were born, it was a warehouse district. Many manufacturers of steel products came to that district to make more products and more money. For decades, business was booming. However, in the late 90s, things changed. Manufacturers left. Businesses died out. For a while, the city tried to fill the location with shops, turn it into a shopping center. After about ten years, that idea died out as well. Now, it was full of clubs and abandoned buildings. Noni hoped the place Bianca had in mind was a club. Abandoned buildings seemed like a place one would go if they were just asking for trouble.

This was the first time Noni agreed to one of Bianca's escapades without complaint. She knew that she wouldn't be able to sleep tonight, so she decided not to torture herself and instead to spend one night out doing something that normal teenagers do.

Charli picked them up in her rust bucket of a car, as usual. "Didn't think you were coming Noni!" she exclaimed as Noni climbed into the back seat.

Noni shrugged, smiling. "I figured one night couldn't hurt," she replied.

Bianca cheered as they pulled off, "That's the spirit!"

The drive took well over an hour, not to mention the ten minutes they spent being lost, due to Charli's poor directional skills.

They arrived at a huge brick building. It was at least three stories high, but only the first floor was in use. There were windows on the third floor that had been busted out, and graffiti covered more than half of the building. To Noni, it looked like it was an old building that was turned into a teen club. Clearly, it still needed renovations because the place was downright sketchy. As the door opened, strobe lights flashed and Noni could see people glowing in the dark, covered in neon colors.

Charli paid for Bianca, and since Noni didn't have her wallet, Bianca paid for her. They all got stamped upon entry and got a complementary *handful* of neon yellow powder on their chests as they entered.

Bianca dragged both Charli and Noni over to the bar which, for the night, had been transformed into a Glow Bar. They bought different color powders to throw on their white shirts, and when they were done, they fit right in with the rest of the crowd.

The music was so loud that it made the walls vibrate. They were at the back of the club, but it sounded like they were a foot away from the speakers, which were blaring a techno song that Noni didn't know. People danced wildly and jumped around, shaking the entire floor. There were girls in the middle of the floor, dressed in all black, with glowing hula-hoops. The motion of the hoops spinning in the dark was almost hypnotizing. Some people's faces were painted, making them resemble animals, clowns, or even skeletons. Powder from all of their clothes covered the floor, creating a collage of neon.

Bianca took Noni's hand, dragged her to the dance floor, and spun her around a few times, causing them to erupt in dizzy laughter. They danced around each other and smeared powder on each other's faces. Noni began to loosen up—something about the energy of the party had invigorated her. As she was dancing, she heard someone shout her name.

"Noni?!"

Quickly, she turned to see Terrell bounding toward her with a smile on his face. He hugged her tightly, picking her up off the ground.

"I didn't think you'd be here!" he exclaimed.

Noni laughed as he set her down. "Neither did I!" She replied. "Bianca dragged me out, as usual."

Bianca grinned proudly. "Life is short!" she announced over the music. "May as well have fun while you can!"

She didn't know how right she was.

Terrell asked Noni to dance—she decided to say yes.

The music changed, slowed down to a hip-hop beat with bass that rattled the walls. Noni and Terrell danced in sync with the beat. He rested his hands on her hips, she pressed her back against his chest as they danced. She didn't meet his eyes, partly because he was much taller than she was, and partly because she didn't want her feelings to betray her. She knew how she felt about him—she just couldn't afford to have those feelings. Not in this lifetime.

Noni let the music carry her away. She didn't pay much attention to the lyrics, but the beat resonated in her chest. She closed her eyes, concentrating on the way that the floor vibrated with the bass. Terrell mimicked her every move. His hips moved with her, his arms swung with hers, and his body swayed in tune. The air in the room was hot and sticky. Sweat made her clothes stick to her body. Noni felt him tighten his grip on her waist for just an instant, and he leaned toward her, his face barely touching hers.

"I'm glad you came," Terrell spoke directly into her ear so that she could hear him over the music. "It's nice to see you out of that ugly green apron!" he laughed. Noni giggled, rolling her eyes. Terrell took her hand and spun her around to face him. She could barely see his face underneath all of the colorful powder, but she could tell that he was smiling. She saw his lips moving, but she couldn't make out what he was saying, because the instant he started speaking, she felt a spike in the atmosphere.

A chill in the air made goosebumps break across her skin. Cold blew across her skin, cooling her sweat. She could sense the aura in the room changing. Darkening. Noni felt like she was suffocating, like the room was getting smaller with every passing second. The stench was what hit her next—like burning, rotting meat. It infiltrated her senses, choking her. Terrell was still speaking but Noni was already moving, pushing him aside. With Terrell out of her line of sight, that's when she saw *him*.

It was as if the whole sea of people parted for him. Noni didn't even think they were conscious of what they were doing. Nobody seemed to see him as he sauntered through. Unlike them, Noni could see clearly; his golden eyes were focused right on her. Her knees tried to buckle underneath her as he approached—an aura of power surrounded him. He was no Halfling. He wore black slacks and a black button down, appearing to be much more formal than any person in attendance. He grinned as he reached her, bowing at the waist, but never breaking eye contact.

"My dear princess—you are as beautiful as I remember."

Noni remembered that voice. Suddenly, she was taken back to the day at the smoothie bar. She remembered now—sitting across from him as he stole energy signatures from her veins. She remembered the way his eyes drew her in. He had stolen that memory from her.

"Noni, do you know this creep?" Terrell spoke up. "Is he bothering you?"

The man rose from his bow smirked as he looked at Terrell, capturing his eyes. Immediately, Terrell's body went lax. He stopped speaking, moving, blinking—everything stopped. His expression was blank and his eyes drained of all life. Terror rose in Noni's chest.

She turned back to the man dressed in black. "I know you," Noni spoke. "*Negus.*" She pronounced his name with such distaste that the man seemed amused.

The music seemed to die down almost completely. It was as if it was just the two of them in the huge room. Noni was sure that no one else knew what was going on.

"Ah," Negus spoke, tapping at his temple. "I see your memory has been restored. Wonderful!" He took a step toward her and Noni took two steps back.

Suddenly, another spike in the atmosphere hit her like a ton of bricks. This time, warmth was restored to the air. Her skin began to tingle, and she knew—she knew it was Alex. She searched around, hoping to see Alex or Ileana, but she didn't. She could sense him, but she didn't know where he was.

Negus shook his head. "Don't worry about your protectors. They are preoccupied."

The way he spoke worried Noni more than she would admit. "What do you want?" she spat. "To kill me?"

Negus shook his head. "Why no, Noni. I could have killed you years ago. I want quite the opposite, actually." His eyes roamed across the crowd, amusedly regarding the teens. He seemed to laugh to himself as he watched them dance. "Humans are such *interesting* creatures," he whispered.

"Why are you here?" Noni bit. She touched the talisman around her neck. She didn't remember much about fighting, but she knew he was dangerous, and she didn't trust his motives. He watched her hand and shook his head at her again.

"I just want to chat. To offer a deal." He paused. "And I wouldn't do *that*, if I were you. This is no place for weapons, you should know that." Noni begrudgingly lowered her hand and Negus smiled. "Good girl." He clasped his hands together, taking another careful step toward her. This time, Noni didn't move. Negus began to speak again. "This deal, my dear, I don't think you can refuse."

Negus waved his hand in the air, in a circular motion, and a cloud of black smoke appeared in the air and settled in his hand. Noni braced herself for the worst. To her surprise, only a black vial was left after the cloud disappeared.

"What is this?" Noni questioned.

"You never were patient. Just like your mother," he noted, rolling his eyes dramatically. "This is for you, Noni. My deal is as follows—all I need is a drop of your blood, and you can continue to live your normal, human life, with your human family, in this forsaken realm."

Noni tentatively took a half step backward. "That doesn't sound like much of a deal." She tried to keep her voice from shaking. "Why would you need my blood?"

Negus' mouth pressed to a thin line. "I know that you would do anything to protect this world, your friends, and your family. I've observed that much. But this realm, Noni—this realm is mine. It is already under my reign and there is no use in fighting. Therefore, to put it simply, I need your Light to complete the transformation of this realm."

"And you think I'd just *hand* it over to you?"

Negus' eyes seemed to scan the crowd again. He stopped and stared at something behind Noni and he grinned. "As I said, I know you would do anything to protect your friends *and* family."

Noni wished she wouldn't have turned.

Behind her, Bianca and Charli smiled joyfully. Bianca looked happier than she ever had, freer than she ever had. She was illuminated in the dark. Terrell still stood beside her, as motionless as ever. He hadn't moved since Negus put him over. She glanced between the two of them and her heart beat frantically in her chest.

"Give me your Light, and I assure you, your family and friends will be spared." Negus told her.

Noni turned back to him and met his cold eyes.

"Disobey, and well, you know how these things go." He held the vial at its neck and extended it to Noni.

For several seconds, she just stared at it. A battle raged inside her while indecision and fear clouded her mind. With downcast eyes and a heavy heart, Noni opened her hand. Negus placed the vial in her palm and he closed her fingers around it.

"Just a drop, Noni. Just a drop and your family will be saved. And you've always wanted to keep them safe, haven't you?"

She didn't look at him, but she could hear the smile in his voice. Negus was gone before she brought her head up.

"Ugh," Terrell groaned, rubbing his temples. "Sorry, didn't mean to zone out like that. I don't even know how that happened."

Without warning, Noni reached out and hugged Terrell. She wrapped her arms around him completely, breathing in his scent. He laughed and hugged her back.

"This has gotta be the best day of my life!" he joked.

Noni shuddered, releasing a shaky breath. He didn't know how wrong he was. She released him and shoved the black vial deep in the pocket of her shorts.

"I have to go," she yelled over the music. She did her best to fight the tears that were building behind her eyes. "I'm sorry!"

She took off before he could say goodbye. She spotted Bianca on the other side of the room and pushed through the crowd to get to her. She was now dancing alone, but Noni noticed then that she had a drink in her hand, and Noni was *very* sure that it wasn't just punch.

"I don't have time for this," she muttered under her breath. She reached out and grabbed Bianca by the arm. The other girl turned abruptly, spilling a third of the drink on the ground in front of her.

"Come on Nons!" she slurred. "Do better!"

"Bianca, we need to go. Now."

"We just got here!" Bianca whined, pouting. "We can't leave. Plus…Charli just went to go get me another drink."

Noni grit her teeth. Why did Bianca have to be so difficult when Noni was trying to save her life?

Before Noni could say another word, a heavy *thud* shook the ceiling. Bianca didn't notice it and neither did any of the other clubgoers. But Noni did, and she didn't need to guess what it was. Another blow to the ceiling shook the building, followed by the sound of wooden beams cracking and breaking. The bass hid the effects of the crash. Noni's instincts immediately kicked in. She knew that if this went on any longer, the ceiling would collapse and everyone could be seriously hurt. There were over one hundred people in this club, and there was no way she could convince the DJ to shut off the music and make people clear out.

Noni combed through the crowd, pushing people aside as she raced to the door. Once she reached it, she did the bravest and dumbest thing she could think of.

She pulled the fire alarm.

Freezing cold water poured from the ceiling. The music cut immediately. A collective gasp escaped the crowd. She braced herself for the onslaught of people that came running toward the door, trying to escape the spray. The bouncers waved people out as they evacuated. Noni, blind with courage and adrenaline, fought against the mass as she went the opposite way. She ducked through the building, careful not to be seen by any of the bartenders or the DJ. It was easy to find the stairs to the second floor. They were blocked off, but Noni hopped over the barriers. She raced up two flights of stairs, finding the third floor in disarray just as she thought. The ceiling was cracking, and the beams underneath were beginning to collapse under the weight of whatever was going on atop the roof.

The final flight of stairs brought her to the door that led to the roof. Noni could hear the clash of metal. She knew that a battle was raging outside. She knew that Alex and Ileana were outside, fighting to protect her. Noni reached up and snatched off her talisman, holding it in her hand. It grew into the bow and quiver full of arrows. She slung the quiver over her shoulder and took a deep breath. She opened the door, took an arrow from the quiver and set it against the bow.

For once in her life, she wasn't afraid.

One after another, Noni's arrows flew through the sky, and one by one, they connected with the enemy. She was spot on, hitting targets as if she'd been an archer her entire life. Her arm moved faster than her eye could keep track. Noni's vision grew sharper, more focused. She could predict the enemy's every move. Shooting was in her muscle memory; she didn't need to think. Noni let her body do the work. She could feel her power building.

The weaker Halflings turned to dust as her silver arrows connected with their flesh. Alex and Ileana fought bravely, destroying every Halfling in their wake. They didn't worry over her safety—she was handling herself. Arrows whizzed past their faces, but they sensed them soon enough to move and let them fly toward their targets. The supply was endless—the quiver was constantly replenished. The Halflings kept coming in flashes of lightning that struck the roof and shook its foundation. Noni never stopped fighting and neither did her friends. The Halflings didn't even have a chance to get close to her.

Suddenly, the roof beneath them began to shake violently, so much that Noni lost her balance. She fell to her knees, dropping her bow in the process. She looked over to Alex, then to Ileana, and saw that they were both on the ground as well. The remaining Halflings were on their knees, fear spreading across their faces. Her prediction was transpiring—the ceiling had caved in. The beams underneath gave; the impact of the fight was too much.

Alex was at her side in the blink of an eye. Noni hadn't even seen him move. She gathered her bow and quiver. Swiftly, he grabbed her by the waist and lifted her off the ground.

"Where's Ileana?" She called out, searching for the woman. She found her on the edge of the roof. This time, she was no longer holding her dagger—a flaming battle axe was raised high above her head.

"She'll be fine," Alex assured her. "She's ending this."

With Noni in his arms, he leapt off the roof. The explosion that followed caused the whole building to cave into itself, and Noni prayed that there had been no one left inside.

Alex landed gracefully. Noni's arms were wrapped tight around his neck, even when they reached the ground. He set her down gently, ignoring the mess of caked up neon powders that covered his chest. Noni wiped her face and kneeled on the ground as she inhaled deeply.

"I don't know how I did that," she admitted, shaking her head. "That was so stupid." She held her head in her hands. It was as if all her adrenaline and bravery had drained away all at once. "I could've died!"

"You did well," Alex commended her. "Come on, we need to find your cousin." He outstretched his hand to help her up.

"What am I supposed to do with these?" she asked, referencing the bow and arrows. "Can't exactly explain it."

Alex took the weaponry into his hands as they began to glow. They lost shape in the brilliance of the light, and as it died down, Noni's talisman was left in his palms. He gave it to her.

"Thanks." She quickly reattached the talisman around her neck. Alex began walking and she followed behind him.

Noni could already hear sirens blaring. Fire trucks had arrived, along with the police and an ambulance. They landed far enough from the building that they avoided the blast, but some weren't so lucky. Noni saw that some people in the crowd had been hurt, hit by flying debris. People were already being taken away in ambulances. She prayed that Bianca, Charli, and Terrell were safe. With Alex, she raced through the sea of people, searching frantically for her friends. After searching for so long, they finally found the others. They were all sitting on a piece of driftwood at the edge of the lake. Bianca was crying into Charli's shoulder and Terrell was sitting with his head in his hands, staring down at the ground.

"Hey!" Noni called out to them as she ran toward them.

Immediately, Bianca looked up. Her eyes were wide with relief when she saw Noni. She stood up and raced toward her, colliding with the other girl as she squeezed her.

"Oh my God," Bianca cried, bringing Noni as close as she could.

"I thought you got stuck in there! They wouldn't let anyone go back in. The whole building collapsed! Noni, where were you?"

The others, Charli and Terrell, were looking to Noni for answers as well. She glanced up at Alex, who stood beside her, but he didn't have an answer for her.

"I went out the back door," she said. "I was in the bathroom and when I heard the alarm, I just went out that door because it was closer."

Bianca was too overwhelmed to find fault in her story. She just hugged Noni again and wept into her shoulder.

Against her better judgement, Noni went home with Charli and Bianca. As much as she wanted to stay with Alex and to see Ileana, she knew that it would be far too strange for her to leave her cousin after all that had happened. Alex assured her that Ileana was fine, despite her not having reappeared. Begrudgingly, Noni climbed into Charli's back seat, followed by Terrell, whom Charli had offered to give a ride home as well. He hadn't been able to find the people he came with and it was late.

On the ride back, Charli played some music to keep their minds off what had transpired. Everyone, aside from Noni, was in shock. But in the middle of their ride, Terrell turned to Noni and whispered something to her.

"Noni, back there, when you said you were in the bathroom when it happened," he began. "that wasn't true. I saw you going up those stairs in the back of the club. What were you doing?"

Noni froze. She didn't know what to say; she couldn't tell a story fast enough. "I can't explain that."

"Okay, then explain this—who was that guy and why did he look so beat up, like he got into a fight?"

She didn't have an answer for that either. "Listen, Terrell. I'll explain another time—I just can't right now. Please, just leave it."

He listened. He didn't say another word for the rest of their car ride. Terrell was smoldering and she could tell; he knew she had lied and that wasn't good. She hoped he wouldn't tell Bianca, or anyone else for that matter. Thankfully, he was the first person to be dropped off. Noni was grateful to have some semblance of peace when he left the car.

Unfortunately, that all ended when they got home. Every single light in the house was on. "Oh no," Bianca groaned aloud. "This can't be happening."

Charli dropped them off in front of the house. "Sorry guys—good luck."

Bianca and Noni got out of the car, soaking wet and covered in neon powder. They looked at one another with pity and fear. There was no time to come up with a cover story. Together, they dragged their feet as they walked to the front door.

It was unlocked.

They braced themselves.

Chapter Sixteen

Grounded. Noni could not remember a time, in the history of her life, when she had *ever* been grounded.

They were not allowed to leave the house unless it was for work. Deidre banned them from the car, and they both had to take the bus. She'd given them a swift tongue lashing the night before, and after it was done, Noni didn't think she'd ever be the same. However, as much as she understood that the consequences for their actions were just, now was *not* the time.

Thankfully, Deidre hadn't taken their cellphones. But with the way she was patrolling the house like a warden, Noni was afraid to even use her cellphone to call Alex and Ileana.

So, the next day, she did the natural thing. She lied. She lied right through her teeth. She dressed in her work uniform—frumpy, forest green apron, slip resistant shoes and all—and lied right to her Aunt's face.

Fortunately, Deidre believed her.

Noni got on the bus and rode it to Alex and Ileana's apartment. As soon as the bus arrived, she jumped off and rushed toward the complex. Their car was in the parking lot, so Noni desperately hoped that they were home. She went up the stairs and didn't even bother to knock. When she opened the door, she was greeted by Ash.

He meowed and rubbed against her legs, weaving between them. Instinctively, she picked the kitten up and carried him with her.

"Guys?" she called out. She heard rustling in the kitchen. She walked into the living room and, from there, she saw a woman whom she'd never seen before. She had dark skin and blazing, sharp, golden eyes. Her hair was jet black, pulled into a tight bun that sat at the back of her head. She wore armor identical to the armor that Noni saw Ileana wearing in her memory. When she saw Noni, her eyes widened with shock. Immediately, she dropped to one knee and rested one hand over her heart.

"It is an honor," she said. Her voice was deep and heavy with an accent that Noni could barely decipher.

Noni was at a loss for words. "Uh...thanks?"

Ileana touched the woman's shoulder. "You may rise, Uma," she announced.

The woman quickly stood up, adjusting the sword at her waist. She held onto the hilt of it as she nodded in Noni's direction. Noni shuffled into the kitchen. Her face was hot with embarrassment.

"I am Uma," the woman said. Noni finally saw her up close. She was at *least* six feet tall. "I am one of the Chief Legion Directors of the First Novaen Army. As I stated before, it is an honor to meet you, Princess Aisha."

Noni nodded once. She didn't know what the earthly equivalent of her position was, but she figured it was pretty high up. She pointed to Ileana.

"What does that make *you*?"

"I am the Leader of the First Novaen Army."

Immediately, Noni was completely taken aback. She couldn't wrap her mind around the fact that Ileana held such an important position in her realm. Noni knew that she was a good fighter—she'd seen that much. Now that Noni knew Ileana was the leader of an entire army, she began to see her in a new light. "Wow."

Ileana shook her head, waving her hand in the air. "It isn't important," she quickly replied. "Noni, what's going on? We were not expecting you."

Noni pursed her lips. Ash wriggled in her arms and tried to claw his way across her sleeve. She set him down gently as she began speaking.

"Something bad happened yesterday," she confessed.

Alex's eyes widened, as if he knew what Noni was about to say; he didn't speak.

"It was him," Noni told them. "It was Negus."

She told them everything. Although she was reluctant to tell them the truth, she knew that she had to. She was in danger, and so were her family and friends. There was no way she could protect them on her own and she knew that. When Noni finished speaking, Uma was the first to respond to her confession.

"It's true that this realm has been tainted by Negus' hand," she announced. "Famine, disease, war—slowly, he has infected this realm for decades. Humans are weak—they cannot resist his influence. And the protectors of this realm..." her voice trailed off as she noticed the pained expression on Noni's face. She lowered her eyes, bowing her head once more. "My apologies."

"What Uma means to say is that this realm is already in danger," Ileana elaborated. "Negus has been here for a long time, it seems."

"What happened to the gods that were supposed to protect this realm?" Noni questioned. "Why aren't they fighting back?"

Ileana shook her head and glanced between Alex and Uma before turning back to Noni. Her expression was grave and almost sad. "We have not been able to locate Taj and Oni for quite some time," she answered, almost whispering. For a split second, Noni felt a familiar tingle in the back of her mind. She knew there was something she was supposed to remember about those names, but, like many of the memories she had attained, she couldn't reach them all.

"This realm is vulnerable. And without them..." Ileana shook her head, taking a seat at the island. "Negus is still weak. He has grown stronger, but he is not at full strength. He's vulnerable and he knows that. He needs your power, Noni, in order to reach his full potential."

"Why me?" she peeped. "I get it. I'm not human, whatever—what makes me so special?"

"You're royalty. Your blood is royal. The Light you possess has been passed down for generations." Alex broke in, unsmiling.

Noni pursed her lips, looking away from Alex immediately. She exhaled heavily and threw her arms in the air.

"I don't know what I'm supposed to do!" she blurted. "I can't let him hurt my family or my friends. I *can't.*"

"No one will be harmed," Ileana assured her. "We will do our best to protect them. Unfortunately," the woman's eyed Noni sadly, and her voice became a low, pitiful sound, "no one will be safe if you're still in this realm."

"*What?*" Noni nearly shouted. "I don't understand."

It was clear that Ileana did not want to continue. The pain in her expression emphasized that much. "Both you and Elijah possess power that does not belong to this realm. Your power is a beacon that draws darkness. As long as you're here, no one is safe. Halflings will keep coming for you; *Negus* will keep coming for you. And if you remain here, you will be vulnerable just like the people on this planet. Humans are susceptible to darkness—they are weak." She shook her head. "You were never meant for this place."

"I don't care what happens to me," Noni argued. "I don't care that those things want to kill me. I care about my family and my friends. I need them to stay alive. I can't—I can't lose another person."

A heavy silence settled in the room.

Noni lowered her gaze, fighting back the tears that flooded her eyes. "I lost my mother and my father, and I was too young to do anything to save them. I can't let that happen again. Nobody else is dying." She wiped her face. Noni wanted to be strong, but her world was falling apart. "I'll do whatever I have to do to keep them safe. And Negus knows that."

"You can't give him your Light, Noni," Ileana warned. "The Halflings are coming. Negus is coming. We can feel it, and I know you can too."

She was right. Noni could feel the shift in the atmosphere. Everything was heavier than usual, even the air.

"With you out of the realm, he won't be able to harm you. As for your loved ones, we'll take care of them."

Noni was quiet. She folded her arms across her chest, becoming tenser with every second. "They'll wonder why I'm gone."

Ileana shook her head. "We'll take care of them. We'll take care of everything."

Noni tried to breathe evenly, but the deep shuddering in her chest kept her breathing erratic. Her throat was tightening as she stood underneath their burning gazes. She brought her hand to her mouth, covering her trembling lips. Her heart beat violently in her chest, her hands felt numb, and she felt a cold sweat breaking across her skin. "I need a minute."

She rushed out of the kitchen, stealing herself away near the front door. She pressed herself into the corner beside the front door, grasping at her shirtfront as she tried to catch her breath. Her ears were ringing. She felt dizzy and a spell of nausea crept through her stomach. Noni held her head between her hands, eyes shut tight, as she tried to ground herself.

She heard his footsteps before anything else. Through blurred, teary vision, Noni caught a glimpse of Alex standing underneath the archway that led to the living room. No words passed between them. He made his way toward her carefully. He placed one hand on her shoulder, as if to ask for permission to touch her. Noni didn't resist her instincts this time. She took a step forward and pressed her forehead against the center of Alex's chest. When he put his arms around her, a sob tore through her body. Alex didn't speak; he just held her, rubbing circles in her back as she cried.

Noni wished that she could stop the tears. She wished that she were like Ileana—she wished she were stronger. She wished she were strong enough to protect everyone on her own. She wished she didn't always cry when everything fell apart, but she did cry. She couldn't protect anyone, and she wasn't as strong as she needed to be. So she was left crying into the shirt of a man who could barely make sense of who she was. *She* could barely make sense of who she was. Nevertheless, she didn't let him go. He cared, and he was warm; Noni could feel the sparks jumping between her skin and his, but she wasn't afraid. It was almost comforting; it was familiar. He held her tight, just the way he held her the night they stood under the moon together. Her tears stained his shirt, but he didn't seem to notice. He kept holding her until the sobs that shook her body died down to sporadic shudders, shortened breath, and hiccups.

"I'm sorry that things had to happen this way," he whispered softly, still gently rubbing her back.

Noni wiped her tear-stained face. "I'm sorry, too," she said. Sadness rose up in her chest again but she shoved it down. "I can't say goodbye to them."

"I know," he responded.

Noni shook her head. "This just isn't—this isn't *fair*. I just wanted to live a normal life. Go to college, start a career, start a family, have a *life*. I had a whole normal life ahead of me and now I have *this*." She wiped her face again, shivering. "I'm so scared. And everything is just falling apart." She felt weak, crying into his shirt like a child. She had never felt so small.

"It won't always be like this," Alex tried to convince her. "I promise."

"You can't promise me that," she whispered. "I know that things are beyond your control. Something tells me that this is just the start. She shook her head, dispelling the awful thoughts that plagued her mind. "Just promise me that everyone will be safe. That's all I want."

Alex nodded once. "I promise," he spoke with conviction. Despite everything, Noni believed him. He had saved her life countless times—she knew he would try to keep her family out of harm's way.

"Thank you," Noni responded. "I know that things have been… weird. But thank you, for trying. For everything."

"I'll always be here for you, Noni. Even when things are *weird*. There are many things I need to consider, and much that I have to work through on my own, but that doesn't mean that I would ever abandon you." He released her, but rested his hands on her arms. "Trust Ileana. She is a strategist. She has a plan. And we won't let anyone else get hurt."

There was no way that Noni could properly tell her family that she would probably never see them again. That was they sacrifice that she had agreed to; it was more painful and more complicated than she could have ever imagined.

Noni would leave, that much had been decided. Ileana and Uma would stay with her and Eli, keeping them safe and getting them out. Alex would stay behind. He'd volunteered to do the hardest job. The memories of her loved ones had to be erased, but only the memories of Noni. Memories, they said, hold power. Memories hold truth. If they didn't remember Noni, they held no connection to her.

As soon as she knew what Alex was going to do, Noni stopped listening. She couldn't bear to hear anymore. They wouldn't know her anymore—Aunt Deidre, Bianca, even Terrell and Charli—they would be wiped of every memory.

It's temporary, Alex told her. Temporary meaning that it would only work for as long as they did not see Noni. *Once this is all over, you'll go home*, he promised, *and it'll be like nothing ever changed.*

However, as Noni approached her home, the same two-story white house she'd known for most of her life, she knew that nothing would ever be the same again.

Everything was a blur after that. She was home and she was grateful to be there. Noni had never gazed upon her home with such melancholy. She had never wanted to *stay* so much as she did now. Home was where only good things happened. Home was where she could be herself—an eighteen-year-old girl who dreamt of becoming a nurse, of helping people, of living a simple life. Home was where her family was, where there was love. Home was safe and stable—*this* home was the only thing in Noni's life that had ever been stable.

Deidre cooked dinner as she always did. With the girls at home, around the dinner table, she was happy. The anger from the night before had almost dissipated from her aura. She seemed to just be satisfied with having her girls together. They all sat around the table and shared a meal. Bianca told hilarious stories about work, and they all roared with laughter. Noni watched them carefully, memorizing the laugh lines around their mouths and eyes, the moles on the sides of her Aunt's face, the freckles around Bianca's nose, the way they both clenched and unclenched their hands as they spoke. She tried to commit their voices to her memory; like her favorite song, she wanted them stuck in her head.

After dinner was over, Noni made the decision to put on her Aunt's favorite movie—*Coming to America*. She suggested that they all watch it together in the living room, the way they used to when she and Bianca were younger. Deidre, though she was exhausted from her day at work, couldn't pass up the offer. They crowded on the old brown couch, and Bianca popped in the VHS.

Deidre ended up falling asleep at the middle of the film, but Noni didn't care. She watched the woman's face underneath the glow of the TV screen. She looked at Bianca, too, and tried to accept that that night would be the last time she saw them for a long time. The movie, which used to feel like the longest movie they would ever watch, ended faster than Noni would've wanted. Bianca left quickly, offering to clean up the dishes in the kitchen. When Deidre woke, she stood from the couch and told the girls that it was time for her to head to bed. Before she could even leave the living room, Noni hugged her. She wrapped her arms around the frail woman, squeezing her ever so gently.

"I'm sorry." She fought back tears.

Deidre, taken aback by the gesture, just smiled and patted the girl on the back. "Oh, Noni, it's okay," she spoke softly. "I'm not angry anymore. I know you girls didn't mean any harm yesterday. I was just worried," she said. She kissed Noni's forehead. "Just promise you won't do anything like *that* again."

Noni closed her eyes, holding the sadness at bay. "I promise."

Deidre went to bed. Noni let her go.

She helped Bianca clean the kitchen. Bianca went on and on about how she was excited to start classes in a few weeks. Her schedule was set, and she'd already received emails from most of her professors. The excitement in Bianca's voice brought Noni so much joy—she knew Bianca would be just fine.

As long as they're happy and safe, she told herself.

The long night stretched on.

Noni sat in her bedroom until dark. She knew she would not be able to sleep tonight. As much as she knew she should rest, her mind wouldn't allow it. The atmosphere was dense, heavy around her. Evil lingered in the air, in the dark, and she knew she wasn't safe. No one was.

She left her bedroom. On the other side of the hallway, Bianca's door was cracked. Noni soundlessly slipped through and whispered her cousin's name.

"Bee?" she said. "Are you asleep?"

The other girl groaned, digging her face into her pillow. "I *was*," she mumbled. She opened her eyes and glanced at Noni who was standing at the door, hugging her body. She sat up. "What's wrong? Did something happen?" she questioned.

Noni shook her head. "No, I just can't sleep in my room," she told her cousin. "Can I sleep in here with you?"

Bianca smiled and rubbed her eyes. "We haven't done this since we were kids," she said, folding the blankets down and making room. "Like when you used to have those nightmares…did you have a nightmare?"

Noni nodded. Everything seemed like a nightmare now. She shuffled across the hardwood floor and climbed into Bianca's full-sized bed. She adjusted the pillows and got comfortable, pulling the blankets up to her chin. Bianca turned onto her side and looked into Noni's eyes. "Is there something else going on, Nons?" she asked.

Noni wished she could tell the truth. She wished she could stay up all night and tell Bianca everything. But if she did that, Bianca would never be safe. She couldn't. She shook her head. "The nightmare really shook me up." She replied.

Bianca nodded, laying her head against a fluffed pillow. "I always thought you'd stop having them eventually," she admitted. "I'm sorry, Noni."

The girls lay there in silence. Bianca's eyes drooped as she dozed in and out. Noni watched her quietly, wishing she could wrap her arms around the girl and hug her one last time. Before Bianca was asleep, Noni spoke once more.

"Bee?"

"Hmm?" The other teen answered sleepily with her eyes still closed.

Noni shuddered, allowing one single tear to fall from her eye. "Whatever happens, I love you."

"Mm, love you too, Noni," Bianca mumbled. Her breathing evened out and Noni knew she had finally fallen asleep. Noni watched her for what seemed hours before she finally rose. She silently crawled out of the bed, tucking Bianca into the blankets. She grabbed the girl's cell phone from the nightstand. She left her door open just a bit, so the sound of closing it wouldn't wake Bianca. Noni checked on her Aunt, just to make sure that she was sleeping. She didn't need to open the door because she could hear the woman snoring lightly. With a nod of the head, Noni walked back down the hallway, to her bedroom.

She began her task.

Every picture with her face had to be disposed of. Alex would get rid of the rest of her things. Noni wasn't sure of the details—she didn't want to know.

She gathered every photo and threw it into a plastic trash bag. Alex told her that everything had to go—the deed couldn't be done if they saw her face. So, one by one, she collected pictures from all over the house. Every family photo album was raided Noni took Bianca's phone and deleted every single picture with her face in it. Noni was strong. She held herself together through the entire ordeal. The one thing that almost triggered her tears was the last picture in their oldest photo album. It was a picture of Bianca, her parents, Noni, and Noni's parents. They all stood, smiling together in the front yard of Noni's old house. They looked happy.

Noni covered her mouth and crumpled the picture with her other hand before throwing it into the garbage.

Noni packed one bag. She pretended that she was packing for a camping trip, just to keep herself sane. She packed light. She gathered the bag of photos, tied a knot in the bag, and dragged it out to the trash bins. The next day was garbage day—no one would ever see those pictures again.

She carried her own cellphone out of her room. She had an unanswered text message. It was from Terrell, a simple "Hey, I miss you" was all that he'd written. She thought of texting him back, but she knew that wouldn't do any good.

They would have to wipe him too.

Noni turned her phone off and disposed of it. She couldn't think about missing him.

After she finished, she waited outside for the others. She didn't have the strength to go back inside.

They came together, the four of them: Alex, Ileana, Uma, and Eli. Noni saw Eli's face; his eyes were red and swollen, and he kept wiping at his cheeks. She couldn't look him in the eye. She knew she would find nothing but agony there. Noni stood and walked over to them. Alex looked at her, pity and pain in his gaze.

"Everything will be fine," he spoke softly. "No one will harm them."

Noni just nodded, walking past him toward Uma, Ileana, and Eli. Ileana nodded to Alex, and he nodded back only once. His eyes lingered on Noni for several seconds before he turned toward her home. Noni watched him walk into the two-story white house, quietly closing the door behind him. Everything was still. Noni looked up and watched Bianca's bedroom window. Ileana rested a calming hand on her shoulder. Suddenly, a bright blue glow erupted behind the window, illuminating the whole room. Noni covered her mouth and turned away from the house.

She never looked back.

CHAPTER SEVENTEEN

The night carried an unusual chill. The wind howled in their ears, a mournful, hollow sound. The lonely croaking of cicadas filled the air. Noni and Eli followed behind Uma and Ileana sullenly, slowly dragging their feet. Neither of them had spoken to the other; only solemn glances had been shared between the two. They stared at the backs of the warrior women before them, trying to remember that they were saving lives.

Their trek was lengthy. Noni was not sure where they were headed, and Ileana and Uma did not inform them. The streets were illuminated by the lampposts. Noni read the street signs. Elm, Grove, Oak, Union, Glenn— the list dragged on. Noni lost count of how many roads they had passed. However, in the distance, a canopy of trees came into view.

The group came upon the city park. Large black metal gates surrounded the area and blocked off the front entrance.

Just as Eli began opening his mouth to ask how they would get through, Uma reached out and grabbed the gate. With one stiff, hard yank, the gate popped open. Pieces of the inside of the lock crumbled and fell to the dirt. Uma kicked the remains aside and held the gate open for the other three.

Noni had never been to the park at night. There was something eerie about the silence, something unsettling about the fact that they heard no animals, no cicadas, and no wind in the boughs of the trees. Noni pulled her thin jacket around her frame, as if to try to swaddle herself. She looked over at Eli again. He was holding something small and round in his hand, turning it over and examining it. It must have been something from home, something to help him remember. Noni hadn't brought any keepsakes with her. They were all in the trash, waiting to be thrown away with the neighborhood's garbage.

They traveled farther into the park than Noni had ever gone, into the wooded area that was usually blocked off to the people. They climbed over barriers and walked past the "Do Not Enter" signs without sparing them a second glance. The trees were thicker there. The grass was unkempt, full of wild weeds and flora that Noni had never come across before. The air was sweeter, too, and the scent was almost calming. Stuck in her reverie, Noni hadn't even noticed that Uma and Ileana had stopped walking. She looked up and saw exactly why.

Before them stood one of the largest trees that Noni had ever seen. Its trunk was thick and solid with dark, deep ridges in the wood. Its dense branches seemed to stretch on forever, and the leaves were so impenetrable that they couldn't see the sky above them. Flowers grew at its base, all blooming even though there was no sunlight.

Eli was the first to speak. "Is this the Yggdrasil?" he whispered.

Ileana shook her head. "No," she answered. "The Tree of Life does not exist on this plane. However, many portals that lead to it can be found, if you know how to find them."

"How do you find them?" Eli questioned.

Ileana stepped forward. She knelt at the tree's base and trailed her fingers through the dirt.

"The roots," She told him. "You follow its roots. They cannot be seen by human eyes, but we can see them. Or rather, sense them beneath your earth's crust."

"You said this was a portal," Noni pointed out. Everyone turned when she finally spoke. Her face grew hot with all of them staring at her. "This portal leads to the Yggdrasil?"

"Yes. And the Yggdrasil will allow us to travel between realms," she responded, "but before we go any farther, I must warn you. The portal to the Yggdrasil is not easy to travel. This is ancient power, something that we can't control. It controls us."

Noni did not like the sound of that. "What does that mean?" she questioned.

"It means that whatever happens, happens. You cannot control what goes on, and you should not try. This power may evoke something within you that you never knew existed. You may see things that you thought were hidden away, and so you mustn't shy away from them. Embrace it. Allow it to happen. And don't fight it."

A single shiver danced along Noni's spine. She looked to Uma. "What happens if I fight it?"

Uma's eyes seemed to sharpen as she spoke. "You will die, stuck forever in a portal filled with your own worst nightmares."

Eli scoffed. "Well that's comforting."

Taking a deep breath, Ileana stood from the dirt. She placed one hand against the tree trunk and closed her eyes. For a long time, nothing happened. Just as Noni began to question whether this was the right tree, the ground began to shake. Ileana's hand was glowing against the trunk, and the glow spread, like vines around the tree. The leaves shivered, detached from the branches, and floated upward, hanging in midair. Light engulfed the trunk. Ileana opened her eyes and looked back at them, keeping her hold on the tree.

"Go ahead," she told them, looking straight at Eli and Noni, "and remember what I told you."

Eli immediately grabbed Noni's hand. He looked at her and she saw herself reflected in his glasses. "Together?"

She nodded silently. They walked into the portal with clasped hands, neither of them knowing what would come next.

Noni woke up in her bed, but it wasn't *her* bed. This bed was a small twin, with a pink canopy that shielded her from the outside world. Through the thin, sheer canopy, she could see the walls by the dim night light in the corner. They were covered with paintings, of castles and worlds that she had never known. There was a green, scaly dragon painted at the base of a castle. In the castle was a little girl smiling and holding a sword in the air.

Tears filled her eyes. She gathered up the blankets around her, clutching them to her chest.

This was her childhood bedroom.

Noni pressed her hands to her cheeks and breathed slowly. She touched the bed again, running her fingers along the cotton sheets. *This is all real. It's all here,* she thought.

Immediately, she jumped of bed and rushed to the door, throwing it open. Noni raced down the stairs and turned left into the kitchen. The lights were dim. The thick scent of food wafted through the air. On the stove, a pot of greens boiled beside a small slow cooker.

Suddenly, it occurred to Noni where she was and what night it was. It was the night before Thanksgiving. She couldn't speak. She turned around and dashed up the stairs to her parent's bedroom at the end of the hall. She opened the door without a moment's hesitation. Both of her parents had been in bed, sleeping soundlessly. However, the moment Noni burst through the door, they both woke abruptly and jumped at the sound.

Theresa gently rubbed her eyes as she sat up in bed. David groaned and rolled over onto his back with a heavy sigh.

"Noni Grace," her mother spoke. "what in the world are you doing up?"

Noni did her best to fight back her tears, but nothing could stop them from rolling in. She rushed to her mother and threw her arms around the woman, embracing her as the quiet tears fell from her eyes. Theresa hugged Noni close, kissing her forehead.

"Oh sweetheart, did you have a bad dream?"

Noni nodded rapidly, hugging her mother tighter.

David sat up in bed, reached over and ruffled Noni's hair. "It'll be alright," he told her, repeating Theresa's gesture. "It's just a dream."

Theresa pushed the blankets down. "Come on baby, I'll put you back to bed, okay?"

"No," Noni finally spoke, shaking her head wildly. "No I have to stay here. I have to stay in here."

Theresa placed a hand on Noni's back and started her towards the door.

"You know your father has to work in the morning. You don't want to disturb him, right?"

Theresa led Noni out of the bedroom and Noni stole a glance at her father before her mother shut the door. He lay in bed with the blankets pulled up to his chin. Noni wished that she could run back to him, but once the door was closed, she knew it was too late. Her mother walked her down the hall to her bedroom. She picked a book up from Noni's bookshelf and walked over to the canopy bed with her daughter. Noni dutifully climbed into bed. Theresa climbed in beside her, kissing her daughter's forehead once more.

"I know nightmares can be scary sometimes," she took her daughter's hands, "but they're just dreams, baby. No dreams can hurt you." She pulled the blanket up, covering both herself and Noni. Noni felt so small, so tiny beside her mother. The woman was still smiling, her high cheekbones so close to her eyes, brown lips spread across her face. Her hair was pulled back into a tight bun and tied under a scarf. She was so beautiful. Noni rested her head on her mother's chest, inhaling her familiar scent, sweet like warm honey.

"How about I read you a bedtime story, hmm?" Theresa asked. "I picked up your favorite book on my way in." She grinned.

In her hands, Theresa held the book *Amazing Grace*. She opened the book and began reading. The soft cadence of her voice lulled Noni, drying up the tears in her eyes. It calmed her heart, and made her feel what home was like, one more time. Noni closed her eyes and tried to memorize the scent of her mother's clothes, the feeling of her warm skin.

For a while, Noni slept, drifting between what was real and what wasn't.

A single sound woke her.

It was her mother, coughing violently.

Noni's heart dropped in her chest.

When she opened her eyes, her whole bedroom was filled with smoke. Theresa was at the door, fanning the smoke away from her own face. She grabbed the door handle but the metal was scalding to the touch. It burned her hand, and she pulled away with a shriek. Noni climbed out of bed and ran to the door, punching and kicking at it, wishing that she was strong enough to break it down but knowing that she wasn't.

Theresa pulled her away from the door.

"No baby, no it's too dangerous!" She pushed Noni into the furthest corner of the room.

From there on, it was just as Noni remembered it.

Theresa ripped a sheet from Noni's bed and began tying it to her bedframe. She secured it, pushing the bed against the wall near the window. She coughed, waving away the smoke as she did. More black smoke billowed out from under Noni's bedroom door. She snuck out of the corner, picked up her comforter from the floor and went to block the smoke from coming in. But before she could finish, a hair-raising sound erupted from the end of the hallway.

It was her father, screaming in agony.

"Dad!" she cried out, running to the door again. Noni went to grab the door handle to try to escape. It was hot, searing, but when Noni touched it, the doorknob glowed a dark, red color and the blast of it threw her back at least two feet. She stood, staggered as she stared at the door. Before she could draw a conclusion, Theresa grabbed her by the shoulder and pulled her toward the window.

"You've got to get out." The woman pushed Noni to climb on top of her bed. "Climb down okay? Remember how Daddy taught you to climb ropes?" Tears had begun to fall from the woman's eyes. Her coughing was raw, rattling her chest. "Just like Daddy taught you— you have to climb down, Noni." Theresa kissed the girl's forehead and pushed her toward the wall. "I'll go get Daddy and we'll both come down right after you, but you have to go first."

"No!" Noni shouted, crying. "I can't go! I can't leave you! I have to ... I have to..." Her voice trailed off as she remembered her duty.

You cannot control what goes on and you should not try...allow it to happen. And don't fight it.

Theresa kissed her one final time.

Noni climbed out of the window carefully. She held onto the sheet and never looked down. She watched her mother's face, watched her tears fall as Noni climbed lower and lower. She jumped down, landing in the grass. When she looked up again, her mother was gone. Noni backed away from the house, watching the red and orange flames dance behind the windows. She couldn't stop crying, knowing that her parents were trapped, knowing that they would always be trapped in this hell.

She heard the sirens before the firefighters, police, and ambulances arrived. An EMT pulled Noni away from the house, carrying her away from danger. She watched as the firefighters began to spray her home with a heavy dose of water, but the flames wouldn't die down. Noni watched the flames growing higher, defying the water that tried to douse them. Black smoke rose and curled in the air, clouding the sky.

In the smoke, Noni saw a figure standing on the roof of the house. She saw him, cloaked in black and hidden by the smolder. She could see his eyes glowing in the dark, even from the ambulance where she sat.

He regarded her for a single moment, and his eyes began to glow even brighter in the dark.

Noni began to scream.

She thrashed and broke away from the EMT, pushing them aside before she took off running. She could see him there, standing at the top of the roof, unmoving. Her scream was a battle cry in the night. She raced through the grass toward her house.

As soon as her feet touched the grass, the ground began to shake. Suddenly, giant roots broke free from the dirt and wrapped themselves around her ankles, tripping her. Noni fell to the ground, using her arms to break her fall. She flipped over on her back and tried to pry the roots from her ankles but her efforts proved futile. More thick roots burst out of the dirt and grabbed at her. In seconds, her arms, legs, and torso were bound. Noni screamed and thrashed, trying to break free, but the roots were too strong.

"I'll *kill* you!" Her throat was raw from screaming, but she didn't stop. The roots pulled her deep into the ground. "Negus! I *will* kill you!" They dragged her beneath the soil, beneath the earth, and her throat filled with dirt.

It was dark, pitch black. Noni kept struggling, but the roots continued to drag her through the darkness. Her breathing was erratic; she couldn't see and didn't know where she was being taken. She couldn't fight back and couldn't escape. She was not in control.

The pressure was almost unbearable. She felt herself being pushed up against the dirt. It pushed against her body, smashing her face and her chest. Breathing was impossible. Noni shut her eyes and mouth tight, bearing the weight.

Suddenly, the load began to lighten. The ground broke apart, and Noni was plunged into the light. She pulled her arms away from the roots, which immediately receded into the ground. Gasping for air, she crawled away from them and collapsed on the ground.

"Noni!" Ileana came running forward. She turned Noni over and propped her up, brushing the dirt away from her face. Noni turned and hugged Ileana immediately, burying her face in her chest.

"You made it. It's okay. Everything is fine." Ileana embraced the teen.

Despite Ileana's consoling, Noni knew that nothing was fine.

Noni couldn't forget what she saw. She couldn't forget the sight of him, of Negus, standing on the roof of her home as her parents burned alive. She knew that it wasn't an illusion—*he* was responsible. That fire hadn't been electrical, as she'd been told her whole life. It wasn't a freak accident. She knew that now.

Ileana helped her get to her feet. Noni brushed off her clothes and took a deep breath. However, when she looked up, she was breathless once again.

It was just as she remembered in her dreams and lost memories.

The Yggdrasil stood tall, stretching high into the sky, so far that all of its branches couldn't be seen. Light-filled orbs circled the tree, soaring around it like bees around a honeycomb. The flora surrounding the tree was immense and dense. There were trees, flowers, and plants that Noni had never seen and was sure didn't exist on Earth at all. Behind the Yggdrasil, Noni saw massive mountains, stretching farther than the mind could conceive. They were covered in what looked like snow, but the glint they gave off reminded her of diamonds. There was no sun, but so much light was shining. Through her feet, Noni could feel the ground pulsating, just like the throbbing of a heart. It beat in harmony with her own heart. Noni took a step forward toward the tree, but Ileana stopped her.

"Not yet," she pulled Noni back. "We have to wait for Eli."

"Eli?" Noni repeated. "I thought he was here."

Ileana shook her head. "No. I arrived at the same time as Uma. Hours later, you appeared. There's been no sign of Eli."

Noni's stomach did a flip. She wondered what nightmare Eli was trapped within.

All of a sudden, Uma walked out from behind the huge trunk of the Yggdrasil. Her sword was drawn and she held a shield in the opposite hand. That was when Noni noticed that Ileana, too was clad in armor. Though her weapon wasn't drawn, she still looked terrifyingly fierce.

Noni paced around, clasping her hands together. Her mind was still racing. She tried to push away what she'd seen and yet, she still committed it all to memory. Rage grew in her chest, hot and ugly. It clawed at her heart, at her mind, and clouded all of her thoughts. She couldn't think of anything without returning to that moment.

Suddenly, Noni heard a familiar sound—the sound of the ground splitting open. Noni saw the roots rising from the dirt, and she started running. She thought that she saw Eli rising from the ground, but when she saw a gray hand clawing its way out, she stopped dead in her tracks. It started happening everywhere, the ground broke apart and the gray-skinned Halflings climbed out.

Uma yanked Noni back, throwing her behind. "Stay back!" she shouted.

Ileana was at her side in a flash and both brandished weapons. Ileana's battle-axe was flaming in the air as she charged toward the Halflings with no reserve. Noni reached for her talisman, but Uma pushed her backward again. "Don't," she said "I will protect you. Go towards the Yggdrasil."

"We have to wait for Eli!" Noni exclaimed.

Uma scoffed. "Don't you see what's happening? There's no time!"

Uma was right. Halflings were crawling out of the ground like insects, surrounding them. Ileana did her best to keep the Halflings at bay, but they were coming far too quickly. Uma, with her sword at her chest, backed Noni toward the Yggdrasil. Noni could feel the tree's power pulsing. It lifted every hair on her body, sent electric shivers through all of her veins. It was calling to her. Noni's eyes darted around quickly as she searched for any signs of Eli. Suddenly, at least fifty feet east, she saw him. The roots lifted him and left him lying still on the ground. Without a moment's hesitation, Noni took off running. She raced toward him with utter disregard for the carnage around her.

Eli sat up and saw her coming. She ran as fast as she could to reach him. His eyes grew large and he pointed and shouted, "Noni watch out!"

Noni turned around and barely missed a dagger to the face. She staggered backward and fell into the grass. The Halfling standing before her raised a knife above his head as he grinned down at her. Before he could bring the dagger down, Noni heard a sickening crack, and the Halfling dropped his weapon and fell to the ground beside her. Ileana's battle-axe was lodged in the back of his head, still flaming. She saw the woman, at least one hundred feet away from him. Ileana nodded to Noni and then pulled two sickles from the sheath on her back. Noni scrambled up and made her way to Eli in a flash. Once she reached him, she grabbed his arm and yanked him up. He tripped over his own feet. She didn't give him enough time to process what was happening. The sky erupted in blue and red lights, Halflings shrieked, and the sound of metal crushing bone echoed in the air.

She half-ran, half-carried Eli to the Yggdrasil. He was muttering something under his breath, but Noni couldn't understand the words. Uma, after bringing a Halfling to a bloody end, snatched them both by their collars and pulled them toward the tree.

"We must go," she ordered. "Now."

"We can't leave Ileana!" Noni protested. "She'll die!"

Uma sheathed her sword. "Ileana is the greatest Novaen fighter. She will not perish at the hands of mere Halflings. You, on the other hand, will. Now go."

Noni and Eli stared at the Yggdrasil. They could feel it pulsating, throbbing beneath them. The ethereal glow that surrounded it seemed to breathe in and out. Eli finally met Noni's eyes and spoke.

"Your eyes, Noni. Your eyes."

She could see them in the reflection of his glasses. They were golden.

The boy shook his head and rested his hand against the tree. "We're going to die," he told her, "I know it." He shook his head and muttered under his breath again, words that Noni couldn't hear.

Uma came up behind him and pressed her glowing hand against the Yggdrasil. "We must all die eventually, child."

Suddenly, a huge force field grew around the Yggdrasil, shielding it from the onslaught of attacks. Noni thought it was Uma's doing, but when she turned, she saw that it was Ileana who had cast it. Her hands were in the earth, glowing beneath the dirt. She gave Noni one final smile before she turned away, back to the fight.

The radiance that erupted from the Yggdrasil was blinding. It spread and shined, engulfing the tree and the three of them. Noni took Eli's arm this time. She didn't look back for Ileana and didn't look to Uma for permission.

She held onto her friend and walked into the blinding light.

Acknowledgements

I will never be able to express my gratitude to all of the people who have helped me get this far. Thank you: Naomi North, for being the best editor I could've asked for and for always guiding me in the right direction. Tom Domzalski, for making me a better writer and forcing me to recognize my own potential. Dr. Tim Murnen, for always encouraging me and giving me a swift kick in the rear when I needed it. Eli, for cheering me on and becoming my best friend along the way. Jay, for feeding me on my hungriest days, for being the best sister I could ever ask for, and for always picking me up and putting me back together. My mother, who always asked, "So, when are you going to write the book?". Karrie, for reading the novel in its entirety and not getting upset when I tried to change all the names—you're a trooper. Barbie, for nine years of friendship, and for always being my sounding board whenever I needed you. And finally, Terah, for inspiring me to continue, over and over again, and for being my best friend, even from 4,000 miles away.